WOMEN EXTRAORDINAIRE

Spanning a saga of three generations and three indomitable women, Suchita Malik draws a sensitive and moving portrayal of change and turbulence and grief and joy set in the backdrop of Punjab and the Partition, and the upheaval in the destinies of a remarkable family whose travails and triumphs we can identify with. A must-read for those who want to understand the unfolding of history not through the pages of textbooks but through the lives of ordinary people and the remarkable resilience they can display in spite of adversity.

—Pavan K. Varma

WOMEN EXTRAORDINAIRE

A NOVEL

Suchita Malik

RUPA

Published by
Rupa Publications India Pvt. Ltd 2014
7/16, Ansari Road, Daryaganj
New Delhi 110002

Sales centres:
Allahabad Bengaluru Chennai
Hyderabad Jaipur Kathmandu
Kolkata Mumbai

Copyright © Suchita Malik 2014

This is a work of fiction. Names, characters, places and incidents are
either the product of the author's imagination or are used fictitiously,
and any resemblance to any actual persons, living or dead,
events or locales is entirely coincidental.

All rights reserved.
No part of this publication may be reproduced, transmitted, or stored in
a retrieval system, in any form or by any means, electronic, mechanical,
photocopying, recording or otherwise, without the prior permission of
the publisher.

ISBN: 978-81-291-3101-0

First impression 2014
10 9 8 7 6 5 4 3 2 1

The moral right of the author has been asserted.

Typeset by Saanavi Graphics, Noida

Printed at Replika Press Pvt. Ltd., India

This book is sold subject to the condition that it shall not, by way
of trade or otherwise, be lent, resold, hired out, or otherwise circulated,
without the publisher's prior consent, in any form of binding or
cover other than that in which it is published.

For

Yudhvir, Surabhi and Vikramaditya—my partners in crime

1

Spring was particularly beautiful in Dera Ismail Khan that year. Tender leaves were breaking out on the branches of trees, their redness lending radiance to the landscape so typical of the season. Rich flowers on the mango trees filled the air with an enchanting aroma and augured a bountiful crop in the days to come. Grooves of mango trees, called *amrai,* situated at some distance from the pavements, offered opportunities to passers-by to relax in their shade and soak in the subtle fragrance of the bloom with the breeze. The full-throated *cooh-cooh* of the ecstatic *koel* lent the music that was enough to send them into deep slumber in the lazy, elongated afternoons.

While the mango trees made their presence known in the spacious bungalows of *zamindars* and the affluent, the periphery of the inbuilt roads, the corners at crossings and the long stretches of the front area looked bright with a sea of golden yellow petals hanging from the branches of thick trees. The *Amaltas* was raining golden leaves and making the dark green of the flora run for cover. The slightest rustle of wind was enough to make the petals drop and the earth was carpeted with blazing yellow, with spots of green peeping through. The spectacle invited many discerning eyes and caused people to stop for minutes on end to enjoy the bounty of nature.

Soon summer came. Leaves began turning dark green and the flowers into fruit. The area was replete with a rich wheat crop and the menfolk seemed proud of their achievements. These were men of understanding, skilful and hard-working, and were content with what they acquired through sheer love of labour. The landscape all around was one of plenty: the fertile earth, the green foliage, the trees laden with fruit, and the sweet smell of ripeness pervading the atmosphere. The sound of honeybees reverberated with strange flurry of activity. Their artful skill, combined with the bounty of nature, produced the sweetest nectar in the world of creation that was inimitable for mere mortals. The golden wheat crop standing across the vast stretches of land matched the golden hue of the equally maturing rays of sun. The time was just ripe for harvesting, ushering in a milestone in the ever-changing cycle of nature.

And so it was in the house of Sardar Jot Singh, whose wife Subhagi was due to deliver a baby, who was not to be her first. The fear of unknown filled his home as the womenfolk sat by the hearth with their fingers crossed, keeping all the utensils full of hot water for the event. A feeling of uncertainty was writ large on everyone's face and their lips moved slowly as if in prayer. They had all been witnesses to the same sequence of scenes, almost a dozen times before, when an infant would be born to Subhagi, seeming perfectly normal; the baby would then hardly survive for more than a couple of days, a week at most. They soon shrivelled up, refused to suckle their mother's milk, then fell into deep slumber and never came out of it. The presence of the most experienced midwives was of no help and every time, no one could explain why Subhagi's newborn died as it did.

There was nothing to bring solace, let alone happiness, to the household of Sardar Jot Singh. None of the physical comforts afforded them by their financial well-being could fill the void left by the one thing they longed for, the most priceless treasure in the entire world: the full-throated cry of a newborn that soon gives way to a child's innocent laughter. He was approaching middle age and so was Subhagi, and it seemed like the fulfilment of their earnest desire to have a child had completely eluded them. Then hope showed itself once more as Subhagi found herself in the family way again. Sardar Jot Singh felt a fresh flow of energy rekindle in his veins. His waning lust for life had renewed itself with fresh vigour.

Life revolved around Subhagi who, once again, had become the centre of hope for the whole family. Her slightest wish was fulfilled as soon as it was uttered; great care was taken regarding her food; pictures of saints and lovely babies were hung on the walls of her room and elderly women were always around to lend their support. As the days passed and the time of her delivery came closer, everyone around Subhagi felt a surge of excitement and uttered fervent prayers to the Almighty that the couple be blessed this time.

The hot afternoon was moving towards dusk when Subhagi's labour pains started. The women laid her down on the bed and wiped her forehead while she grunted and tossed around. Subhagi clenched her fists, let out a sharp cry and the pain passed on this time. She rested for a while and, as she had always done during those other labours at the urging of her caregivers, slowly paced the room between the pains. It was soon dark and the women set up lanterns in the room and the adjoining veranda. They kept pots of warm water and tea ready.

The pains were coming more frequently now, ten minutes apart. Relatives and the neighbourhood women stroked her limbs gently while Subhagi let go of all restraint and screamed loudly through the fierce pains.

'*Jiji*, take it easy. It is only a matter of minutes now,' said Burfi, her sister-in-law, holding her hand.

'Everything will be alright this time,' said another voice.

'The fruit of hard labour is always sweet.'

'Pray to God for safe delivery!'

The screams continued for some time until at last silence fell. The shrill, squeaking cry of a child went up in the air which was fetid with the smell of birth. Subhagi heaved a long sigh and lay tired of the ordeal while Burfi fanned her face with a piece of cardboard. The rest of the women busied themselves with other chores.

Sardar Jot Singh, meanwhile, had been pacing the front courtyard of the spacious *haveli*. An elderly woman left her work at the labour room and walked up to him. Keeping her lantern down, she pulled him by the elbow, looked at him for a moment, her eyes wide and mouth breaking into a smile.

'Sardar Saheb, *mubarakan*! Your dynasty may still prosper and flourish. You have got a beautiful daughter. She looks like a princess. Mother and the baby, both are doing fine.'

'*Sacche Badshah, tera shukria* (God Almighty, I thank you!).' He knelt as if in a prayer, raising his hands towards the sky as a mark of his thanksgiving to the Almighty. Then Sardar Jot Singh got up slowly to his feet and went to the door. He wanted a glimpse of his daughter. Subhagi looked up drowsily at the face of her husband as he took the lantern from the floor and held it up against the face of the newborn, though from a distance. Sardar Jot Singh's eyes sparkled with joy as he looked at the sleeping face of his lovely daughter. Tender feelings surged through his chest as he looked lovingly at his daughter and then at the tired face of his wife.

'What do you want to call her, Subhagi?'

'*Ji, jo tusi chaho* (Let it be your choice)!'

'She is going to be my Kaushalya, my little gem. She will be brought up like a princess. *Allah mehar kare* (God's blessings are sought).'

'*Aapki marji ji* (Your choice),' said Subhagi, and dozed off.

Sardar Jot Singh ordered his men in his loud, thundering voice,

'*Sare shahar mein laddoo baton* (Distribute laddoos across the whole town). Unto my family an heiress is born.'

As Sardar Jot Singh's joy leapt, knowing no bounds, he could not help but think of how kind his life had been. He had started as an ordinary clerk in the local court. He had been a hard-working lad with an intense desire to always make something better of his life. An uncanny ability to sense opportunities at the right time and the foresight of turning the tide in his own favour were the hallmarks of his character. Age was on his side and so was his determination, as also his family's support along with a sense of pride and ambition to become someone important.

People from different walks of life visited the local *kachehri* (court) to sort out a whole range of issues and problems. Jot Singh, with his amiable manners and a natural inclination to help others, always lent a hand to anyone who came to him for simple, routine work. He became the most sought-after *mulazim* whom people trusted and depended upon. It was only a matter of time before Jot Singh established a whole lot of important contacts and started nurturing hopes of establishing a flourishing business of his own. Opportunities were aplenty and the enthusiasm of the boy elicited eager response of his acquaintances and friends. Jot Singh started considering various options, keeping in mind his own interests and entrepreneurial skills. His work in the *kachehri* had taught him to weigh the pros and cons of any situation before taking decisions that may have far-reaching consequences. He was comfortable with the idea of taking risks if it held prospects of doing well by dint of sheer hard work and a bit of luck.

Offers came his way, seeking his help to consider joint ventures that promised a whole lot of profitable situations. But Jot Singh was cautious and bid his time. He wanted to take charge of a good business opportunity, put all his energies into it and make it a profitable venture under his own supervision. Being worldly and coming from a respectable family, he could afford to wait, until fate intervened and opened opportunities to give shape to his dreams.

Soon that opportune time knocked on his door. He came to know of a printing press which was running on losses and was on the verge of closure. The prospects were dismal but challenging. Jot Singh toyed with the idea for some time, imagining a successful venture out of the printing press and battling contrary voices inside his own head. Eventually he made up his mind to accept the challenge and plunge into the fray. Things were not easy but Jot Singh was determined and industrious. Things began falling into place and he steadily made progress. Soon the foundation of 'J.S. Sant Singh Printing Press' was laid: it printed literature in Urdu and Arabic as well as sacred Hindu scriptures and texts like the *Gita* and *Ramayana*. The success of his venture quickly became Jot Singh's passion. His business was growing quickly and his books were in great demand. Success and prosperity added greatly to the confidence and personality of Jot Singh.

Jot Singh's was a large joint family and they all stayed together as was customary then. Their ancestral *haveli* was big, divided equally into five sections, where all his younger brothers, four in all, lived happily with their families. Jot Singh was the eldest of them all, definitely the most responsible, successful elder brother who liked to take good care of his younger siblings. He was an extremely caring elder of their *kunba*. There were a lot of children in the family who kept the old *haveli* bubbling with fun and activity; each brother's family had three or four of them. Jot Singh's household had remained barren of this blessing until now. It was not that Subhagi was unfit to bear children. After all, she had borne him children almost every alternate year but they wouldn't survive for one reason or the other. It was as if a curse prevailed on their life and he prayed for *waheguru's mehr*. They had taken recourse to religious blessings at many places and sought *mannat* from God but their dearest wish had remained unfulfilled so far. A *fakir* had once come travelling in the neighbouring area and happened to pass by their *haveli* when Jot Singh, who was coming out of his house on his way to work, saw him and invited him respectfully to grace his *haveli* and bless his cheerless home. Jot Singh and Subhagi sat at his feet with folded hands, their eyes full of pain and longing. They got up only when the *fakir*, taking pity on this childless couple and moved by their reverence, decided to bless them. It is said that a sage's blessings do not go to waste. In a couple of months Subhagi conceived. She bloomed even in her middle age.

And that, the parents believed, was how Kaushalya had come into this world.

2

As soon as Kaushalya was born, Jot Singh and Subhagi knew their daughter was a blessing. Their previously dull and insipid existence was awoken and their house came to life once again. The printing press began doing exceptionally well too and Kaushalya's birth was hailed as the coming of Lakshmi (Goddess of wealth) in the entire household. She became the prized possession of all those near and dear. The little girl who had inherited her father's vibrant disposition and her mother's sweetness of nature soon became common property of the ancestral *haveli*. Her name was shortened to Koshi and she became a great favourite of all the children of the *chachas* (uncles) living at the big house. She was growing up fast and showed an animated interest in everything that caught her eye. Her own household, for lack of company, was never enough for her ever-widening world of imagination and Kaushalya, after eating her food in the morning, would totter towards the other side of the *haveli*, which was always beaming with life and activity. She would then spend almost all her waking hours in the company of her cousins.

For Jot Singh and Subhagi it was a fresh lease of life; they glowed with happiness. Kaushalya, after all, had come to their life after their youthful phase had ended. The fulfilment of even the slightest of her wishes had become the most important purpose of their lives; they believed that she deserved nothing less than being treated like a princess. Jot Singh was already making plans about her future education, choosing the best school in the entire town, defying the common tradition of keeping a girl child inside the *dahliz* of her house. For Jot Singh and Subhagi, it was unthinkable to deprive their daughter of education for small as she was, Kaushalya already showed a keen intelligence and an innate curiosity to learn. It did not escape Jot Singh's attention, for example, that Kaushalya was very fond of accompanying her mother or other women of the house to the *Gurudwara* or temple when they went in the evenings to offer their prayers. People would often look curiously at little Kaushalya, dressed in beautiful frocks made only of the finest fabric, plush, *bosky*, *shanil*, or velvet with exquisite embroidery or sequins on them. She would listen attentively to the religious preaching, even if these were not really intelligible to her young mind. Anywhere she went, she showed a particular interest in looking at picture books or any kind of written word.

In time Kaushalya was admitted to Victoria School, the best English-medium school in the town, usually reserved for the children of privileged classes. Dressed in her latest English-cut frocks, her golden hair falling beautifully on her slender shoulders, little Kaushalya never lacked the eagerness to go to school. She loved playing with her classmates, reading and writing, looking at pictures; she had a vivacious laughter and was clearly the favourite of all the teachers. She was a keen student and had an extraordinary memory. Deciphering letters and gradually putting them together to make words came easily to her. Her sense of curiosity was sharp and grew stronger day by day. Her small world was expanding at a rapid pace and nothing delighted her more than the world of books and knowledge.

Every day during mid-break, Subhagi would come to the school to bring Koshi's food; usually milk, fruits, and some sweets. Seeing Subhagi, simply dressed and unassuming as she had always been, Koshi's school friends would ask who the lady was. The little girl, unmindful of the affectionate motherhood which is the greatest blessing of the world, would blurt out, 'You know, she makes food at our house!'

The general disparity about her manner of dressing and demeanour would clinch the issue and Kaushalya would send her mother back after eating her food. Days passed in absolute peace and happiness and it seemed like Kaushalya was living a fairy tale. Upon coming back from school, she would immediately seek out her cousins and spend the rest of the day with them. She was particularly fond of Prem Singh, the son of her uncle Sant Singh, and treated him like a real brother, looking up to him for protection and support. She would also tie a *rakhi* on his wrist. Prem Singh reciprocated the love, making everyone around them happy.

Months passed by, then a year, and then another and yet another. Kaushalya had grown up, turning nine on her last birthday, and her love for knowledge had not waned. She still spent all her spare time reading. She already had a library larger than that of anybody else in her neighbourhood, and she seemed to only want more and more books. It was, in general, learning that she yearned for and she sought it out in various ways.

The *Arya Samaj* was fairly active in that area, thanks to the influence of Swami Dayanand Sarswati. The town was caught up in its wake and teachings. Kaushalya seemed to be a child prodigy and would attend some of these *sammelans* at that age. Women's education was one of its main tenets and women were gradually starting to come out of the shadows of their homes. There would be large *sammelans* organized by the *Arya Samaj* every now and then where men of learning would talk about the teachings of the great social reformer Swami Dayanand and the need for social change. As Kaushalya would attend these gatherings, she would imbibe some of these *sanskars* and revolutionary ideas that were being soaked in the inner recesses of her mind.

It was interesting that while Kaushalya was witnessing the changing norms of orthodox society on one hand, her English-medium schooling exposed her to another level of education that gave her personality a new facet altogether. It was paradoxical and yet complementary. The opposing strands of tradition and modernity had woven a wide canvas in Kaushalya's young mind on which she was free to paint her own pictures using her own paintbrushes, her thoughts and convictions. All this had a great impact on her mind and her voracious tendency to lay her hands on all the books that came her way added to her storehouse of ideas. She was, quite certainly, the most well-read of all the children and siblings around her. She was like a star which shone the brightest; a source of inspiration for others, she wanted the younger ones to take to books and open their minds.

Jot Singh was immensely proud of his daughter and her character, already obvious to everyone around her at such a young age. He took special note of her intense curiosity to read and her achievements. Her word was the ultimate commandment for him and her wish, his greatest priority. There was nothing that Kaushalya wanted that wasn't procured immediately. She was given pocket money of one rupee every school day to buy and eat whatever she liked but the young girl would always come back with a handful of books instead.

One fine evening, Jot Singh happened to come home early and found Kaushalya, then twelve years old, immersed in her books. He sat with her and they talked about general things: the happenings around the family and relatives, and the family business, too. Slowly the conversation came to the kind of books

Kaushalya liked to read and Jot Singh could not help but be amazed at the depth Kaushalya had attained as a result of her constant drive for learning.

Jot Singh asked his daughter, 'Koshi, what else do you want? Is any wish of yours still unfulfilled? Tell me truthfully and I will fulfil it at once.'

Kaushalya fell silent for a minute, her eyes twinkling with joy and mischief. Her mind was weighing the options; she wanted to carefully measure her words before speaking them out before her father.

'Koshi, tell me,' coaxed Jot Singh. 'What else do you want? Don't hesitate.'

'Really, Father, will you agree to what I say or ask?' Kaushalya was hesitant.

'Ask once and see for yourself!' Jot Singh was eager to know of her daughter's wish.

'Father, I want to go to *Vilayat*.'

'Where?'

'*Vilayat*!'

It was clear to Jot Singh that Kaushalya's imagination had been stirred by whatever she had read about the foreign land. 'Whatever you wish, my darling, will be done!'

Kaushalya was overjoyed. Her father did not even hesitate before saying yes. But how could he? Kaushalya had been God's gift to him and that too, after a long wait. Her wish was sacred to him.

In the next days, Jot Singh quickly set out to do all the preparations for his journey with Kaushalya. The paperwork did not prove to be highly difficult given his influence and resourcefulness. Kaushalya too put her mind and heart into the preparations. New clothes had to be purchased, as were a whole lot of other things. Her mind was brimming with extraordinary ideas and her imagination soared with fantasies of the new lands she was about to see. She had been reading a lot of books and had formed her own perception of *Vilayat,* as she called it, or whatever had naturally occurred to her mind as a result of hearsay. She had always been an object of envy among the children of her age; given her circumstances and the privileges of being the only child of rich parents and the sole inheritor of her father's family business. Added to all these were her own abilities to read and write and develop literary capabilities. She had grown up in an extremely secure and affectionate environment and had been completely unaware of the ways of the world, as also the tough reality that lay outside the doors of her sheltered existence. She looked forward to all the new and varied experiences that would expand her mind's reach. The journey she was about to undertake with her father, for instance, had made her very eager. She grew more impatient for their departure and a peculiar restlessness had taken over her in the last few days. Her father had finalized almost all the arrangements and was busy giving instructions to his brothers who would be taking charge of the printing press in his absence. He wanted all loose ends tied up. He was, after all, not certain about when he and Kaushalya would be coming back home from their sojourn of unknown lands.

On the eve of their departure, as the house was abuzz with a mixture of excitement and anxiety, Jot Singh felt particularly tired and decided to take a nap.

'Father, why are you sleeping at this time?' asked Kaushalya.

'Oh, nothing, dear. Arrangements are all complete. Since we have to start tomorrow morning, I think I will take some rest before such a long journey.'

'All right, Father. I will go and meet my friends and cousins.'

'Take blessings of the elders too, Koshi.'

'Yes, Father!'

Kaushalya went towards the other end of the house while Subhagi came in to see her husband. 'Shall I get some milk for you, *ji*? You look very tired.'

'No, I am fine. Only my head aches a little,' said Jot Singh. He reclined on a pillow.

'Shall I massage your head with a little oil?' asked Subhagi, lovingly.

'No, no. I'll sleep for some time and it will be fine by evening.' Jot Singh ended the conversation.

'Take care of yourself, *ji*! You have a long journey ahead. Kaushalya is also very young.' Subhagi realised she was getting a little apprehensive.

'Don't worry, Subhagi, I'll be fine.'

Jot Singh eventually fell sleep.

An hour went by and Jot Singh continued sleeping, and then two. Subhagi checked on him twice and both times decided not to disturb him. The afternoon stretched towards evening and still there was no sign of Jot Singh waking up. He sighed and grunted occasionally in his sleep. It was evening when all the brothers gathered around Jot Singh, collectively beginning to worry about their brother's seemingly prolonged sleep. Sewa Singh, one of his brothers, felt his forehead and discovered that he was running a high fever. Jot Singh stirred and asked for water. After a draught or two, he dozed off again making no attempt to get up or talk to anyone.

'Let's call a *hakim*,' suggested Sewa Singh. One of the younger brothers immediately left to summon the *hakim* who lived about an hour away.

Subhagi took a small towel and some cold water, placing the piece of cold cloth on her husband's forehead and repeating the process every few minutes.

Soon the extended family had all got together. Jot Singh's fever showed no signs of retreating.

As his fever burned, Jot Singh started blurting out gibberish in his unconscious state.

Kaushalya, though too shocked to speak, was able to fathom the gravity of the situation. None of the home remedies helped, and her father gradually fell into a coma.

Unable to do anything else, all the relatives sat together and spoke in hushed tones.

Kaushalya had been sitting by her father's side, fanning a *punkah* and looking at everyone's grim face with a blank expression. Her face wore a faraway expression which was beyond the realm of fear but trying to penetrate into the sphere of eternity.

The night was falling and everything was still in the house. Everyone sat silent waiting for the *hakim* to arrive while Jot Singh lay still on his bed and Kaushalya held his hand in a tight grip.

By now, the relatives feared the worst and avoided looking at the peaceful face of Sardar Jot Singh.

The *hakim* arrived after a couple of hours, examined Jot Singh, and declared that he was dead. He told them that he had died of *Sarsam,* a kind of high brain fever.

Shrieks burst out in the house of Sardar Jot Singh, the head of his family, who had just passed away on the eve of his departure for *vilayat* to fulfil the wishes of his one and only dear daughter.

Fate had struck its first cruel blow upon the innocent life of Kaushalya. Her world, once simple and secure, had fallen apart in an instant.

Tears rolled down her tender face. She broke into uncontrollable sobs as Subhagi sat still, stone deaf and herself blind with tears.

3

The sky greyed slowly as the crowd gathered outside the house of Sardar Jot Singh. The atmosphere was one of shock and disbelief. Despite the stillness of the night and the paucity of time to send messages, word of the sudden demise of Jot Singh had spread like wildfire. People thronged Jot Singh's house, not bothering about looking dishevelled for having rushed out of their homes as soon as they heard the news. With his kind and amiable nature, Jot Singh had been extremely well-liked and respected among his clan and neighbourhood. People flocked to him in need and he had never been known to say no.

And now Sardar Jot Singh was no more. People found it hard to believe and prayed that the news had been wrong, even as they realized as they reached his house, perfectly quiet and still, that he was indeed gone. But how could it be? He had been in perfect health! He was preparing enthusiastically to go to *vilayat* with young Kaushalya! How could God be so cruel? What a twist of fate for the young daughter! What will she do? How would she come to terms with this tragedy? Would her fortunes remain the same? Who would take up the family responsibilities? Would the elders in the family set-up take the same care of her wishes and accord her the same status and privileges that she enjoyed during her father's time? What about Subhagi? Poor woman! She would have to be at the mercy of her brothers-in-law for running the printing press and for the sustenance of her household. Having a young daughter would add to her responsibilities. Everyone felt sorry for Subhagi and Kaushalya. Lightning had struck their lives. Who could understand the ways of God which would always remain incomprehensible?

Subhagi and Kaushalya sat by the side of Jot Singh's body, dazed, unable to control their tears. Her happy childhood flashed before Kaushalya's eyes: a doting father always ready to fulfil her slightest wish as soon as she uttered it; his ripened face, the flowing beard, the affectionate look, generous hands and an overprotective possessiveness. The memories danced in Kaushalya's mind's eye and she knew that life would never be—rather, could never be— the same for her again. Gone were the carefree childhood and the fancies of school days, recollections of what had been dearest to her. And then she had a glimpse of her own face, glowing with girlish beauty. The joys of the past came swimming back to her mind again and again and got mixed with the gruesome reality. She looked at her mother, sitting next to her, clutching her hand fiercely and turning to her for protection and reassurance. She imagined that her mother was probably undergoing the same feelings, traversing her own memory lane. Subhagi, well-stricken in years, had seen more of life. Her eyes looked dim and blurred, with an acute awareness of what Kaushalya's life would have been if Jot Singh had been blessed with a long life.

What brought them back to reality was the sight of Sardar Jot Singh's body lying in the front veranda of his own house. All the relatives and townsfolk were assembled to witness his last rites.

In the grey light of dawn, Sardar Jot Singh started his final journey. The house had filled up with people during the latter half of the previous night and the rituals were completed in the early hours of the morning. It was time for the last rites to be performed and the final journey to begin. All eyes were moist and hearts heavy at the enormity of the tragedy. The cremation ground was packed; everyone who could be there was present. 'It is a strange phenomenon, this death,' people whispered among themselves. 'When the soul leaves the body, no one wants to keep it inside the house for long, not even for a day. There is always an urgency to cremate the body as soon as possible. Any amount of love for the person is not able to keep it inside beyond a few hours. How strange but unavoidable!'

Sardar Jot Singh's remains were consigned to the fire and his name became a part of history. The morning passed and people came back to his house and sat on the floor in the front courtyard. Slowly the relatives started moving about the house, undertaking the necessary chores and looking after Subhagi and Kaushalya and planning the impending activities. The mourners sat in utter silence and gradually started departing after some time. They were replaced by another set of people who had come to offer their condolences. Kaushalya sat in the middle, as if still in a daze; she didn't like company in grief and would have preferred to be alone. Subhagi sat along with her, her head covered and eyes downcast. She wouldn't say a word or respond to any gesture. Silent though, mother and daughter had never felt so close to each other in the earlier days.

'Time,' people said, 'is the greatest healer!'

'Was it?' thought Subhagi.

Only time could tell. But could it also erode memories for all times to come? Subhagi could not think any more and closed her eyes. Kaushalya was her sole world now and her future, her utmost priority!

Sardar Jot Singh had left behind a large family; all staying in the ancestral *haveli* but in different demarcated parts of it. As such, Subhagi did not face an immediate sense of financial insecurity because Jot Singh's brothers were already working in the printing press, which was presently doing roaring business. The charge of the press was immediately taken over by his brothers who ensured that it functioned as smoothly as it had when Jot Singh was alive. Womenfolk at that time never used to step out of the house or interfere in a man's domain and thus Subhagi was hardly aware of the workings of the family's business. She was content in the knowledge that the press would continue and the legacy of Jot Singh would remain well protected in the family. She was confident that Kaushalya's future was secure.

Days passed and life was slowly limping back to normal. Subhagi realized how amazing it was that human beings adapt themselves to new situations and become tougher and more resilient in the process. Her world now revolved around Kaushalya, her well-being and interests. She had resolved in her mind never to let Kaushalya feel that she was deprived of anything because she lost her father early in her life.

Kaushalya, for her part, matured beyond her years following the tragedy. Slowly she began recovering her zest for life and insatiable thirst for knowledge. She plunged herself wholeheartedly into her world of books. Her longing for travelling had remained unfulfilled and she sought refuge instead in the world of knowledge. Nothing much had changed apparently for her; she did not want for anything she longed for, her lifestyle remained the same and so did her privileges. She continued with her schooling.

Years passed rapidly and Kaushalya turned fifteen. She had already completed middle school and she wanted to continue with her studies. She had blossomed into an extremely beautiful young girl with excellent taste for the finer things in life. Interest in books and an exposure to literature had lent a grace to her personality and sharpened her communication skills. Her literary abilities were penetrating and her understanding of the matters of the world was also insightful. She was certainly a cut above the rest among her peers and cousins. And when it came to lineage, she stood the highest above the rest; a rich heiress, an exceptionally beautiful, educated, accomplished young lady. Without doubt, Kaushalya was the priceless jewel of the family.

Subhagi would look at her daughter lovingly and admire her beauty and pleasant persona. For the past year or so, she was getting circumspect about Kaushalya's future, given the societal norms. Relatives and neighbours had been throwing hints that it was time for Kaushalya to settle down in matrimony and have a family of her own. Subhagi herself had been toying with the idea and was aware that she could no longer avoid the issue for long. It saddened her heart sometimes! Kaushalya was her only emotional bond and the thought of being away from her for the rest of her life brought tears to her eyes. Her life had lost its moorings after the death of Jot Singh and it was the face of her innocent daughter that had saved her from sinking into the pit of depression. But then, she thought, who has been able to keep a daughter forever in one's home? This is how life is and one can only pray for eternal happiness for one's daughter. 'May God give her everything she desires in life and let the future unfold itself in its normal course,' Subhagi muttered as she let out a deep sigh. Whenever Subhagi felt sad or worried about anything, her mind went deep into a reverie and she would see Kaushalya as a little baby who had brought immense joy in their household; the subsequent years filled with her childish laughter and her gradual growing up into a fine girl. Her heart filled with tender feelings for her daughter and she knew that she would give up her life if it could buy Kaushalya eternal happiness. 'Koshi! My dearest Koshi! May God give you all his choicest blessings! I must look for a suitable match for her…' Subhagi was still lost in her thoughts when Kaushalya, crossing from the other side of the *haveli*, came rushing towards her and gave her a warm hug.

'Look Ma! What have I got for you?'

'What is it, Koshi?'

'A book! I am going to teach you how to read and write.'

'Me? At my age?' laughed Subhagi.

'Why not, Ma? It is never too late! Swami Dayanand also believed in women's education and empowerment. Do you know that he described women as '*matri-shakti*' (power of mother)?'

'Koshi, it is time for you to teach your own young ones now. You should be getting married soon.'

'No, Ma, let me study a little more. Maybe my education will take me around the world at some point in my life!'

'Shhh... Koshi! Don't mention that again. You have not let go of that dream till now.' Subhagi's eyes were brimming with tears.

'All right, Ma, please don't cry. I will always do whatever you wish me to do from now on. I just don't want to leave you alone. I will take you along wherever I go.'

Koshi hugged her mother.

'We'll see about that later, dear. Let's have our food now. I have been waiting for you.'

Subhagi, controlled, walked quickly to the kitchen and was smiling, genuinely pleased by Kaushalya's answer.

'You know Koshi, when you were born, I almost wished I had a son who would inherit our legacy and would look after me in my old age. But I realized soon enough that a daughter can be company in a way no son can ever be. A daughter can be a real companion.'

Kaushalya was taken aback. She had never seen her mother articulate her thoughts in such a free manner before.

'Oh, Ma you are so sweet!'

'I am getting old, Koshi. And I have learnt to take things in their own stride rather well. I feel like talking and talking for the first time in many years. Old age can be a blessing only if things turn out the right way.'

Subhagi put food in Kaushalya's plate and wanted to feed her with her hands that day.

Taking their time, they continued talking to each other, bound by an intimacy that is possible only between two women whose fates were so intertwined with one another.

The two women had only each other to hold on to, whether in good times or bad. Such was their destiny.

4

Autumn foliage was slowly withering away or getting buried into the muddy earth and the air was ready for a change. The winter was harsh, keeping people indoors most of the time. The cycle of nature was naturally yielding to an imminent makeover when spring, the season of colours and sweet smells, would fill the motherearth with myriad hues and varied fragrance.

Spring was in the air and a huge area surrounding the *haveli* was now full of colour and the scent of flowers—roses, dahlias, and marigolds. The creepers planted along the outer walls of the house were climbing up aplenty, swinging their tender leaves and hanging several feet above the ground, providing a shade to the house from the warm rays of the sun. Their branches happily embraced bougainvillea vines that were standing tall along with them bearing brilliant magenta leaves. The atmosphere was rich and blooming though the house bore a haunted and dreamy look. It was the oldest and biggest house in the town, surrounded by numerous *pucca* houses on each side.

As the objects of nature bore a festive look, Kaushalya too was blooming. She looked forward to the new season, her imagination soaring to fanciful worlds where she was the object of interest of a male figure. Such thoughts, and more so their articulation, were anathema in an orthodox, normal household. But Kaushalya was different, having been born to her own, extraordinary circumstances. Her privileged upbringing and access to the male-dominated world of knowledge, along with uninhibited interaction with society like any head of a family, had always defied any attempts at conformity or stereotype.

One day, feeling a peculiar restlessness and a sense of anxiety, Kaushalya asked her mother, 'Ma, I don't know what is happening to me these days. I am unable to concentrate on anything!'

'I have been noticing, Koshi. It is all very natural, darling,' Subhagi said with a smile.

'My books also fascinate me only for a limited time. After that, I just want to dream and dream.'

'Oh, Koshi! I have been thinking of talking to you seriously for a few days now. I have been receiving many good offers for your hand, my dear. It is just the right time for you to have a family and children of your own.'

'But what about you? How can I leave you alone?' Kaushalya began getting emotional.

'I am not alone, Koshi. Your father's family is there to look after me. Don't worry about me. So tell me, Koshi, do you have any specific ideas about the kind of family you want to belong to or perhaps the kind of life partner you want. Don't hesitate at all. You will only help me and make my work easier.'

Subhagi took Kaushalya's hands in her own.

'Ma, nobody can decide that for me better than you. Education and knowledge have always held a superior interest to me than material riches. I believe that marriage would sustain better if life partners have similar interests and can relate intellectually too.'

'Koshi, my dear! I will certainly keep that in my mind. God bless you, my child!'

Kaushalya tiptoed into her room, feeling dreamy and elated. A whole new world of thoughts and dreams was unfolding itself in her mind and she felt her imagination encompassing new people and visions. She imagined herself draped in beautiful clothes trying to catch somebody's attention with both her beauty and brains. Dreams of a new home and new life were capturing her mind with an intensity she had never before known or cared for. It was as if some frenzy had overpowered her imagination and coloured her single-track mind with different hues of the life beautiful. Suddenly, life seemed interesting and fascinating and conjured up images before her that she would love to come true.

Youth, it is said, thrives on dreams and hopes; it fills people with fervour that makes them forget about life's tragedies. More so it was with Kaushalya, she who was blessed with such a powerful imagination. Subhagi's suggestions about her future had kindled in Kaushalya a love for the unknown and distant happiness that she believed was her future.

Offers poured in from well-respected and wealthy families for the hand of the beautiful Kaushalya. Subhagi found it difficult to make a decision. Many *khandani* families had many things: a good lineage, well-established businesses, sprawling houses, and responsible sons to look after the family affairs and traditions. Subhagi had been keen to finalize the talks of a marriage with a family where education or the acquirement of knowledge played an important role in their lives. Subhagi, though herself illiterate, had always understood and respected Kaushalya's immense love for books and knowledge and she knew that only a like-minded family would be able to understand Kaushalya's literary leanings. She missed her husband sorely at this stage of her life. If Jot Singh were around, she thought, decisions would have been easier and perhaps more balanced. She let out a deep sigh as tears welled in her eyes. She could not help but feel sad about soon letting Kaushalya go to join her future husband's home. 'Who says there is no difference between a son and a daughter?' she thought as she continued crying silently. 'Only if Kaushalya had been a son! She would have lived with me all her life. My old age would have been a boon with a flourishing business and an expanding family. My little grandchildren would play and live with me till the last breath of my life! Oh my dear Koshi! May God give you all the happiness in the world! May destiny give you everything that I could not!'

One day Subhagi received an unusual proposal for Kaushalya's hand. It came from a family that had ordinary, middle-class roots and whose eldest son was highly educated. Ram Chander, the handsome young man, was a BA Hons, with a first class first from King Edward College, Peshawar. The family's lack of excessive material wealth was amply compensated for by the zeal of the young man for education. Subhagi had little doubt that his interests would match Kaushalya's, inch by inch, and that she would be an equal to him in her relentless intellectual pursuits.

Of course, Subhagi also thought of the other aspects of the prospective match. Kaushalya had had a luxurious life and had never had to do any work at home. Would she be able to adjust in her future home? Subhagi knew she needed more time to think. She had never been so unsure. There was no precipitating hurry to begin with and such an important decision should be made to wait. Subhagi consulted the other members of the family, whose diverse views helped her see things clearer.

'Only if Kaushalya's father were alive,' Subhagi thought again and again. 'Who says nobody in the world is indispensable? It may be but then, it isn't the same ever or cannot be! The world no doubt moves on and the memory might dim with age but the void remains unfulfilled ever!' Subhagi's solitude had become her preserve where even Kaushalya had a limited entry.

Days passed and both families waited for the other to make a move. Meanwhile, talks were also ongoing with some other families; Subhagi wanted to widen her options. Utmost care was needed in selecting Kaushalya's future home. She needed to ensure that Kaushalya's future family would appreciate her for everything that she was and recognize her worth.

People say that when a girl is born, she brings her groom along, tied to her plait; that their union has already been willed and blessed by the Almighty, and all that human beings need to do is execute God's divine design. It was also believed, by Subhagi too, that all relationships were God's way of paying or repaying our previous birth's rewards and punishments of our *karma*. For Subhagi, losing her husband at a juncture when she needed him the most had made her a staunch fatalist and a believer in the divine, mysterious ways of God. She waited with bated breath for events to unfold themselves, show her signs along the way, and help her make a decision that would prove wise if not now, then in time.

And so did it prove right in Kaushalya's case. While there was no dearth of rich or educated families or boys, it was destiny in such cases that took one to the doorstep reserved for the person by the omniscient power. One by one, the prospective grooms fell by the wayside for one reason or the other. In some cases, the boys were no match for Kaushalya in any way; in others, their families' value system did not sit well with Subhagi and Kaushalya. Subhagi, mindful of the implications and consequences of her vital decision, did not want to make a decision too quickly. All divine signs seemed to be pointing to one direction. Only if she could be sure! Only if somebody could give her a guarantee of her daughter's happiness! 'Our ancestors were right,' thought Subhagi. 'Marriage is indeed a gamble and rebirth for the daughter. Who knows what the future will bring in its wake? The scales of happiness in a marriage are in the hands of the goddess of luck who is blind to any discrimination or favour on account of beauty, lineage, or riches.'

One day Subhagi sat down with Kaushalya for a talk.

'What is it, Ma?' asked Kaushalya. 'You have been thinking a lot these days.'

'I have been thinking about you, Koshi. I have received an offer of marriage for your hand from a family which is not very rich but their eldest son is exceptionally meritorious and has academic interests that can match your own.'

'What are your reservations, Ma?'

'You have lived a very comfortable life, my dear. There may not be small luxuries around. Would you feel a misfit?'

'Ma, how could I belong to a family which may not appreciate or approve my interests?'

'Koshi, you don't know how you have lifted a great burden off my shoulders!'

'Ma, I just spontaneously said what I felt. You have always encouraged me to speak my mind and follow my dreams.' Koshi leaned her head against her mother's bosom.

'May God always bless you, my child!' Subhagi hugged her lovingly.

5

The day of Kaushalya's marriage was drawing near and the wedding activities were gaining momentum in the *haveli*. Sardar Jot Singh's daughter, heiress to the family fortune, was going to be married and the festive mood was palpable. Happiness was beckoning once again at his doorstep and everyone was praying for a happy and prosperous marital life for Kaushalya. Her imagination, romanticized with youthful dreams, was making her hysteric with sweet visions of a new life. Everything around her seemed beautiful as she walked in and around the *haveli* with a spring in her step, wearing a shy smile of contentment on a face that radiated with inner beauty. Her present life had suddenly transformed itself into a moment of eternal spring. Kaushalya still believed in the possibility of happiness that may descend unobtrusively from heaven and warm her nest in the coming years.

Her trousseau had been chosen and prepared with utmost care. It was a feast for the eyes and inspired intense admiration from friends and relatives and anyone who saw it. The womenfolk of the household had let their imagination run wild on her bridal clothes and their skill with needlework had wrought exquisite embroidery on the entire ensemble. The best fabrics available in the market, whether Indian or imported, had found their way to the old *haveli* where elaborate plans for its adornments had been undertaken with love, enthusiasm and an urgency that is typical of a household that is about to marry one of their own. The trousseau was like a bevy of flowers; myriad colours and different shapes embellished with exquisite embroidery and sequin work. Fantastic strokes of gold thread made artistically had resulted in a splendour that lent a special charm to the chosen apparels. Kaushalya would cast a demure look at these garments and would be completely taken in by the lavish richness of the exercise, its radiant colours and the luxuriance of imagination. She would imagine herself wearing those dresses which, in a peculiar manner, seemed to express the attitude of her spirit and the range of her own imagination.

Kaushalya had always been ladylike; tall, with a perfect, elegant figure and a richness of complexion that spoke volumes about the feminine gentility of her lineage. Her dignified demeanour was impressive; her hair light-coloured, abundant and glossy. A delicate grace marked her entire persona and her beauty shone out in indescribable dignity. Anyone would have stars in her eyes in such circumstances and surroundings; so it was with Kaushalya. A look at her wedding wardrobe had sent her into a swoon and Subhagi's choice of her jewellery collection had brought tears to her eyes. There was pure gold; gems and jewels collected over a lifetime when Jot Singh had been alive and indulged Subhagi with numerous, precious gifts in the form of jewellery. Subhagi had brought out all her ornaments which would match Kaushalya's dresses and suit all occasions in her new household. These were exquisite pieces; heavy gold sets studded with rubies and emeralds for an ornate look. Kaushalya was particularly fond of the glittering *kundan* (burnt gold) set that outshone almost all the other jewels. This heavy neckpiece was made of six *kundan* strands with a stunning pendant of *polki*, aesthetically set in the middle. It could be worn with many *resham* saris and a few *lehangas* too. The lightweight gold sets for ordinary wear were also numerous and unique in their design.

These handcrafted pieces of exquisite craftsmanship had been designed with an indulgent eye and a richness of imagination that would suit all occasions and dresses.

The bangle box, too, was brimming with pieces of various shapes and designs to adorn Kaushalya's delicate wrist. Subhagi imagined Koshi wearing these lovely symbols of married life and experiencing bliss in her new life. These matched very well with the gold sets; the *jadau,* the *kundan,* the glittering pure or the oxidized gold one or the ones intricately set with rubies, diamonds, and emeralds. Worn with or without the gold sets, these were all artistic pieces that stood out for their sheer aesthetics. Complementing these were the numerous rings, set with precious stones in various designs and put together intricately by craftsmen to suit the dainty fingers of the heiress. Kaushalya had always been fond of the rings with big stones surrounded by various small gems. These had been carefully matched in design with various other earrings that were also an integral part of the gold necklaces. The choice of ornaments for Kaushalya was plenty and she could suit every occasion, mood, festival or apparel. Subhagi's affection had tried to match the range of her daughter's imagination. This was probably Subhagi's last responsibility towards Kaushalya in her maiden home and she would not fall short of anybody's expectations, especially her own. She had been relentless in her efforts to oversee all arrangements and vowed not to make any compromises. She had been happy assembling Kaushalya's trousseau and whenever she looked at it, her heart would beam with joy and pride. A silent prayer would always engage her mind and her hands would naturally fold themselves as an offering to the Almighty.

Every morning without fail, Subhagi organized a *havan,* offering prayers to ward off the evil eye and ensure the success of the auspicious occasion. Kaushalya herself was an eager part of the sacred morning rituals, invariably followed by the offering of food and old clothes to the poor whose blessings, in turn, would be solicited for the happy event.

Besides ornaments and jewels, there were other fine, precious things that Subhagi had taken keen interest in buying for her daughter's future home. She purchased various household items which she wondered if Kaushalya even knew how to use. 'This new chapter of Koshi's life,' thought Subhagi, 'must begin on a note of plenty. She must not want for anything or miss the comfort that she was used to in her parental home.'

Thus it was all bought for Koshi: home linen, furnishings, furniture, kitchen items, household ornaments, and the best clothes available in the market for all her would-be in-laws. Subhagi had thought of the likes of Kaushalya's would-be brothers and sisters-in-law when she had selected gifts, jewellery and clothes for them. Subhagi hoped that Koshi, with her warmth, gracious laughter, and intelligence, would quickly endear herself to her new family and would truly belong to them.

The flurry of activities was picking up every day and everyone in the *haveli* was busy, everyone except Kaushalya, who always sat quietly in a corner where she would eventually feel strangely restless. She was undergoing a myriad of emotions where her entire childhood would flash before her eyes. She would see the affectionate face of her father, doting on her every demand and making sure she had a carefree upbringing. As the moment of leaving her maiden home was drawing closer, she suddenly realised what she would leave behind: an entire phase where she had never known even a single moment of insecurity, pain, or neglect, where everything happened with her comfort and happiness in mind. All her young life she had known only affection, love and intense satisfaction, save for when her father had passed away. Yet even that episode had had a dreamlike quality and would be left behind for a long time to come like a faint or half-remembered dream.

Kaushalya thought about her mother, Subhagi, and her life and could not help but feel a tinge of sadness. 'Poor woman!' she thought. Her whole life had been spent in service of others, whether her husband, other family members and relatives. She had never thought of herself as an individual—ever. She belonged to that generation of Indian women who were not encouraged to do so, and instead were taught to put family over and above themselves. Willingly and happily they did so.

For Jot Singh, Kaushalya's mother was a pillar of strength and a source of steady support in all of his endeavours, especially the family's printing press business. Subhagi dealt with the loss of her husband sagaciously, keeping family ties intact and acting upon wise decisions regarding family business. As far as Kaushalya was concerned, her mother had never allowed her to feel the absence of her father in any way. She never let the trials she faced in life daunt her spirit; rather, she made those adverse situations render her more tenacious. After her father's death, Kaushalya more explicitly felt the calm strength possessed by her mother.

'Only if I could stay with my mother forever,' thought Kaushalya, 'only if I could serve her in her old age and be of some support, physically and emotionally.' Kaushalya felt helpless, strangely helpless, for the first time in her life. She found the enormity of the circumstances beyond her control. Nostalgia had overcome her.

Soon she heard a cacophony of voices nearby and saw people coming towards the corner where she had taken refuge to snatch some quiet time. She became the centre of attention once again as relatives and cousins gathered around her, vying with one another to bring her out of her sombre mood and apprise her of impending rituals for the would-be bride, as there was going to be a ceremony every day. Kaushalya's sombre thoughts were lost in the din of the various occasions; the engagement, the *geet*, the *haldi*, the *puja* and, finally, the marriage. The day dawned with the chirping of the birds. The sky looked lovely with the gentle rays of the sun spreading its crimson radiance. The air was soft and fragrant and the leaves looked glossy in the brilliance of the morning light. The arrangements had been completed the night before and the *haveli* itself looked decked up like a bride with fresh marigold blossoms.

Subhagi had seen to it that every place Kaushalya would walk on her marriage day would be decorated with flowers. Her room emanated a fresh fragrance in the morning; her toiletries would not be complete without the use of flowers. The passage outside her room leading to the verandah and the inner courtyard where the *vedi* was erected were exquisitely adorned with flowers of various hues; the house itself looked like a valley of flowers in full bloom. A long, open passage way was specially created from the *vedi* leading to the front door where a majestic palanquin lay in waiting for the bride. Flower petals of all colours were spread on the path that would symbolize Kaushalya's transformation from a young maiden to a ravishing bride and a new wife.

Fresh flowers and human tears marked the wedding day of Jot Singh's Kaushalya who was all set to traverse the path of the extraordinary destiny laid out for her by the Almighty.

6

Kaushalya's new home was a *pucca* structure, though made of mud and tartar. The palanquin had stopped in the street before a square brown house that looked rather damp with yellow flowers and leaves that were used to decorate the house in an old-fashioned way. The narrow pavement had some parched grass and mud. Out of the thin veil of the palanquin, Kaushalya saw that her new home was merely a larger version of similar-looking mud houses that were unprotected from the vagaries of changing weather. The settlement comprised about one hundred houses and a large number of people had huddled together to welcome and catch a glimpse of the beautiful bride, who they all heard belonged to an influential and wealthy family. Clad in colourful clothes, the women of the house and the neighbouring huts gathered outside the door eagerly to help Kaushalya come out of the *palki* and observe the rituals associated with the *grih-pravesh* of the newlywed. Singing folk songs and *badhai* of marriage ceremony, the women led Kaushalya to the front porch and asked her to immerse her hands in mustard oil, brought before her by the elder daughter of the house. Kaushalya did as she was told and then put her hands on the front door leaving behind an impression of her delicate hands; a ritual considered auspicious before entering a new home and life.

The traditional welcome thus over, she was led inside by the jubilant ladies amidst a lot of noise and laughter. After crossing the small courtyard, Kaushalya was taken to her room and made to sit on a charpoy and offered sherbet and sweets. Feeling shy but curious, Kaushalya tried to lift her *ghunghat* a bit and have a look at the women who were now her relations and an integral part of her life and family. She beheld simple but affectionate faces, eager to please her and serve and make her feel comfortable and at home.

It was now time for the welcome ceremony of the bride or the *muh-dikhaai* to take place. The elderly women explained to her that every Indian bride, on entering her new home, is accorded this traditional welcome when each member of the family as well as the close relatives bestow her with gifts of jewellery or clothes, have a look at her face, and introduce themselves. The occasion goes a long way in thawing the ice with the new relatives and taking away the initial hesitation and feelings of unfamiliarity in a new setup. Kaushalya realized that she now belonged to a large family: two brothers-in-law and three sisters-in-law, besides other distant relations. It had always been Subhagi's wish to marry her daughter into a large family where she would feel secure in the warmth of an affectionate household. Kaushalya had been her parent's only child and longed for siblings of her own. As luck would have it, she was now part of a family that was not materially rich but compensated for that with its value system and an affectionate and caring attitude. Kaushalya was showered with gifts by her mother-in-law, brothers- and sisters-in-law, who hovered around her to see to her needs and make sure that she was absolutely comfortable. Kaushalya was overwhelmed by their love and concern. She was particularly touched by a thoughtful remark by her mother-in-law, who said to her, '*Beti*, I have given you my son in *muh-dikhaai*, take good care of him; take good care of the family too because you are so well-educated. For us you are like the avatar of Saraswati and Laxmi both. It is our good luck that you have come to our house.'

Feeling choked with emotion, Kaushalya got up and touched her mother-in-law's feet as a sign of respect. Geli Bai hugged her, holding her tight against her bosom.

Kaushalya was exhausted and wanted to escape into her own world of thoughts and rest. She also wanted to have a view of the house and her own room where she was expected to now live for the rest of her life. Though she felt pampered by such a loving reception in the family fold, Kaushalya's mind was in a tizzy as the difference in their family status and living conditions gradually started sinking in. The differences were obvious as she gazed about the courtyard and the adjoining rooms. Their simplicity or, worse, dismal state, dawned on her: the awkward shape of the inner house, the plain washing area, even the carelessly dumped water pitcher in one corner. She could smell the odour of the cattle too and she guessed that a cow was tied up at the rear of the house. She heard a dog's barking in the background.

'Oh, God!' Kaushalya shuddered. She felt dismayed at the strangeness of the house and wondered if there was even enough space for all the things that her mother had given her for this union. Kaushalya remembered that her mother, who had perhaps visited this house a couple of times before the marriage, had taken note of everything that this house needed and had ensured their availability to see to her daughter's wants and needs. Subhagi had gone out of her way to give Kaushalya a lavish dowry, even by the standards of their own house. 'But will they be used here, where living is so rustic?' Kaushalya thought. Her mind was in a state of extraordinary activity when she heard whispers among those present inside the house.

'Where do we keep all that?'
'They have given a lot!'
'We have to find a way out soon!'

Kaushalya's mother-in-law, Geli Bai, came up with a solution. 'Let's keep the things at our immediate neighbour's house for the time being,' she said as she wiped the sweat off her forehead with her *pallu*. She then gave instructions to her daughters Lakshmi, Chetni, and Hukmi, to make arrangements for food for the family, while she herself led Kaushalya to show her to her room.

Kaushalya discovered that her room, though small, was the best one in the house. The antique furniture was covered in pale brocade and the linen on the bed had a rather musty smell. There was a table and a chair kept neatly on one side. And on the other side, easily the best part of the room, stood huge wooden racks filled with books so neatly arranged that you would like to grab one and read.

'These are your husband's constant companions, *beti*,' said Geli Bai. 'If you will have any competition, it will be from these. You will have a tough time snatching Ramchander from these!'

'I, too, love books, *Maji*,' replied Kaushalya. 'They will also be my companions. We will all live together in harmony.'

Geli Bai heaved a sigh of relief as she came out of the room.

Alone at last, Kaushalya sat on the bed and looked around. She felt peace and contentment descending upon her as she looked at the family relics and thought that these were going to be her friends for a lifetime. She felt a little uneasy; she had always heard that a new bride should feel coy and demure but Kaushalya felt no such emotion. Strangely enough, she felt like an equal partner to her husband, in marriage, mind, and spirit. She felt nervous when she thought of Ramchander, 'What would he be like?' She hoped their common love for reading would quickly make them comfortable with one another.

'The way to his heart has to be through his mind,' thought Kaushalya as she removed the heavy pieces of jewellery from her forehead and adjusted her heavy bridal garments. 'I don't know how to cook or do other household chores. Maybe I'll learn later. But the initial bonding has to be on account of books. They have been my friends since childhood and I guess the same is true for him, too.' Kaushalya's mind raced.

The house had been in the throes of a lot of excitement and activities since the new bride had arrived. Kaushalya could hear the jubilation outside her room and savoured her solitude. It had been a hectic day for her, after all. She reclined on her bed and tried to empty her mind of all meandering thoughts. But the enormity of her loss dawned on her with a clarity she did not understand before. Putting her hand over her eyes, she tried to suppress a sob that choked her throat and blinded her eyes but it was irrepressible and she gave in. She missed the comfort of her own home, the feeling of plenty and security. She missed her mother, the familiarity and routine, the *haveli*. She missed her cousins! Kaushalya was homesick. The roller-coaster ride of her emotions lulled Kaushalya to sleep. Soon Lakshmi, her eldest sister-in-law, gently woke her up as it was time to eat.

Kaushalya quickly realized how much better she felt after that nap. She eagerly came out of her room, with her earlier homesickness and troubling thoughts composed. She greeted everyone respectfully and sat down to a simple but hearty meal, which she enjoyed despite feeling quite conscious as they all viewed her with intense curiosity. She knew that to them she was an enigma; an interesting *bahu* who can inspire awe and be a role model. She was beauty and brains combined; like a dream come true for them. They looked at her with admiration, offered delicacies prepared specially for her, folded their hands in respect and made her feel extremely welcome in their simple home.

Kaushalya, deeply perceptive of their affection, responded gently and with a tender grace typical of a new bride. Being a *bade ghar ki beti* as well as the *badi bahu* of a middle-class household gave her more responsibility. She vowed to be one of them and fulfil their expectations, to make her love larger than their financial disparities. They seemed sincere and kind-hearted and Kaushalya began imagining ways of giving back their warm embrace. Education was one, she thought. She would work to bring education to the whole settlement. She would take care of them, their interests and their future, and along the way, she hoped, her husband would support her. She was aware of the need for her to be patient with her relatives, to not criticize anyone for their lack of education. She knew that the desire for change must come from their own hearts first. 'Perhaps God has willed me to be the medium for their wider awakening,' she mused.

All evening Kaushalya was pampered by her in-laws and started feeling at home. But she longed to have a glimpse of her Prince Charming!

7

Late at night, Kaushalya heard footsteps treading the courtyard, sounding closer and closer towards her. Drowsy and confused from her interrupted sleep, she listened to the door as it creaked open and heard someone fumbling in the dark through the inner door panels. She hurriedly sat up, drawing her *ghunghat* a little on her forehead. The earthen *diya* lying on the side table was still flaming and spreading a dim radiance that lent a charming glow on her face.

'Sorry to keep to you waiting, Kaushalya!' said a male voice, husky and with a tone which sounded so familiar that it made the awkwardness of the moment go away. 'I am sure the hectic day must have tired you out by now.'

'No, no, I am fine!' muttered Kaushalya, fidgeting and attempting to conceal her nervousness.

Kaushalya stole a quick glance at the profile of the man who was supposed to be her soulmate. Ramchander stood near the table and was looking outside through the window. He looked tall and healthy. There was a determined sharpness in his eyes; an air of purposefulness around him gave a force to his personality that Kaushalya had never felt before with anybody else. She felt his eyes on her; they expressed a strange earnestness, compassion, enthusiasm; they seemed gentle yet full of life. Kaushalya was mesmerized. She sat rooted, waiting for the next part of the conversation. He turned around, came near the bed and said to her, 'So I have heard you can read and write well and are very fond of books, is that correct?'

'*Ji, haan* (Oh, yes)!' replied Kaushalya, betraying her enthusiasm. 'I never had brothers or sisters of my own. Loneliness at times drove me to books which have been my faithful companions in moments of solitude.'

'They make the best of friends, don't they?' Ramchander took her hands in his own.

His electrifying touch sent Kaushalya into a swoon and she could barely speak. 'I have been having a look at your books during the day. They are so neatly arranged.'

'Literature is fascinating. It may combine geography and history and can transcend through times, barriers of caste, creed or religion.' He admired the rings on Kaushalya's hand and smiled.

By then Kaushalya's nervousness had disappeared and she felt her normal self once again. 'Literature looks deep into human nature and portrays it like nothing else can. Characters become puppets in the hands of the writer and he highlights different traits and human instincts by way of their characters.'

The night was young and so were the newly-weds. They had fallen in love at first sight and tonight, on their first conjugal night, their bond was obvious to them both. Even as they talked about books and reading, they shared an intimacy that was special. The light of the moon filtered through the window and fell gently on their cot, lending an aura to both their figures and making everything around them minutely visible too; the quaint objects of domestic use, the antique chair and the centre table, a faded table lamp, the book racks and the carefully kept volumes of books and a family picture on the freshly painted wall. The candlelight added to the ethereal effect, mimicking the smouldering of a fireplace. The result was a dream-like setting between dream and reality.

Kaushalya and Ramchander stood next to the window, hand in hand, enjoying the cool breeze and watching the moon, watching each other. She looked at him coyly with the thrill of subdued joy. He reciprocated with a tender glance.

'You can lighten the burden on your hair, Kaushalya. Remove these clasps and ornaments that bind your hair and feel free like this breeze. Should I help you?'

'No, no, I'll do it myself,' whispered Kaushalya. She slowly untied her long plait and removed the adornments. She felt relieved. As she removed the last of them, the embellished *dupatta*, her hair fell upon her shoulders like a cascade till her slender waist, dark, rich, glossy and abundant, lending a charming softness to her features. A crimson flush glowed on her cheeks and her youth exuded the richness of her beauty and the essence of womanhood. Ramchander, filled with awe for her exquisite beauty, vowed that he would never be able to live without her companionship any longer. He felt truly blessed, in mind, spirit and heart. His heart was filled with passion for his new bride.

'Kaushalya!' he said, pressing her hand and drawing her near.

'*Ji, haan!*'

'You are beautiful...ravishing, indeed!'

Kaushalya stood demure, spellbound.

'Kaushalya, I'll take care of you in the best way I can. We all will see to it that you do not want for anything in your new home. We may not be able to give you the lavish comforts of your parental home but we'll make up for that with our love. Do not hesitate to ask for anything you need, dear. It will be easier for us if you tell us what you like or dislike.'

'I just want to be a part of you. I want nothing more than to belong to your family,' said Kaushalya.

'Well, my dear, you have me and my whole family with you. I am yours entirely. All of my flesh and blood and spirit! I will always belong to you and to nobody else.' Ramchander's voice choked with emotion. 'It's a beautiful night, Kaushalya. Let's make it perfect by making a vow to be forever sincere and loyal to each other.'

'I am fortunate to be here with you and will always belong to you, come what may. I own you and your family with all my mind and heart.' Kaushalya's tears of joy streamed down her cheeks. She bent down and tried to touch his feet but he quickly stopped her. 'Oh, no, not at all! You are my equal, dear. In you I have found a soulmate, a companion with whom I can share everything, all my thoughts and ideas that I have kept confined for so long. You are an asset in my life. You are somebody who can share my responsibilities completely, with your capabilities and a liberal mindset. Kaushalya, I will treasure you in the deepest recesses of my heart. You are the breath of my life, my entire being, my dear. Come here, come to me entirely now,' whispered Ramchander in his deepest voice and drew Kaushalya near. 'Let us make each other happy and and both our families too.'

Kaushalya was deeply moved by his humility and clung to him wholeheartedly. She found strength, courage and kindness in her man; he was like a sought-after refuge from an indifferent world.

And the newly-weds became lovers. They fell asleep in each other's arms, lost in the silent darkness of the night.

The day dawned for Kaushalya and Ramchander with the chirping of birds and sounds of life outside in their courtyard. The room's curtains were still drawn, keeping the sunshine out, and all they could see of each other was their silhouettes. Kaushalya got up and walked to the window to have a look outside. The sun had risen beyond the land, making the sky look beautiful in the pure light of its rays. Ramchander joined her, and for a long time they merely stood by the window, admiring the freshness of the morning sky and the specks of grass scattered in between the houses. They looked at each other and smiled contentedly with the newfound joy of newly-weds. They were aware of their bond and felt blessed by the grace of God.

'I will have to go now, Kaushalya,' said Ramchander and laid the back of his hand against her cheek as she looked at him with adoring eyes. She wondered if he could see the bit of impatience in her eyes.

'Take care of yourself during the day. I don't expect you to like everything immediately but I will appreciate it if you would understand that here we live a very simple and carefree life. What is most important for us is that we are in the company of our loved ones. Try not to be over-sensitive about anything that may not come up to your expectations, dear.' Ramchander was wonderfully discreet but affectionate. 'My mother was widowed early, as you know, and she made sure to raise us with simple needs. She taught us to live with honesty and dignity, even in the most adverse of circumstances. She inculcated in us the right values and the importance to live in harmony and with love towards each other.'

'*Ji*! I do understand very well. I also lost my father when I was very young. Though she was well cared for financially, I saw how my mother toiled through a lonely existence and faced the tough task of raising me as a single parent. In her life I felt the courage and tenacity of being a woman and I will respect your mother as much as I respect mine.' Kaushalya held his hand tightly and snuggled near him. 'I must ask you though, to give me some time to adjust.'

'You have all the time in the world, dear, and me as well.' Ramchander looked deep into her eyes as they cuddled each other. He would have wanted to stay that way longer but realized they had to join the rest of the family. Kaushalya also prepared to step out of the bedroom.

She felt ready to begin her new life in her new home. It would be wonderful, she thought, to make a snug nest of her own where everyone could live with an understanding of one another's needs and interests. Having a large family made it a real home in the true sense. Constraint of space in her new home would make certain things difficult but she resolved to make it a happy place. For the first time in her life, she realized, she had thought about the convenience of her immediate family instead of her own. And that too, on her own accord!

Kaushalya stepped out of the bedroom and looked around. Wearing a bright red sari and matching jewellery, she looked regal in the milky brightness of the morning. Glowing with the unique happiness of a new bride, she stood quiet for a few moments as she viewed the house from an opposite angle than what she had seen the previous day. It had a square, old-fashioned structure and the mud coating gave it a brown tenor. She was facing a large, open *aangan* which was the hub of activity in the morning. Her eye caught sight of a small pillar-like pedestal that was sporting a plant or a shrub with leaves falling all around it. She saw Geli Bai, her mother-in-law, standing behind it with her face towards the front door, humming a tune and offering water to it with folded hands. With a keen look Kaushalya realized that it was a *tulsi* plant, the worship of which is considered sacred in Indian households in the mornings.

'Wow,' admired Kaushalya, 'how traditional!'

From the corner she heard the crackling of fire and turned to see it. She discovered some billowing smoke and the peculiar odour of a hearth coming. There was Hukmi, her youngest sister-in-law, lighting the mud *chullah* and putting wood sticks deftly in its hollow bottom and resuscitating the nascent fire with her own breath through a long stick like an iron rod. Not far from there sat Chetni, her middle sister-in-law, making some dough, among other things, which Kaushalya guessed was meant for the menfolk's breakfast before they had to leave for work. She then spotted her eldest sister-in-law, Lakshmi, coming from the rear door carrying a big bucket of milk and hurrying to where Chetni was making food.

'How romantic!' Kaushalya thought. She could not blame herself for what she realized were her romanticized notions of the village and the lives of its people. After all, she had seen these scenes in her books, and she was a young, inexperienced *bade ghar ki beti* to boot. She gazed intently at what appeared to her as a spectacle.

'What a close-knit family and what bonhomie among one another!' she thought, as her gaze fell on the big cot lying near the front door. She saw Ramchander engaged in serious conversation with his younger brothers, Ganpat Rai and Arjun Dev, who were listening intently.

The mere sight of Ramchander once again catapulted her into her world of fantasy. 'Was this a dream or a dream-like reality?' wondered Kaushalya. 'I belong to them now. They are mine, wholeheartedly.' She remembered her vow. As she made an effort to come forward, the rustle of her dress and jewellery caught everybody's attention and Geli Bai, along with her daughters, rushed to welcome her.

'Come, *beti,* join us for breakfast. Why, you are up very early!'

Kaushalya knelt to touch her mother-in-law's feet. Geli Bai returned the respect and warmth with a blessing, '*Sada suhagan raho, dudho nahao, puto falo* (May God give you eternal marital life, with lot of sons and prosperity!).'

Kaushalya was deeply touched. And yes, she thought, these were her realities now. All else had vanished like a dream.

8

Before she realized it, she and Ramchander had been married for two years. Time seemed to fly as the two of them lived in marital bliss. Kaushalya thrived in her conjugal abode, filled with affection from her new family and love and understanding between her and Ramchander. While the household was run efficiently by Geli Bai and her daughters as before, Kaushalya was given enough opportunity to follow her own interests and adjust accordingly. She was not entrusted with any responsibility in the home management nor was she expected to do any household chores. Of course, out of her own will, she had always happily extended a helping hand.

Kaushalya, ever mindful of their generosity and goodwill, had taken to her new life with a wholesome frankness. Each day had cemented her emotional bond with them; she no longer felt bothered by the lack of spaciousness of the house or the family's modest financial means. She came to hold the view that happiness and money were not necessarily interdependent.

She thought of surprises, new ways of educating, entertaining and helping her family. Besides reading, Kaushalya had grown very fond of knitting; she had gifted them beautiful mufflers, scarves, and socks on various occasions and her skills had become the talk of the neighbourhood. Often she received visitors to their house who wanted to have a look at her fantastic creations with wool and thread. Kaushalya would always have some knitted items ready so she could gift them to the small children who came visiting. Women marvelled at her skill with needlework, too. The simple and coarse linen of the house was replaced by soft quality linen and embroidered with exquisite, beautiful designs and motifs. There were cushions, tablecloths, pillow covers, *dupattas* and handkerchiefs, all of them boasting of her skill and deftness of fingers. There was one piece that was closest to Kaushalya's heart: an embroidered tablecloth for Ramchander's table where he kept his books and papers and which was her first gift of love to her husband. She had also given him a crocheted covering bordered with lace which he used for his book racks.

Over the two years of being husband and wife, Ramchander had grown even more proud of Kaushalya's virtues and skills. It was in Kaushalya that he had found a mate for his intellectual interests. They loved engaging in discussions on social, political, and academic issues, and Kaushalya proved herself to be highly capable in sorting out her opinions and offering analysis. Ramchander was overjoyed; in the person of his lovely bride he had found an equal partner, a soulmate, and a dear friend, all in one. Kaushalya had also never failed to show respect and affection towards his family.

She had also, in the past two years, made changes to the house that gave it a more vibrant look. Every time she thought of some new thing to do, she would politely ask her mother-in-law for approval. '*Maji*, can I change this setup a bit?'

'Yes, Kaushalya, it is your own home, *beti*. Do with it whatever you want. And do adjust everything that your mother gave so lovingly. We have chanced upon a *hoor-pari* (beautiful damsel). We feel so blessed indeed.'

And so Kaushalya made adjustments here and there, giving the small *baithak* a fresh perspective. The small details made a lot of difference: pictures on walls, earthen lanterns on small tables in the main corners, beautifully laced curtains, even book racks placed at an angle that provided cover to private quarters. She also made the *aangan* more habitable and appealing to the eye. Barring the utility area that was used as an open kitchen and the frontal *tulsi* pedestal, she put a mix of cots and easy chairs on the big, unused side area, with a centre-table in between, and made it more people-friendly. She used *chatais* and small druggets to enliven the area. She removed the carelessly kept earthen pitcher and the *surahi* from the front door and kept them properly in the corner near the indigenous kitchenette. This arrangement was not only convenient but also took away the emptiness of the corners. Kaushalya put a colourful drugget in front of the book racks, along with a few cushions that immediately appealed to the eye and invited the guests for a casual look. The books gave character and soul to the otherwise routine interiors of a pastoral setup.

Geli Bai and the rest of the family were thrilled. Ramchander, too, appreciated it. 'It does look a lot better,' he said. 'I am amazed how the very same things can make the place look either beautiful or ugly. Kaushalya, you have come as an angel in my home and in my life. I am indebted to you indeed.' His praise filled Kaushalya with happiness and her love for her partner increased manifold.

Spring had come and the blades of grass were slowly turning green. A palpable change could be felt in the ground and the sky. Spots of colour could be seen raising their heads at random in the form of flowers and the days were being filled with a languorous stupor enhanced by the amorous calls of the birds. The dawning of the new season heralded the beginning of new life all around.

Kaushalya, too, felt a change coming over her as new desires welled up within her with a force she couldn't control. She felt a life energy taking hold of her body and emotions. The physical vibrations, she noticed, were penetrating deep into her consciousness as well and even her face, her cheeks showed a crimson glow these days. She surfed with new energy and enthusiasm. Geli Bai was quick to notice this and asked her daughters Lakshmi, Chetni, and Hukmi, to take special care of their *bhabhi*.

One day as Kaushalya was reading a book, her sisters-in-law sat close to her and began teasing her. Chetni said, '*Bhabhi*, why, you look so lovely and happy these days! It seems our brother is taking good care of you.' Lakshmi chimed in, '*Bhabhi*, tell us some good news, will you?'

Kaushalya was amazed that her sisters-in-law knew. She blushed and tried to evade their eyes. She had wanted her husband to be the first to hear the good news and the revelation before her sisters-in-law had caught her off-guard. She felt extremely coy, though happy in the warmth of their affection and understanding.

Geli Bai was overjoyed. She knew that a baby was on its way and that Kaushalya needed all of their care and support. She had a new reason to celebrate! Every morning she blessed Kaushalya profusely, fretted about her health and gave instructions to prepare food and delicacies that would suit her daughter-in-law's tastes and mood swings. Subhagi's visits, too, increased. She ensured that Kaushalya remained in the best of health and spirits.

Days passed and Kaushalya started feeling the growth of the new life inside her body. She was nauseated every morning, and the daily morning sickness would then pave the way for a period of inertia and boredom. She did not move around as much as she used to, and she wondered whether her increasing immobility was making her the centre of advice (and gossip!) amongst the neighbouring women.

And so Kaushalya sent word out to them that she would like to teach small children their alphabets and some other general knowledge. Children could come to their house in the afternoons after school and Kaushalya would love to help them with their lessons and tell them stories about the lives and adventures of some of the greatest patriots and warriors from history. All the fascinating tales that she had read in her childhood came back to her from memory. And the children would listen in rapt attention. Her stories, interesting and told in her gentle manner, made her a favourite of all the children in the neighbourhood. Kaushalya was filled with a deep sense of contentment and happiness, feeling totally at peace with herself and her surroundings.

Days came by fast and soon Kaushalya could no longer recognize herself in the mirror. She didn't like how she looked, 'like a bloated balloon,' she thought, unattractive and different from her old self. Quickly, though, her heart would fill with only the most tender of emotions for the new life growing within her, made of her own flesh and blood.

Kaushalya didn't have to wait too long. The baby was born in due time without much difficulty and to the utter delight of both the families. It was a healthy baby boy who announced his arrival with a loud cry, more like a roar. Jubilation broke out in Geli Bai's house. Relatives and neighbours expressed their happiness by beating drums and breaking into a dance. Womenfolk assembled in the *aangan*, procured a *dholki* from a nearby house and sang songs of *badhai* and prayers for long life for the infant. Subhagi was ecstatic. A male heir had finally come to her family, something her beloved Jot Singh had longed for when he was alive. The newborn's aunts, Lakshmi, Chetni, and Hukmi, busied themselves making *laddoos, kheer,* and other sweet dishes for the guests who quickly streamed in to congratulate Geli Bai and Subhagi on the birth of their grandson. Kaushalya, though drowsy with exhaustion, was aware of all the sounds of merry-making around her. She cast a look at her sleeping infant and saw his strong-looking limbs, black hair, and chiselled features. She thought he was fair like her, and he had taken his overall appearance from his father. She forgot all the pain of childbirth and her heart welled up with a strong instinct that she knew was typical of a new mother. Kaushalya loved the life that lay before her, so innocent, sombre and sound in sleep. Her heart was overwhelmed. She softly uttered a prayer of thanks to God Almighty for such a gift of love. She marvelled at the miracle of procreation and nature's bounty.

The child was named Ved Prakash. He lit up every corner of the house with his funny antics and sheer energy. He grew into a robust, healthy child, with obviously strong bones and a perfect posture. Before Kaushalya realized it, he was two years old, already showing that thoughtful, casual look that he had inherited from his father. Kaushalya loved him for it, and for many other reasons besides. It seemed like nothing else existed for Kaushalya; he was the centre of her universe. She enjoyed motherhood to the hilt. Ved Prakash was the object of her future hopes, the disciple on whom she could experiment with her educational ideas and vision. She couldn't take her eyes off him. She made him sit with her when she did *havan* in the morning, told him stories of warriors and heroes, knit for him countless beautiful sweaters, socks, and caps. She designed his baby linen, wove intricate embroidery on his clothes, and gave him a piggyback ride whenever he wanted. She had no apparent desire unfulfilled and she found her home almost like a shrine: she was the devotee.

And then, at times, Kaushalya also thought wistfully about her parental home, the one she loved dearly and was her world until a few years back. When Subhagi, her mother, came for a visit, the memories became fresh too. At such times, she would look at Subhagi's face and then understand a mother's heart. She also came to understand why Subhagi frequently visited her home. She had discovered, with the coming of her own child, that the bond of a mother's love was strong and unbreakable, that it survived many years, generations even, and remained immeasurable.

9

At times Kaushalya felt trapped. Motherhood brought with it various mundane concerns and limitations and her life had changed in many ways after the birth of Ved Prakash. Yet she always ended up with the happy discovery that she would not exchange motherhood—and the never-ending cycles of demanding and receiving love—with living a dull and stagnant life. While books stimulated her mind and taught her many things, raising her child filled her heart and soul with contentment. It was a meaningful, interesting life that she lived, ensconced in Ramchander and Ved Prakash. She shared an almost mystical relation with them. She felt she was in paradise. Raising Ved Prakash had also brought her closer to the family, as she depended on them more and more for the smallest of things where Ved Prakash was concerned. They offered her advice on various things, from her own diet to how to raise Ved Prakash well so that he would grow up to be a healthy and well-mannered human being.

Ramchander, too, partook of the happiness that embraced the family upon the arrival of Ved Prakash. Though overtly calm, Ramchander would occasionally pick up his child and play with him.

'What a naughty child, Ma!' Ramchander told his mother as he thrust him on her lap one day. 'Is he a pleasure to live with or a nuisance? He must be giving all of you a hard time. I think he takes after me!'

'Oh he's an angel,' Geli Bai replied as she gave her grandson a kiss. Geli Bai knew that Ved Prakash had given their lives a new vigour. He was growing up into a fine boy. His blue eyes, mirroring his personality, were never still. They expressed perpetual wonder, curiosity, and amusement. In his young age he showed a keen interest in learning, which Kaushalya responded to most enthusiastically.

Days elapsed, and then months, and soon the year was quietly coming to an end. One day Ramchander came back home early in the afternoon from work, feeling particularly tired and wanting to get some rest. He had been feeling unwell and losing his appetite in the last few days. That day particularly he felt listless and was pale. As soon as he reached home, he put his charpoy aside and lay on it. Everyone was caught up in their own activities, unaware of his having come home. He fell asleep. A bout of cough, however, woke him up and alerted everybody around of his presence. Geli Bai came running to him. 'Ramchander, son! Is that you? What happened? Are you alright? How come you are home at this hour?'

'I am fine, Ma! I just felt a little tired and feverish. I wanted some rest. It looks like the usual cough and cold. Don't worry.'

'You work too hard. You need to take care of your health, my child. You have not been eating properly.' Geli Bai was in a mood to give him a long lecture, and so continued. 'Kaushalya, too, has been busy with Ved Prakash. I will remind her to look after you also the same way. But she can do that only if you come home on time.'

'Ma, don't worry about me! I am just feeling a bit sluggish. Rest will put me back in order.'

'*Beta*, why must you combine work and studies? Your preoccupations never seem to end. You have even been neglecting Kaushalya,' Geli Bai whined.

'Ma, Ved Prakash keeps her busy and she seems to get along with all of you very well. These days she hardly even finds time for her own hobbies. Her books are gathering dust, imagine that.'

'God bless her! Nobody in our neighbourhood has got such a beautiful, educated and accomplished daughter-in-law. She commands respect wherever she goes or whoever she talks to. We are very lucky indeed!' The conversation had taken a different turn altogether.

In the following days Ramchander kept coming home from work in the early afternoon. His coughing did not get any better; the first thing he did upon coming home was to lie down on his cot. He ran a mild fever the whole day and would get irritated whenever anyone enquired about his health. He was not eating well, and soon his energy was drained and he clearly showed signs of fatigue. He turned pale and grew increasingly disinterested in his surroundings.

All of it caught Kaushalya's notice and she grew extremely worried about her husband's health. She decided to seek medical help and asked relatives to summon a few well-known doctors to check on Ramchander. Not one of the doctors succeeded in figuring out what was wrong with Ramchander; their medicines offered neither cure nor relief. Geli Bai turned to the gods, and performed a puja for her son's recovery. But Ramchander did not get any better. He continued getting thinner day by day, his coughing more and more sporadic.

The household, once blissful, suddenly felt anxious and Kaushalya especially so. While making the bed one morning, Kaushalya noticed spots of blood on Ramchander's pillow cover. She asked Ramchander about the blood stains, and he admitted that it was not the first time he had coughed blood in his phlegm. He said he brought it to the attention of the doctors who saw him.

Kaushalya's heart sank. She spent the next few days running from pillar to post trying to find the best medical intervention for her husband. Soon the family was able to confirm that Ramchander was suffering from tuberculosis. The dreaded disease had struck at their door like an unwelcome guest and showed no signs of retreating. And the doctors said there was no cure! The only option was to move the patient to a region with cleaner air, so that his pain could be alleviated, and to pray to God for mercy.

The family considered shifting Ramchander to the distant hills or a well-equipped sanatorium. But Ramchander did not agree, and said he needed some more rest before undertaking a long journey. No matter how hard Kaushalya tried to convince him, Ramchander was adamant. He put his charpoy in the backyard, where it got direct sunlight, and confined himself to the area. He did not want his family exposed to his infectious disease.

It was a harrowing time for Kaushalya and Geli Bai. They shared duties, keeping a round-the-clock vigil on Ramchander, administering his medicines, making healthy food, boiling his drinking water, and burning his phlegm-stained cloths. There were countless tasks, and the two women did them all. They were the ones who were most affected by his disease, after all. For Geli Bai, he was the eldest son and the head of the family; for Kaushalya, he was husband and soulmate. Their lives depended on him and so did the future of the family and Ved Prakash. They did their best to snatch him from the clutches of the deadly disease: their weapons were sheer determination and unconditional, endless love.

Ramchander showed some signs of improvement as days went by. He seemed in better spirits too. He took some books out and kept them next to his charpoy. He would read as much as possible without straining his eyesight or mind. Friends and acquaintances came to enquire about his health and he engaged them. It did not escape his notice, of course, that his visitors always refused any offer of food or drink. This fear—of being infected by his tuberculosis—pained him to no end. He resolved to get well. And soon too. He needed only to look at Geli Bai and Kaushalya, working tirelessly to keep the household together and take care of him, to draw courage to fight his disease. These two women were tenacious.

Meanwhile, Ved Prakash was left to the care of Subhagi, his *nani,* and he shuttled between his paternal and the maternal homes. He seemed to enjoy the setup, learning new things and picking up new words with his naturally inquisitive mind.

Their lives had fallen into a pattern. Ramchander's younger brothers, Ganpat Rai and Arjun Dev, helped the family with running various errands even as they continued with their schooling. The younger sisters ran the household and they did so efficiently and impeccably.

Everyone prayed for a miracle. Geli Bai would always make her daily morning offerings of water to the *tulsi* plant. She was also the one to light up the evening *diya* as the day fell.

One evening as she lit the *diya,* she heard Ramchander let out a mild groan. Quickly she ran to him and found him panting for breath. She felt his forehead and discovered that he was running a high fever. A severe bout of coughing gripped him as he turned aside to look at his mother. Their eyes met and a wave of helplessness coursed through them.

'Ma, take care of Kaushalya and Ved Prakash when I am not there. It is a cruel world!' He spoke with much difficulty as he gasped for his next breath.

'You are going to be alright, Ramchander. God is kind and merciful,' whispered Geli Bai, her sobbing uncontrollable.

By then Kaushalya had heard the commotion and, all dishevelled, she came running to the room. As she sank near his feet at the charpoy, other members of the family joined them in the room and stood watching Ramchander, motionless and helpless.

Geli Bai raised her hands towards the sky and muttered, most of her words incomprehensible. Kaushalya found herself rooted to the ground, unable to do anything but look at Ramchander whose eyes were expressionless.

Kaushalya sensed that her husband was passing on and wanted to hold his hands and tell him how much she loved him, that his death would devastate her. Kaushalya could feel her heart breaking. 'How could this happen to me?' she thought in despair. 'He can't leave me alone, I'm still a bride! How can I live without him? What will happen to Ved Prakash? How could God be so cruel? First, my father and now Ramchander!' She uttered a frantic prayer. She sobbed uncontrollably, her eyes blinded by tears.

Ramchander saw his wife and wanted to get up and say something to her. But he was too weak, and quickly he was overpowered by a fierce bout of coughing. He sank back to his bed and quietly gasped his last breath. No one stirred or uttered a word. Not his mother, nor any of his siblings, his wife Kaushalya, son Ved Prakash, nor the elderly neighbours and friends who sat with folded hands and a prayer on their lips. They bid goodbye to Ramchander, a beloved member of their family and perhaps the most intellectual of his generation.

As the night darkened, the flame of the *diya* lit near the *tulsi* plant burnt itself out and Geli Bai's home was plunged into darkness. It was a darkness that their hearts and minds would never really grow out of.

For the second time in her young life, Kaushalya had fallen on hard times. The princess of Jot Singh had lost her moorings.

10

A pall of gloom descended upon Geli Bai's house. The entire town was in shock and disbelief as the news spread like wildfire. People flocked to join them in their grief, sitting quietly and not finding the need to speak. For what was there to say? The tragedy was enormous, overwhelming. People looked up at the sky with a prayer as if trying to evoke the mercy of God. 'Strange are the ways of God,' one of them said. 'He might do the right things but with crooked hands!' They knew that destiny leads one by the nose but takes one meandering through dark alleys and in the darkest of hours. Who can fathom? And who can fight? Human beings were mere puppets in the hands of the Almighty whose power can be felt in each moment. Life was a mystery and death, an enigma, a riddle nobody has ever been able to comprehend or solve.

Kaushalya sat in the middle of the front courtyard surrounded by Geli Bai and her family. Her mother Subhagi was on her side with Kaushalya's son Ved Prakash in her lap. Clad in a white sari with her head covered, Kaushalya's gaze was elusive. She was oblivious to her surroundings and did not respond to anyone who extended their warmth and sympathy. A whirlpool of memories swirled in her head, taking her back to that moonlit night when she sat in her room in this very house waiting for Ramchander, then her new husband. She remembered his gentle eyes, his loving manner and husky voice. She could almost feel his electric touch on her skin. She remembered standing with him next to the window, watching the moon and taking a vow to be always together in this mortal life.

'How real it seems even now. Wasn't it all only yesterday? Kaushalya thought. 'Where has Ramchander gone? Maybe he has gone on a long journey and would be back soon.'

Kaushalya's eyes turned towards the door and she suddenly became aware of the hoards of familiar faces sitting all around her, glum-faced and ashen-eyed. What were they all doing in her house? Why did they all look so sad? Why was everybody wearing white? What had happened? Where was Ramchander? She could see everyone except her husband!

She noticed that everybody was sitting on the floor. She became aware of the grief-stricken faces of Geli Bai and Subhagi, both trying to hug Ved Prakash as if he had lost his father.

'Lost his father!' Kaushalya snapped back to reality. The scene of the dreadful night flashed before her eyes and the truth struck her like lightning. I am a widow! A shriek came out of her throat and rent the air. Perplexed, suffocated, she broke down loudly and ran to her room to seek shelter from this cruel twist of fate.

The people were grieved, looking at Kaushalya, remembering how she was once so young and beautiful, the happy bride of a wonderful young man who was well-loved in their neighbourhood. Today they could all see how Kaushalya had lost interest in life. They could not blame her, losing the love of her life at such a young age. Every time she would look at the innocent face of Ved Prakash, she would only remember Ramchander.

For Kaushalya, her brief married life now seemed nothing more than a distant dream, something she would always remember. Her eyes roamed the house without locking on anything: she seemed to not recognize anybody. Flashes of grief would overpower her iron will and calm strength so strongly that she would retreat into her own self where everything appeared bleak. Her body quivered while her lips tried so hard to resolve, 'I am done with my tears! Even they refuse to come anymore. Ramchander wouldn't have liked to see me in this condition. I am going to take charge of my life once more. Oh God! I hope no other living being ever has to feel my pain!' Quickly, however, she would once again sink back to the refuge of her innermost sadness and fear, and utter despair, 'This is too much for me to bear. Oh God! What did I do to deserve this? Why has my fate been so cruel to me? How can I live my life? What will I do?' Again she would cry, pushing her resolve back.

Through her sadness and depression, Kaushalya's family stood by her side and gave her all their support. Geli Bai also ensured that Ved Prakash would always be around his mother and be her anchor. One day, Geli Bai thought, time will heal the wounds of her daughter-in-law. After all people say time is a great healer.

Slowly, Kaushalya showed signs of improvement, although her mind remained full of negative thoughts. 'Does time make you forget memories or does it make them sharper with each passing moment? Is it easy to suppress your memories and move on as if nothing had happened? But life is not a book where a few pages can be torn off without them leaving a trace. Alas, if only life were a fairy tale that ended in happily ever after!' Kaushalya heaved a sigh. Her mind went back to the various tales in the books she had read during her childhood. God or the forces of nature always tried to test the spirit of human beings by pitting them against all odds and making them walk a tightrope. 'Experiences make a man,' Kaushalya remembered having read somewhere. 'These determine his character.'

Every day, Kaushalya spent most of her life sitting and thinking. She had abandoned her hobbies, even the daily rituals that used to make her happy. While she responded to Ved Prakash, it was only mechanically, out of duty. The boy reminded her so much of Ramchander that it pained her to even look at him.

As Kaushalya took her time to grieve her husband's death, Geli Bai worked each day to put the house back to normal; soon, things limped back into a routine. Subhagi made her visits more frequent, helping Kaushalya heal and come out of her cocoon. Kaushalya knew that life had to move on, that she must accept God's will and try to make of her life whatever she can. She still had her whole life ahead of her! She had a four-year-old child to look after. She had to get out of her depression, and quickly.

Subhagi made a suggestion to Geli Bai, '*Jiji*, let Kaushalya and Ved Prakash stay with me for a while. Her cousins are there and they would surely help her feel better. The change of environment would be good for her.'

'Why not?' agreed Geli Bai. 'We will miss Ved Prakash but it would be good for Kaushalya.'

Thus Kaushalya went back to her parental home. It was her refuge, the place where she would have her mother, whose unconditional love would certainly help her get back on her feet. It would give her the change she needed.

And that's what Kaushalya did. The one-year mourning period came to an end and she could hardly believe that she had survived it. She acknowledged all the help from the two amazing women in her life: her mother, Subhagi, and mother-in-law, Geli Bai. They were a great support and a source of courage. They rallied behind her.

Kaushalya was now convinced that her life should not revolve only around one person. 'I still have Ved Prakash and Ramchander's entire family to attend to. I can't desert them. After all they have lost their son. Ramchander's responsibilities are mine now!'

She returned to her own home and began to take interest once again in household affairs. Then one day, Geli Bai said to her, 'Kaushalya, those little children you used to help with their studies sometime back were remembering you fondly. Would you like to see them again? It would be a diversion for you too.'

'Yes, *Maji*! They are always welcome. And Ved Prakash would have playmates also.'

So the children came in the afternoons and Kaushalya got busy again. She also took to visiting the nearby *Arya Samaj Mandir* occasionally, along with Subhagi, in order to rejoin the community. Relatives, friends, neighbours, and acquaintances extended their sympathies to her and treated her with utmost respect.

It was only a matter of time before new proposals of marriage came Kaushalya's way. To each of those families, Geli Bai responded maturely, 'Isn't it too early yet? We'll see later.' She knew, though, that the proposals would crop up again.

Subhagi, for her part, felt more receptive to the proposals. She waited for an opportune moment to convince her daughter about weighing her options carefully. That moment came soon when, during a visit to Geli Bai's house, she witnessed an irritable Ved Prakash pestering Kaushalya, 'Ma, where has my father gone? Why doesn't he come back to us?'

Subhagi looked at Kaushalya meaningfully and whispered, 'Koshi, the time is ripe to think about your own life once again and Ved Prakash's too.'

'What do you mean, Ma?' Kaushalya was aghast.

'Koshi, proposals are coming your way once again. All of them are from very good families. Why don't you think about it carefully and take a decision?'

'Ma! How can you even suggest such a thing? I can never forget Ramchander or desert his family. It is my moral responsibility to live with them.'

'Koshi, the older generation will go one day and the younger ones will all be busy with their own lives. You will be left all alone. How will you live and what will you do?'

'But, Ma, I have Ved Prakash. He is the one I look forward to. And I am not alone!'

'Koshi, a son can never fulfil the role of a life partner. He can only look after you but can never be a companion. It is a very long life, dear. One needs the protection of a man.'

Geli Bai overheard their conversation and joined them. While she agreed with Subhagi, she was unwilling to let go of Ved Prakash, who was the only remembrance she had of her eldest son.

Over the next few days references to Kaushalya's remarriage kept being made, causing quite a stir in the otherwise placid household of Geli Bai.

Subhagi, Kaushalya, and Geli Bai were all adamant in their positions while being careful not to hurt each other's feelings. Subhagi wanted to rehabilitate her daughter's life and secure her future. Geli Bai would not hear of parting from Ved Prakash, her only grandson and a living reminder of her son. And Kaushalya would never agree to remarry on the condition of leaving behind her dearest Ved Prakash.

As luck would have it, a suggestion came up from the *purohit* of the *Arya Samaj Mandir* that Swami Dayanand Saraswati had advocated not only the concept of the education of women but also widow-remarriage, preferably with the younger brother of the deceased husband, if any *devar* also could be interpreted as the 'second husband'. The suggestion evoked approving response from the members of the family as well as from amongst the townsfolk. The unanimous sentiment was that it was the best option for Kaushalya.

It was Kaushalya's mother, naturally, who was given the daunting task of getting her to agree to such a proposal.

'Koshi, this suits everybody's needs and requires the least adjustment on everybody's part,' Subhagi said to her daughter.

'What about my feelings, Ma? How can I accept Ganpat as my husband? It is absurd. Outrightly disgraceful!'

'Life is a compromise, Koshi. Do agree for everybody's sake, if not your own. What do I do, my dear?' Subhagi's helpless eyes tugged Kaushalya's heart.

'As you wish, Ma!' Kaushalya fell into Subhagi's lap and wept uncontrollably. 'God only knows, what he has in store for me!'

'God bless you, my child. Everything may yet turn out right for you!' Subhagi tried to control her tears.

The two women were bound to each other with the thread of life and love till death would do them part. They made a decision to not go up in arms against their fate; they shall share their agony and face it together.

11

The marriage of Kaushalya to Ganpat Rai, the younger brother of her deceased husband, was solemnized in the *Arya Samaj Mandir* in a simple manner. Only close relatives and friends were invited to bless the couple, as well as a few respected members of the town. As the ceremony ended, prayers were uttered invoking the blessings of the Almighty. Rose petals were showered on the couple while Kaushalya sat still with downcast eyes and folded hands. Ved Prakash sat next to her, holding her hand and looking at her with eyes that were innocent and inquisitive at the same time. Kaushalya pressed his little hand and hugged him closer. Ved Prakash felt reassured by his mother's embrace. He looked around at the assembly, seeing some familiar faces and wondering why they had gathered. Soon he got bored and started scampering around.

Kaushalya did not want her every emotion to show; she drew her sari to cover half of her face as she got up from the *vedi* with Ganpat Rai. She remained silent, pondering her surrender to the will of God. The desperate weariness she had experienced a week earlier had mellowed down into a kind of calm stoicism. She longed to get home, to familiar surroundings, the usual rut, and the refuge of the commonality of existence. In a strange way, she was happy that nothing else changed—and nothing else would. As far as adjustment with Ganpat Rai was concerned, it could wait and take its own time. He would understand and so would everybody else. Kaushalya no longer felt guilty. She had gotten over the initial shock and her eyes were once again full of tenderness and compassion.

Kaushalya came back to the same home, again as a bride, and again as Geli Bai's daughter-in-law. The change in circumstances and its effect was writ large on everyday's face. Elderly relatives tried to make the atmosphere normal by their kind words and normal behaviour. Geli Bai and the sisters-in-law welcomed her and gave her blessings. Though there were a few tears and an occasional sigh escaped the lips of a few people, the general impression was one of happiness and acceptance. Well-wishers of the family heaved a sigh of relief as they prepared themselves to depart after having the customary meal.

For Kaushalya, the homecoming was almost like silent mental torture. All she could think about was Ramchander, and the happy times they shared. With Ramchander, it had truly been a fusion of mind and heart. Who knows what level of understanding she would be able to reach with Ganpat Rai? No, she said to herself, she could not possibly fall in love with him. She had always liked him but in a different way. He was shy, almost reclusive. Kaushalya still could not believe that she was now married to him. But it was her reality and she would have to accept it sooner rather than later.

She did not feel any romantic love for Ganpat Rai; she did not think that would happen any time soon. Yet she also knew that being married meant there was a home and possibly other children in the future for her. 'Isn't that what every woman needs at the end of the day?' she said to herself. 'It is difficult to sustain love anyway. It has to deal with many obstacles in its way, human or divine. The world would have come to an end if all marriages were to be based on love. Love! Oh! When has that been the end-all of a successful marriage?' Kaushalya could feel a change coming over her, as if she had matured beyond her years.

She thought about society's constructs of marriage. It was a social business or necessity perhaps. Marriage had helped build societies or races and extend boundaries of land as well as culture. The world had survived and prospered on the basis of the concept of marriage. It could not be looked down upon or taken lightly. It kept a family together and helped build relationships. It enabled couples to have the constant companionship and emotional support needed in order to face life's difficulties, and at the same time share its joys too.

Kaushalya knew she would have to be strong. While God had taken away Ramchander from her, society had given her another chance to rebuild her life, and around the same family as well. She had got a new lease on life, and her son, Ved Prakash, had been given one too. He would have a father-like figure who would care for him, look after his interests, and play with him. And she would remain the eldest *bahu* of the family.

She prayed, 'Let bygones be bygones! Let the past not haunt me again and again! Oh God! Help me come out of the crisis of my life without any hard feelings.'

Slowly Geli Bai's house came back to normal. They had responded to an extraordinary situation in an ordinary way and they had come up with a viable solution that suited everyone. Strange, though it might sound, Ramchander's absence became a thing of the past. The sole reminders of him were his books and Ved Prakash, who himself was expanding his new childhood memories with a wide range of activities. No other member of the family would refer to Ramchander in any way, least of all Geli Bai who wanted to help Kaushalya and Ganpat Rai take to each other and live together if not in romantic love, then at least in friendship and harmony.

Ganpat Rai and Kaushalya still felt awkward in each other's company. A wall of inhibitions stood before them and neither wanted to make the first move. The mantle of an uncertain future had fallen on their shoulders and their unwillingness enhanced its burden manifold. They were poles apart in their temperaments, interests, and attitudes. Ganpat Rai was more down-to-earth and less interested in academic activities, milder in nature and more interested in the practical aspects of life. At times he veered towards the spiritual and believed in facing life as it came to him. Though tall and well-built just like Ramchander, he lacked his elder brother's aura and keen mental abilities. He belonged more to the practical world and believed in adjustments for the sake of the greater good. The interest of the family was dearer to him than his own aspirations. He was particularly deeply attached to his youngest brother, Arjun Dev, and was always ready to walk an extra mile to make him comfortable. He would indulge in occasional reading; the books that interested him were those of religion or spirituality. He could also read balance sheets or papers containing financial information. He was frugal in his habits and believed in living a simple life. He could be an ideal life partner for an ordinary girl but Kaushalya was different. They traversed different mental regions; while one was fond of the fine and aesthetic things in life, the other was yet to find his particular interests and leanings. The disparities were marked and constant; and subconscious comparisons with Ramchander rendered the task of adjustment a rather long process. If it was a marriage of convenience for Kaushalya, Ganpat Rai had agreed to the proposal purely out of a sense of duty or responsibility. The question of love had never occurred to either partner and could never be the basis of their union. However, Ved Prakash was and still would be the cementing force of their marriage. And so would be their entire family.

Both found ways to keep themselves busy in order to avoid awkward situations and allowed life to take its own course in a normal routine. Kaushalya resumed teaching small children in the afternoons, besides taking active interest in her social life concerning the *Arya Samaj* and propagating the importance of women's education. She enjoyed the support of Geli Bai and her sisters-in-law, who never bothered her with any of the household chores. Ganpat Rai, meanwhile, found a stable job in a nearby bank and continued with his studies in the evenings. Days would dawn with a purpose for both of them and end with a sense of satisfaction in the pursuit of their routine affairs. Both got used to the habits of their existence. When left by themselves, they had nothing to say to each other. They remained self-conscious in each other's company; rather sensitive, making an effort to understand each other's separate world without really poking their nose in.

In the privacy of their own thoughts, both Kaushalya and Ganpat Rai wondered whether their relationship would ever move forward. Right now, they knew, their marriage was more of a 'facade', although credit had to be given to them for their mindfulness of each other's needs. Geli Bai, refusing to continue being a mere silent spectator to the distance between the two, began passing subtle hints in the hope that Kaushalya and Ganpat Rai would develop a liking for each other. Almost a year had passed since their wedding and they still took every opportunity to ignore each other. They lived side by side in harmony, but not *with* each other.

Ganpat Rai tried to accept and appreciate Kaushalya's high-profile lifestyle, her love for books and beautiful clothes, and her fondness for interaction within the society and her desire for social reform. He was different. He thought a woman's role in life was to stay within the confines of her own home and be the procreator of progeny, just like his own mother. He secretly wished that Kaushalya would lend a helping hand to his aging mother and look after the family a little more. Women, he believed, should be followers of the traditions of her husband's family rather than try to set their own examples and be a leader. Kaushalya, on the other hand, thought just the opposite. She reasoned that women were the most potent drivers of change, and that their ability to combine the virtues of head and heart gave them an edge over men. Why should they lag behind? Society, for its sustenance, depended more on women and they should exercise their right not only in its formation but also for its development. Change was a cycle of nature and society should also experiment with its norms and effect a change wherever required.

She often wondered if marriage required like-mindedness or whether that was a concept found only in books. She thought of the couples around her and asked herself, 'Where is the like-mindedness?' She saw men being the breadwinners and their wives the keepers of the house and mothers. Children, she reckoned, were the only common ground.

The change in circumstances with a difference in outlook had made Kaushalya more contemplative, rather, cynical. She told herself to stop thinking about these issues. 'Let fate lead me wherever it deems fit!' she said aloud. It was clear in her mind that the search for a soulmate was futile in her case and life had to be a compromise in order to pursue a larger interest.

One morning, Kaushalya was tidying up the drawing room when Ganpat Rai came out of his room and looked towards the kitchen. Finding no one there, he looked around and spotted Kaushalya.

'Kaushalya!' came a call softly.

'*Ji!*' Kaushalya was a bit startled.

'What are we having for food today?'

'I'll call *Maji* or Lakshmi,' replied Kaushalya. She was a bit annoyed.

'Aren't you supposed to know?'

'Why me? I have never prepared food in my life.'

'There is no harm in learning it. In fact, that is the first skill a woman should know. Besides, it will help my mother too. She is getting old and needs help.'

'She has Lakshmi, Chetni and Hukmi to help her. I can take care of other things.' Kaushalya was clearly miffed.

'What other things?'

'Don't you see the changes in the house? I also help with the education of the neighbourhood children. House work is much more than mere cooking and cleaning.'

'That, in my view, is the primary work, Kaushalya.'

'Well, I know enough of housekeeping and contribute my bit in my own way.' Kaushalya avoided his eyes and felt hurt.

'But you do not get my point at all. You bother too much about your books and these issues of women's education, and so on and on. I was only giving you a suggestion. I didn't mean to argue.' Ganpat Rai held on to his views. They had no choice but to end their conversation when Geli Bai came in through the front door. She had gone to a neighbour's house to tend to an ailing child on a request by his mother.

Geli Bai quickly understood that she had interrupted a serious conversation. She tried to lighten the mood by offering them food. 'Kaushalya, Ganpat... come to the kitchen! See what I have made for you today!'

The three of them then sat for a meal, and with that over, both Kaushalya and Ganpat felt momentarily free and went on with their respective routines, finding refuge in the luxury of their own thoughts. Kaushalya returned to her library, rebelling silently against the drudgery of her domestic situation. She was not mentally attuned to enjoy only the pleasures of a simple, insipid domestic life. Her ambitions and outlook varied a great deal as compared to Ganpat Rai, and she refused to follow customs regarding the role of women in society passed down over the centuries by the patriarchy.

She made a decision that if she and Ganpat Rai did not come to an understanding of each other, then arguing and debating would only be a waste of time and energy. 'Let things continue the way they are,' she said to herself.

In another part of the house, right at that moment, Ganpat Rai too was making the same resolution.

They were like two heterogeneous elements yoked together by both society and their fate.

12

Kaushalya tried to appear content with her present situation; so did Ganpat Rai. It was a contradiction of sorts, given their opposite temperaments, but both were keen to move on with their lives. A new tract of life had opened before them and both grappled with the unknown traits of each other's personality. They treated each other with respect and kindness, their eyes sported a look of silent appeal in pure humility. Sometimes Kaushalya made a sincere effort to seriously open her heart to him. He would listen with deference but without understanding the intense longings of her mind. Ganpat Rai was too polite to articulate his disapproving opinion after they had had an argument about Kaushalya's lack of knowledge in the kitchen. He would not like another one if he could help it. Sometimes he would grow restless in the absence of an emotional bond with his wife and found simple happiness in the little jobs that never seemed to finish at home. Ganpat Rai was a remarkably useful man at home; he could make or mend anything with his hands and found pleasure in work and work alone.

As days passed, everyone in the family noticed the emerging feeling of empathy between Kaushalya and Ganpat Rai. Harmony and goodwill prevailed in the house, generating an air of positivity all around. Kaushalya and Ganpat Rai had become more tolerant of each other; in fact they even appeared rather happy in each other's company at times. Neither cared whether they loved each other in a romantic way or not; right now, it was not necessary.

They had to undergo a full gamut of emotions or cross various stages of ebbing sentiments before their relationship could actually reach the stage of fruition. But it was clear to everyone that they both were making a genuine effort in that direction. And that was what mattered!

It was only a matter of time before Kaushalya and Ganpat Rai would be blessed with a child. Lady luck had smiled on this simple household once again and Kaushalya bloomed. Ved Prakash, too, was excited at the prospect of having a sibling with whom he would be able to play. In the seventh month of Kaushalya's pregnancy, the air was thick with excitement as preparations were arranged for a quiet ceremony of the daughter-in-law's *godbharai*. Subhagi came with numerous gifts and blessings and so did other relatives and women of the neighbourhood.

Two months later, Kaushalya bore another son without much difficulty. The baby was very beautiful, with dark hair and large blue eyes. Geli Bai named her grandson Anand Prakash as he had brought a breeze of joy once again to their lives. Kaushalya loved him passionately and he quickly became the little darling of the entire household. Ganpat Rai taught Ved Prakash how to play with his little brother.

Ganpat Rai looked after Kaushalya well as she recuperated slowly. Kaushalya, of course, appreciated all his efforts but still felt a tinge of sadness. She felt lonely with him; his presence reminded him of Ramchander and how different the two of them were. Kaushalya felt herself miles away from his mental and emotional world. It was difficult for her to imagine how two well-meaning persons could be so different from each other and yet evoke feelings of goodwill from those around them. But Kaushalya loved the child more than her own self. He had been born at a time when her faith in life had been dwindling and her soul felt empty and bereft of life. She had come a long way from her years of girlhood and seen much more in a short span than many of her own age. She was now a mother of two sons and had enough on her hands to keep her busy. Where was the time for her to think or delve into her own world of ideas? Her priorities had changed and so did her objects of attention. The household ran smoothly and she was happy busying herself with the needs of her small children. The days would pass quickly but she often longed for like-minded company. Lacking that, she would often grow restless and turn to walking around the house to soothe her distraught nerves.

On one such evening, Kaushalya stood in the small side-garden and looked around. There was no noise anywhere and she got lost in her own reverie for a while. She then decided to take a few rounds of the garden, occasionally stopping to look at the rose bush that was blooming with velvety red roses. She touched the petals with her fingers and smelled the scent, sweet and invigorating. She felt the calmness of the atmosphere enveloping her consciousness and making her delirious with a deep contentment. She walked up and down the garden path and watched the sun go down, filling the sky with its melting radiance. She imagined the dawn as well as the dusk and their mysterious brilliance.

Kaushalya realized she felt at peace with nature but forlorn in the world of men and its complicated affairs. She became aware of the fast descending darkness and quickened her steps towards her home where her children would be waiting for her with their arms spread wide wanting to hug her with all their might. As she entered through the front door, she saw Ved Prakash and Anand Prakash playing tag with their grandmother. Geli Bai seemed to be enjoying her grandchildren's tricks, saying all kinds of sweet nothings and showering them with kisses. Kaushalya's heart warmed at the spectacle. She left them alone and moved on to the little tasks that had remained unfinished in her absence.

Ganpat Rai came home rather late in the evenings; he barely made it for the evening meal and often found the children asleep. He would be too tired and wish to sleep after having his supper. Kaushalya would make an effort at some communication but would give up as he did not hide his indifference. She knew him well enough now and understood that the gentle smile on his kind face asked only that he be left alone, and he rather preferred to sink into the world of deep slumber rather than respond to her exhortations. Kaushalya realized how he needed this after a day's hard work. Nothing else, at that time, gave him more pleasure and Kaushalya had made peace with the routine.

Time quickly flew by. Ved Prakash was now eight and Anand Prakash, two. Kaushalya felt that the boys were growing up too fast, keeping the family on their toes most of the time. Both the boys were highly active and the house constantly reverberated with their energy, its every nook marked by sounds of activity. A growing restlessness was visible on the faces of the children as their world widened, now not only confined to the interiors of their home. Little Anand Prakash would take the hand of his elder brother and nudge him out of the house along with him. The two brothers were each other's perfect companions. Contentment flowed in Geli Bai's household.

There was also quiet anticipation as Kaushalya was once again in the family way. She often felt too heavy to move about, so she sat alone and pondered over things that interested her. When the children would be in bed or occupied elsewhere she would do her sewing, knitting or embroidery. She was highly skilled and had no intention of doing away with her hobbies throughout her pregnancy.

Kaushalya longed for a daughter this time. She uttered fervent prayers to God to bless her with a baby girl. She was already imagining making beautiful frocks for her daughter, decorating them with intricate lace and embroidery. She also imagined that her daughter would inherit her beauty, even her intellect and aesthetic sensibilities. Her daughter would also grow up to be a real companion for her mother; she will not be lonely.

Ganpat Rai, when at home, tried to help Kaushalya in every possible way. The silences between them had grown into a kind of quiet bond where both made an effort to be kind, humble and polite to each other. Yet there was a space between them, a kind of emptiness which had not been fulfilled in either's life. Even when together, they enjoyed themselves alone, working, thinking, or simply being. Their relationship was based on trust, tenderness and tolerance, rather than romantic love or passion. The inclusion of children in their private world had brought them together in a way that cemented their varied outlook. Kaushalya looked forward to adding another child to their brood.

And soon she gave birth to a baby girl. Kaushalya's intense wish had been fulfilled. She felt nothing but eternal gratitude. Her baby girl was very pretty, plump and fair, with a mop of thick black curls, large eyes and thick eyelashes. Giving birth to her was the happiest moment in Kaushalya's life. She named her Shobhna, a ray of hope. She looked at the child and she felt instantly warm. She also felt an immediate bonding with Subhagi, her own mother, who had braved everything to give Kaushalya a comfortable life. A wave of motherly love overpowered her heart and she held the child close to her breast. She gazed at the sleeping beauty and longed for the day when her daughter would be old enough to be able to talk to her in a sweet prattle. Kaushalya lay reclining on her bed, keeping her infant close in her arms and feeling that integral bond that united the two. She could not do anything else by way of diversion or undertake any form of exercise till she felt strong enough to do so. She kept the window of her room open and would watch the sun going down gradually, filling the sky with its crimson flush. The late evenings always generated feelings of nostalgia in her throbbing heart when a peculiar heaviness would combine itself in her, along with a zest for life, and prod her soul to move.

Kaushalya discovered that she no longer resented anything. Instead she felt warm and secure in her nest and naturally the feelings percolated down to all the family members. She wanted her children to grow up fast and Shobhna, who was now three years old, was the focal point of her life now onwards. Since becoming a mother of three, she had forgotten her own little fancies and interests and barely had time to attend to her own whims. Yet she did not miss them. Instead, the little things about her children made her happy. It gave her pleasure to walk around the vicinity of her house with little Shobhna in tow. Clutching her little hands with her strong grip, she walked past the dusty track, crossing narrow lanes and reaching the small green patch of land that bore the semblance of a garden. Spotting a few neighbours, Kaushalya stopped to have a word with them while Shobhna, freeing herself from her mother's grip ran around wilfully in search of flowers or objects that caught her attention. Kaushalya found herself rejoicing in all the pleasant things around her: the cool shade of the trees along the road, the bright sunshine falling on the leaves and the brown wood, the floating birds in the sky, small children running after curious objects and the tiny beds of seasonal flowers. She bathed in the bliss of her everyday life, savouring the friendly things in her pleasant surroundings. She was happy.

One day as she walked back home with Shobhna, humming a tune in a leisurely mood, she suddenly remembered her father. She remembered her own carefree childhood under his benevolent eye; he was always ready to put everything at stake for her happiness. She missed his strong presence, his never-say-die attitude, and his fierce courage of conviction. A strong father figure was lacking in her life; an anchor who could draw her out by his bold personality, and could fascinate her mind with stimulating ideas and make up for her lack of interest in the mundane.

Quickly, though, she realized how she was being unfair to her husband. She was dismayed at her own train of thought. Though she remained uninterested in him and found him too virtuous, she had learned to be happy with Ganpat Rai. Her sense of guilt had also made her more attentive to him and his needs, even though she mostly wanted to be left alone in her own fanciful world.

Kaushalya was thinking ambivalent and she did not like it. She told herself to shake off her obsolete ideas and move with the times.

Suddenly her thoughts were interrupted by the cheerful voices of children greeting her; she and Shobhna were back home. The gentle, smiling face of Ganpat Rai welcomed her, 'Where have you been, Kaushalya?'

13

Kaushalya's routine was packed and interesting. Their children were growing bigger and stronger by the day and they kept her occupied. She gave all that she could—time, strength, and energy—to the family she loved deeply. Their home had become the dearest place on earth for her; she loved the little *baithak* and the quaint kitchen where children tramped about; the dim lighting of the books area; the peculiar silence of the corners where the table lamps stood. She loved the appetizing aroma of the wheat *rotis* coming out of the smouldering *chullah*; the cosiness of their family. She loved Geli Bai, her mother-in-law, with her worldliness and practical wisdom; and her sisters-in-law, with their unflinching support and affection. She loved Ganpat Rai for his cooperation so that she could have her way in most things; and most of all, she loved her children, who were all equally warm, lovable and loving, who lit up the house with their uninhibited laughter. Kaushalya would not give up this bliss for anything in the world.

The next seven years saw the births of three more sons, one after the other: Harsh Prakash, Abhay Prakash, and Vijay Prakash. The boys had inherited the family lineaments: a fair colour, greyish blue eyes, long lashes and a good build. They all had a happy manner in them that was easily noticeable. It was obvious, too, that they did not care much about their studies and, much like their father, were more inclined towards sports, music, and manual work. The large family pampered them, making much about their liveliness and their mere presence. Kaushalya tried to inculcate in them a fondness for reading but they simply did not have the interest.

'Goodness gracious!' exclaimed Kaushalya one day to her mother, who had come visiting. 'How can my boys not love books and the written word? It is so disappointing!' She was clearly dissatisfied. 'It is only through education that one can move ahead in life or move with the times. It was the only saving grace for the middle classes if they hoped to make their future and make it well!' Kaushalya tried to make Ganpat Rai look after the boys but he never had the time. He was too occupied, not only with his own job but also with looking after his younger brother, Arjun Dev, who had become heavily dependent on him, especially now that his marriage had been fixed. Preparations for the marriage, though a simple affair as the bride belonged to an ordinary family, had been keeping the family busy. As such the children were mostly left by themselves, with minimal supervision and free play. This often led to bickering between Kaushalya and Ganpat Rai.

'They have been whiling away their time in useless pursuits,' remarked Kaushalya one day with a bit of bitterness in her tone.

'What's wrong with that?' Ganpat Rai replied. 'Childhood has to be carefree and relaxed. They have enough time on their hands to learn things.' He watched his sons, their faces rugged and happy, and felt satisfied.

'But sons do need the constant and firm tutelage of their father, too. A mother's love alone is not enough for a strict upbringing. Can you please try to spend more time with them?'

'Let's get over with the marriage first. I shall see later.'

Kaushalya fell silent. Secretly she detested the easy-going attitude of Ganpat Rai when it came to bringing up their children. She could see that he behaved more like a friend to the boys. She wanted them, however, to feel the iron hand of their father; she wanted Ganpat Rai to remain vigilant and watch their manners and correct them when they needed to be. The bond of love between Ganpat Rai and Arjun Dev was another cause for concern for Kaushalya which often cast a dark shadow on their family life. Kaushalya could not find fault with Ganpat Rai over any apparent reason. He had an impeccable character, was gentle and kind towards everybody and sported a happy and benevolent disposition which made him a favourite of all the people around. He possessed the virtues of a saint but lacked the vibrancy of a common man and Kaushalya sorely missed that. She missed a soulmate and the emotional bonding. She longed for a cathartic communion and so she turned towards the children. But her boys disliked following her instructions and she simply could not cope with their energy.

Yet life went on. They shifted to a bigger house in Model Town, Lahore, where Kaushalya and Ganpat Rai had constructed a reasonably big house that would befit their growing family. It was not easy. She had had to sell a good lot of her jewellery in order to raise enough money for the new house. It was a two-*kanal* house with a small lawn in the front and a big garden at the back. The house in the middle consisted of many rooms and there was comfortable space for each member of the family. Kaushalya's sisters-in-law had also been married during the last decade and had joined their conjugal homes located in nearby towns, leaving the house empty for Kaushalya and her children. In the rear garden there were many fruit trees which the children climbed when they wanted to run away from either Kaushalya or Geli Bai, their grandmother. They would stay propped high up on a tree, for an hour or two, savouring the tree's succulent fruits. Whenever they did that, Geli Bai would run after them with a cane in her hand and summon them down. 'Come down and go back inside the house, have your milk,' Geli Bai would call. Eventually they would listen to their grandmother, get down from the treetop, and drink their milk.

Milk was one thing their household never ran out of. At any one time they always had either a cow or a buffalo and milk was always abundant. Geli Bai's mornings were spent in milking the cow, and then putting the milk on a slow fire for a considerable part of the day until a thick layer of cream formed on the surface which she would then collect and make into butter. The remaining buttermilk would be stored separately to be distributed to the poor people who would form a queue in front of their house. The children had never tasted buttermilk. They grew up thinking it was fit only for the poor.

In many ways Kaushalya's children and Geli Bai lived a privileged, carefree life. Their summer holidays were spent going for picnics or excursions near the canal. They would take along their food and a big basket full of mangoes which they would put in the cold canal water to be eaten later and spend the entire day relaxing, eating and playing. They would run and chase each other, play *gulli-danda*, eat cold mangoes, take a dip in the water and spend the entire day in the lap of nature. They would come back home in the evening, totally exhausted but rejuvenated. Other family members accompanied them sometimes, leaving the house in the care of Geli Bai and their dog, Tiger.

It was on one of these occasions when the boys were frolicking on their own that Shobhna, now ten, expressed a desire to visit her grandparents' house in Dera Ismail Khan. She also wanted to meet the daughters of her paternal aunt, who were almost of her own age and who lived not very far from their ancestral house. 'Ma, let's go and meet everyone there. It will also be an outing for me. We will see our old home too,' coaxed Shobhna excitedly.

'Ah, yes! Why not?' replied Kaushalya. 'You must see your *nana-nani's* house too and realize what roots you come from, dear.' Kaushalya sighed at the poignant thought.

Shobhna ran towards her siblings to share her news. Being the only sister, she was a great favourite of all her brothers and cousins as well. She was full of excitement and it showed in her voice. It was true! She was going to visit her ancestral home along with her mother!

Their plan was finalized on the same evening after consulting the other members of the family. Shobhna was ecstatic and she immediately set down to help her mother with the preparations.

A week later, Shobhna and Kaushalya began their journey. Shobhna relished the experience, every bit of it, even holding her mother's hand while walking amidst the hustle and bustle of the platform crowd. As the train left the station, Shobhna, clutching her bag of food with her arm, became more interested in looking out of the window and taking in the view. The train and the moving objects outside seemed to be racing each other and vanishing in the blink of an eye. The novelty of the experience and the vastness of the expanse outside rather intimidated Shobhna who tried to soak in the new impressions with a certain reserve. The train journey came to an end as they neared the periphery of the Sindh River. A new experience awaited Shobhna as she boarded the steamer that would take them through the river to the other part of the large land that contained the memories of her forefathers' lives.

'Mother!' exclaimed Shobhna, 'the river is so big and deep. Everything around looks so beautiful! The whole world must be so large and a challenge for the human mind to understand. I wish we could go around. Maybe later?'

Kaushalya gazed at her daughter, startled! It was as if she was seeing her young self in front of her. If she heard Shobhna right, her child had the same dreams as hers, and it left her speechless. She wondered if this is what people meant when they said that we pass our longings on to our children. 'Is this how history repeats itself?'

Shobhna was excited throughout the sea journey. She paced one end of the deck to the other, quietly watching the scene. Kaushalya, meanwhile, stayed in her seat and watched the sunset, which to her appeared like a ball of melted lead. She felt as if she had crossed eternity in trying to get back to her roots. She had come a long way and felt much older. She looked at Shobhna and felt like crying. She wanted to protect her; protect her against all the uncertainties of life. She wished she could stay with her forever or keep her for all times to come! Her eyes were welling up with tears. She reasoned with herself to stop, to remember that her daughter had her destiny charted out, and that what she needed to do was pray that Shobhna would have only roses in her way. They were nearing their destination and a deep pain took hold of Kaushalya's heart. She was rediscovering her loneliness and felt a peculiar fascination for the old, uninhabited place and its historical significance. She was being drawn to her past.

The next day, Kaushalya and Shobhna walked hand in hand through steep and narrow lanes around their old home. Kaushalya took Shobhna to her ancestral *haveli* that stood like a monument and retained its aristocratic aura. Everything shone softly in the sun as Kaushalya gave Shobhna a guided tour of the *haveli*, describing to her some of the fondest memories of her childhood days. She stood in the courtyard that was witness to not only some of the happiest moments of her life, but also the saddest. The dim atmosphere, the greyish walls, the empty rooms, the dilapidated roof—they spoke and said it all. Kaushalya stood rooted to the ground, eyes moist and overwhelmed with nostalgia. Unable to stay longer, she came out and visited the neighbours. She still found familiar faces amongst them who were delighted to see her after such a long time.

They had their lunch and then set out to see the other house where Kaushalya had stepped in as a bride. The solitary mud house, though old, was closed but looked neatly structured. The glittering afternoon made the house appear golden as a vision.

Shobhna felt a strange bond with the house. It was the house, after all, where her ancestors had been born and lived. She belonged to them as much as they belonged to her. Fascinated, she watched the interiors of the house and the surroundings in the faint brightness of the atmosphere. Shobhna felt a strange emotion overcoming her spirit, the dormant love for her roots becoming active suddenly in a moment. Kaushalya watched he daughter's face intently and understood the feelings writ large on her face. She had also always loved the house, for it was here that she became a wife and a daughter-in-law. Kaushalya and Shobhna, both were bound to the same house like an infant to her mother with an umbilical cord.

They continued their sojourn to a nearby town called *Bannu*, which was known for its *Pathan* habitation. Kaushalya's sister-in-law, Lakshmi Devi, was married there to a *thekedar* by profession and it was obvious that Kaushalya would want to meet her along with Shobhna, who looked forward to meeting her first cousins. The visit was memorable for Shobhna, although she could not roam the town as freely as she had wanted to. Such movement of women outside their home was not encouraged as it was believed that Pathans were fond of beautiful women and would whisk them away. On one occasion, as Shobhna got ready in her finery, thinking that they would go in and around the town for sightseeing, her aunt suggested to her, '*Beti*, don't wear beautiful clothes in this place. There is always the risk of being kidnapped by *Pathans.*' Thus Shobhna had to content herself with visits to relatives who lived nearby and welcomed them with open arms. It was an interesting experience for her to get to know many of her first or second cousins and spend time with them.

Soon enough the fortnight was over and it was time for Kaushalya and Shobhna to journey back to their home that beckoned them with all its responsibilities.

14

The way home was much the same. They began their journey back on a warm evening. The steamer started with a loud sweep, leaving the sandy shore behind where the relatives saw them off. Soon the foam along the coast too became invisible and not a figure could be seen. A deafening silence but for the sound of the sea waves intensified the misty atmosphere. People stood on the deck watching the blue sky turn crimson with the rays of the sinking sun that was staring at them from the other end. Kaushalya and Shobhna stood next to each other, inhaling the fresh air and enjoying the whispering sea. Soon the sky started turning grey and people streamed inside to make themselves comfortable.

Looking towards the shore, Kaushalya wondered if her past life had been a dream. She had walked so far away from her young days that she couldn't remember when she used to run so carelessly in those very lanes more than a decade ago. How time flew! She resented it somehow. But just as quickly she realized that it was the same with everybody else: nobody could comprehend these eternal mysteries. Light was fading fast and Kaushalya went indoors, taking Shobhna by the hand. A couple of hours passed listlessly and suddenly the speed of the steamer started getting noticeably slower.

Passengers began to murmur, 'What is happening? What has happened?' Awaking from their lethargic stupor, people started assembling on the deck to see what was going on. The steamer coughed a few hiccups and then came to a sudden halt. It stood still. People quickly got scared, especially with the darkness descending sharply on the atmosphere. The sky had started twinkling with tiny stars that were throwing dim glares of light in all directions. The sound of restlessness and commotion became more and more audible as people slowly started thronging the deck.

'How can the steamer stop in the middle of the river?' one passenger asked frantically.

'What has gone wrong?' another one spoke. People looked at each other, waiting for any reassurance from anyone that there was nothing wrong with the boat.

They saw the captain coming towards them, looking concerned but composed. He bore an undecided look as people looked at him, expecting an answer.

'The water level of the river has gone down considerably since we crossed it last. I believe we can't do much about it. Nature is truly unpredictable,' he shrugged his shoulders.

'What are we going to do?' asked one passenger.

'There has to be an alternative,' said someone else.

'I have heard that the surrounding forest has a *gurudwara* somewhere in the middle,' the captain replied. 'If we can get across to the shore to find our way to this shrine, we can spend the night comfortably. Something can always be worked out tomorrow.'

'It is for you to get us across safely to the shore,' shouted a man to the captain.

'He's right! He's right! You should get us safely to the shore!' came a chorus of voices.

'Well, we have a few boats and rafts aboard,' said the captain. 'Menfolk can help get the women, children, and the luggage across the river.'

Prayers were uttered urgently. 'God Almighty save us!' they said.

They then gathered courage and commenced the process of getting to the forest. Boats, one after the other, were lowered into the water along with women, children, their luggage, and a few escorting men and floated towards the shore. There were about three to four hundred people aboard and the whole operation took a few hours till the night was thick with darkness. The shore was suddenly seething with anxious people who had been waiting for everyone to assemble together so that they could go farther in search of their destination.

The journey ahead was arduous, uncertain, and dangerous. Tottering collectively through an exhaustive, lengthy march, they finally found the *gurudwara*, where a hospitable shelter awaited them under the affectionate care of members of the Sikh community. Food was provided as well as rooms to rest for the night. People thanked their stars and blessed their hosts wholeheartedly. Sleeping sporadically through half the length of the night, they got up at the break of dawn and prepared to continue their journey back to their respective homes. They marched towards the Multan Nagar station which was quite far away, but the lack of any other alternative only strengthened their resolve. Their hosts had made arrangements for their journey by providing a few camels which came as a great relief to the women and children. A survival instinct and hope to reach their homes safely became the guiding spirit throughout the tedious journey. Crossing many obstacles on the way and roughing out the odds, the multitude finally reached the railway station in the late hours of the morning and heaved a collective sigh of relief. Many of them took recourse to sending telegrams to their near and dear ones about their safety and the probable time of their arrival. Nodding happily at one another and saying goodbye, they dispersed and went their own ways. After a harrowing experience in the night which was followed by a long journey, the tired crowd made an interesting scene at the platform. While men hurried towards the ticket counters, women flocked to the waiting room and every possible nook and corner where they could make themselves comfortable. Small children, excited with the novelty of the experience ran from one end to the other, vying for attention and demands to buy things that caught their fancy.

Kaushalya, taking Shobhna by the hand, first sought out the post office so she could send a telegram and tell Ganpat Rai that they were safe. They then searched for the right train to Lahore.

'Ma, I will never forget this experience in my whole life,' said Shobhna to Kaushalya as their train began its journey. 'If we hadn't found the *gurudwara* last night, we would have been stranded in the steamer!' The thought still scared Shobhna.

'Well my dear, God doesn't come himself in times of need but he sends his representatives in the form of other people to help those who need it,' said Kaushalya. 'He is the preserver and the destroyer both. Nothing in this world moves without his will!'

They reached the Lahore Railway station and lost no time in finding a *tonga* to take them first to Budin Road before heading towards Model Town, Lahore. It was on Budin Road that Arjun Dev, Kaushalya's younger brother-in-law, had opened a general merchant's shop and where Ganpat Rai also lent him a helping hand whenever needed. Kaushalya wanted to tell them that they had arrived safely.

Everyone was happy to see them. The boys listened closely as Shobhna told them about the steamer incident. How much they wished they had been on board! They pressed Shobhna for more details till she was left with no more stories to tell.

'There's nothing more to tell, nothing at all. Stop pestering me now!' she shushed them with a smile. 'Now, you tell me whether all of you have finished your school homework. The holidays are coming to an end. It is time to get back to the old routine.'

'Ha, ha, you're the one who needs to beware! Father says you will study only till class eight. It is going to be the end of school for you. You won't be allowed to study further.'

Shobhna was shocked by what she heard from her brother. She ran to her mother.

'Ma, why can't I study further?'

'Of course you can, dear. As long as you want!'

'But my father doesn't want it!'

'Who told you so?'

'My brothers! They are having a good laugh at me right now.'

'I will certainly talk to your father.' Kaushalya's eyes shifted to Shobhna's face and rested there. They seemed exhausted and full of anxiety.

Kaushalya could not believe what she had heard. Her darling Shobhna won't be allowed to study further? She had always been a champion of women's education, taking pains to teach the basics of literacy even to the domestic help who used to look after the younger boys, and now her own daughter would be deprived of schooling? She herself had continued with her passion for education despite being a mother of six children. Her family life had not stopped her from successfully passing the *Prabhakar* examination, which happened to be the highest degree in the Hindi language. All this had taken place under the encouragement and able guidance of their neighbour, Pt. Bhagwad Dutt, who was a prominent *Arya Samaj* leader as well as an eminent historian, author, and intellectual. His wife was also a professor of Sanskrit in a college at Lahore. They held free classes for *Prabhakar* at their home in the evenings; it was a boon for Kaushalya. She faced veiled resistance at home for continuing with her education and despite the odds her determination always saw her through. Their neighbourhood was full of such like-minded people who wanted to contribute their bit to the welfare of the society.

The *Arya Samaj Bhawan* in the vicinity often saw the congregation of eminent people of whom Kaviraj Harnam Das was one such personality. Rai Bahadur's wife Smt Vidya Wati, Kaushalya, and a few other women belonging to good families had gotten together to raise funds for the construction of the *Arya Samaj Bhawan*. They also opened an *Arya Pathshala* for educating young girls in the premises of the *Bhawan* itself. Kaushalya had been entrusted with the responsibility of the girl's school, of which she became honorary in-charge. With a lot of persuasion, she was able to enrol three girls of her own relatives and pushed the school through its humble beginnings. The drive picked up fast and many more families began enrolling their children and providing financial assistance as well. Kaushalya had put her head and heart together for this noble cause and had won the admiration of all those around her. The thought of her own daughter not being allowed to continue her studies was intolerable!

As soon as they got home, Kaushalya tried to reason with Ganpat Rai about Shobhna's schooling; she was calm yet vociferous. But Ganpat Rai did not relent and soon Shobhna was pulled out of school. Even the principal expressed sadness that such an intelligent pupil was being made to stop going to school but Ganpat Rai was adamant.

As luck would have it, a job offer came Ganpat Rai's way. Rai Bahadur Wali Ram, Kaushalya's maternal brother-in-law, owned an *Ayurveda* College at Nisbat Road in Lahore. He was on the lookout for an honest and hard-working manager and Ganpat Rai's profile was best suited for the position. Ganpat Rai did not take long to accept the offer and had Kaushalya's wholehearted support.

Ganpat Rai joined the college and found out that the minimum qualification for admission to the college for girls was a pass certificate of the tenth standard. The medium of instruction in this medical college was Hindi and Sanskrit. Ganpat Rai suddenly felt a pang in his heart. If only Shobhna had completed her tenth standard! She would have been eligible for admission in this college and could have become a *vaidya* in her own right. He felt guilty. He resolved to find out from the authorities if an alternative was available. The principal offered to examine Shobhna in the languages of Hindi and Sanskrit and if she passed, promised to admit her as a special case.

Thus Shobhna appeared for a test, then an interview, and passed both with flying colours. She was offered admission in the college of *Ayurveda*. Kaushalya's joy knew no bounds; she still could not believe that her daughter would one day become a doctor in the stream of *Ayurveda*. There were, of course, problems initially, but Kausalya saw them only as minor irritants which could easily be taken care of. Lahore was at a distance of at least five to six miles from Model Town but they could get the seat reserved for her in advance in the local bus and take care of the commuting problem. Mother and daughter were both elated at the turn of events. The hand of destiny was guiding them.

The desperate restlessness that Kaushalya had felt for months began going away. She felt at peace. She thanked God again and again wondering whether it was at all possible for the human mind to understand the subtle ways of the Almighty. She had to remind herself that indeed, all rational thought falls flat when pitted against the mystery of the universe. She realized that change was the only constant in life and one should welcome it with an open mind. Who really knows for sure whether things will take a turn for better or worse? Kaushalya's eyes shone bright.

15

It was sunny that day. Geli Bai had slept a little longer than usual and the morning routine inside the household had lagged without her. She got up and prepared to start her day; she was silent and reserved. She looked gaunt and haggard. Ganpat Rai was concerned.

'Mother, you do too much work at your age. Give some extra work to the children. They are big enough to help.'

'Oh! I am all right!' Geli Bai picked up the pail and went to milk the cows.

'Ma, you are ruining your health,' said Arjun Dev, visibly upset. They had often asked Geli Bai to rest more, given how she had bouts of asthma, but she would not listen.

'I am a little tired, that's all. Go and do your work. Don't waste time on me.' Geli Bai dismissed them with a wave of her hand.

They listened and went back to their work. The boys got ready for school and Shobhna helped Kaushalya with making breakfast.

The household was in the throes of the morning rush and Geli Bai wanted to be part of it. Her whole life had revolved around her home and work and she took pride in her energy even at her age. She never grumbled nor resented her lot. Instead she was a pillar of strength for the family. She had battled so many odds in her life.

Today, her steps were heavy as she went about the house, looking for things to do. She realized that she was having difficulty and gasped for breath. She prodded on, heading towards her animals, her constant companions who understood her deeply and with whom she felt warm and motherly. Their shed had been her cherished refuge, a sort of a haven. She longed to be with them that particular morning.

Kaushalya called out to her, '*Maji*, I have prepared the food. Come and eat something.'

'You go ahead, *beti*. I will eat after a while. I am not hungry right now.' She walked to her favourite spot.

'*Maji*! Call me if you need me for anything.' Kaushalya turned towards her room to get ready. She had made a list of a few things she needed and intended to go to the bazaar. On her way back, she could visit one of her relatives and still come back in time for when the children would return from their schools. It had always made her happy to spend her mornings running errands and doing some shopping and social interaction.

As she got ready, Kaushalya could hear Geli Bai's affectionate muttering towards her animals, although her voice was low and her words sporadic. She thought that perhaps the heat was making it difficult for Geli Bai to breathe; or the odour of the animals, even. In a way, she felt indebted to her mother-in-law: she had been a big support in her family life. 'God save my mother-in-law and give her a long life!' A wish escaped her lips.

Kaushalya carried the string bag that contained her essentials and her umbrella and came out of her room. She decided to peep through the shed to have a look at Geli Bai, and tell her that she would be back in a couple of hours. Kaushalya reached the open courtyard and called out, '*Maji*! Where are you? I am going for a while.' There was no response; instead, an eerie silence. The animals too looked sullen. Kaushalya took a few more steps and looked around. She saw Geli Bai, in one corner of the shed, lying unconscious. For a moment, it looked as if she was sleeping; worn out, perhaps with exhaustion. Kaushalya ran towards her, took her head in her lap and tried to wake her up, stroking her, first gently and then a bit harder. Geli Bai did not respond, her eyes remained shut. A shudder ran down Kaushalya's spine at the mere thought of having lost her. Utter disbelief and panic overpowered her. When the truth finally sank in, she got up hurriedly, gently setting Geli Bai's head down on the floor. She ran out of the house, shouting for help. A few people showed up at her first call.

'What is the matter Kaushalya*ji*?' asked one neighbour.

'Something has happened to *Maji* and I am all alone. Come, please!'

They ran inside the house with Kaushalya, who took them to the shed where Geli Bai lay unconscious.

They surrounded her and one felt her pulse while the rest looked for some sign of life in her. But they all knew she was gone. 'God bless her and give peace to her soul!' one of them led a prayer, and the rest joined in chorus.

One elderly woman said to Kaushalya, '*Beti*, she has left for her heavenly abode. Her journey in this life is complete. Let us call the family members.'

They all helped Kaushalya lift Geli Bai and bring her inside the house. A white sheet was spread on the floor—in the middle of the house that she had headed for a long time. They laid her body down. Two men went out to summon Ganpat Rai and Arjun Dev from their shop. The children would be home soon.

The whole neighbourhood started gathering, with the elderly women taking charge of the necessary rituals that had to be performed. Kaushalya was still in shock and could not take lead; she would rather follow their instructions for now. Everything had happened too suddenly and she had yet to come to terms with it. She awaited the return of her family desperately. The boys were the first ones to come back home. On seeing a large gathering, they ran inside and saw their grandmother lying on the floor. They went to her and touched her body. Finding it cold and motionless, they looked for their mother who sat in her own mute world looking helpless, her hands folded on her lap. They all burst into loud cries and huddled towards each other, seeeking comfort and reassurance. One of them stood by the door to watch out for Shobhna's return and as soon as he saw her at a distance, the boy ran to her and gave her the sad news. She was led into the house from the rear door where some women took charge of her. Soon Ganpat Rai and his younger brother reached home. They were sullen and dishevelled, out of breath.

'Oh! Mother!' Ganpat Rai shrieked. 'So sudden! What will we do without you?' He softly put his hand on her forehead.

Arjun Dev whimpered, 'Mother, come back to us! Please!' He wiped his tears.

The family sat together in the courtyard, united in grief. Geli Bai rested in the middle of the front veranda and lay like a historical monument. Never again would their household be the same without her formidable presence, her quiet strength and her uncanny commonsense. The spoke of the wheel in their household was gone. She went away after laying down a firm foundation for the progress and growth of their family.

Geli Bai was cremated before sunset in the little *ghat* that looked over the fields and houses on the other side. It was a warm day—and a cruel one for the family. The entire neighbourhood, friends, and relatives, mourned the death of Geli Bai, the stoic lady who dared to meet the challenges of life with her sheer grit.

Kaushalya and Ganpat Rai worked in perfect harmony for some time after the death of their mother. The mantle of running the household had fallen on their shoulders and they had to fill the vacuum; they had no choice but to set their personal differences aside.

Kaushalya was the one who felt the deepest void left behind by Geli Bai's passing. She looked around the house and, without Geli Bai, it was empty; it was immobile, bereft of all activities. Kaushalya had little idea of how to run the household. Geli Bai had never bothered her much about the day-to-day functioning of the house.

The animals also felt the impact of Geli Bai's passing. Kaushalya simply did not know what to do with them. Ganpat Rai and Arjun Dev tried to take up this responsibility and help as much as they could but they had little time. They decided to sell the rest of the animals except one cow whose yield they reckoned would be sufficient for the family. Gone was the surplus milk that was then made into butter and ghee.

Kaushalya felt a pang in her heart. How she wished Geli Bai was still alive! She realized her worth now, after she was gone. She longed to tell her mother-in-law how much she respected her; she wanted to chat with her about casual, mundane things; she wanted to spend time with her, enjoy her company; she wanted to touch her feet, for once, not out of formality but respect. Only if she could do it once, it would make up for her indifference towards her in the past. Kaushalya wanted to atone for all her neglect of homely duties. She regretted not letting Geli Bai know how much she respected her, how much she depended on her. Geli Bai was the sun around which their family revolved!

The mere thought of their future without Geli Bai, caused Kaushalya to be thoroughly petrified. She would have to manage things singlehandedly from now on. Shobhna was there, of course, for company and help. But she too was raw for matters of the home. She thought of the good old times when her sisters-in-law were always there to look after everything, so willingly and happily. She could never repay her debt to Geli Bai and her sisters-in-law for having made her life easy and comfortable as long as they could.

Geli Bai's sudden death had unnerved Kaushalya; she felt shaken to her core. The house seemed empty, listless, and bereft of benevolent forces. The boys felt anchorless and were irritable at the slightest provocation. Shobhna had always been closer to her mother but she too missed the stick-wielding female touch in an otherwise insipid household. Ganpat Rai and Arjun Dev tried to drown their grief with work. They all felt the same: the quiet and peace in their household was deeply annoying.

Soon, Kaushalya's sadness gave way to loneliness. She felt trapped. She was not used to spending the whole day at home. Before Geli Bai's passing, Kaushalya had found for herself a group of like-minded people who were involved in various issues of social emancipation. Her interests lay somewhere else; she had always found housework dreary.

She wondered if she would manage when she did not even know how to get the boys around.

An overwhelming feeling overpowered her heart. Suddenly, she thought of Subhagi, her mother. She had an instant longing to visit her and unburden her heart. Subhagi would no doubt understand her pain. She would tell her mother all about her situation, how she had suddenly become the man of the house.

She had a little breakfast and finished her tea, then set off for her mother's house. She was exhausted when Subhagi met her at the door.

'Oh, Ma! How I've missed you!' Kaushalya sobbed as Subhagi composed herself, completely taken aback at her daughter's unannounced arrival and outpouring of grief.

Subhagi led her inside and made her sit down. 'Change and death are the law of nature, Koshi. Even the Almighty can't change that, my dear.' She lifted Kaushalya's delicate face with her small but work-hardened hands.

'It's hard, Ma. How will I cope?'

'I know it is a great loss, Koshi. You feel a gap that will not be filled so easily. But you need to be brave now. Parents do not stay forever.'

Kaushalya looked at her mother; a little, frail woman who had weathered many storms in her life with her subtle, quiet strength. Her heart ached for her.

'Oh, Ma, I love you so much! Don't you ever leave me!' Kaushalya's sobs became louder and more irrepressible.

They talked and talked, sometimes aloud and other times, in whispers. They shared what was inside their troubled hearts and tightened their bond of love. They both were surprised at the ease with which their hearts were unburdened. The cloud of gloom on Kaushalya's heart had dissipated and she felt relieved and full of energy. She was ready to face life once again.

16

The months passed slowly. Kaushalya gave in completely to the management of the house, wondering how it might have been for Geli Bai to have spent a lifetime at home trying to work the family and its system.

One day as Kaushalya took a break from housework, she sat brooding. She thought about her sons and her daughter, and their future. They were all closely bound and it brought a smile on her face. Her sons were tall, rugged and in perfect health. They were very handsome, were fair and had curly black hair and full, red lips. They had inherited the chiselled features and greyish blue eyes of their mother and the build of their father. Shobhna, too, was fast growing up into a beautiful young girl. The images of her family filled Kaushalya with a sense of pride.

Kaushalya decided that they needed to hire a servant so that she could have help in the housework. Ganpat Rai quickly shot down her idea. 'Nonsense!' he said. But Kaushalya was determined to act independently about the matter. She was, after all, now incharge of their home affairs, especially the children. Ganpat Rai remained, as always, preoccupied with his work and his younger brother's affairs. Kaushalya sighed as she thought of the antagonism between her and Ganpat Rai over his brother. She had long felt that her husband cared more about Arjun Dev than their own children. Kaushalya wanted Ganpat Rai to share greater responsibilities towards their brood.

One day, she asked Ganpat Rai, 'Did you give permission to Ved Prakash to go to Nagpur in connection with his work with *Rashtriya Swayamsevak Sangh*?'

'Why should I?' replied Ganpat Rai. 'He never asked me. I have no idea about his programme.'

'The boys are getting out of hand. They don't have their heart in their studies. They don't listen to me either. You should interact with them more often and teach them to focus on their studies.'

Ganpat Rai didn't reply. Kaushalya continued. 'Maybe you can take more interest in the future of your children rather than your brother's shop.'

Ganpat Rai was livid. 'I suggest, Kaushalya, that you spend more time at home than in your *Arya Samaj Mandir* or pursuing your studies. That might help too.' His tone was icy.

It was clear they were angry with each other. After a few exchanges of some strong words, they both fell silent. They were both aware that a lack of understanding between parents often resulted in a lack of direction for their children.

Despite Kaushalya's refusal, Ved Prakash continued on his trip to Nagpur for his social work. His studies suffered and he failed his high school examination. Anand Prakash, who was in the eighth class, was also unwilling to continue with school. He told his mother one day, 'Ma! I don't want to study any further.'

'What? But why?' Kaushalya was aghast.

'I want to work in Uncle Arjun Dev's shop. I want to earn my own money. Why should I study? I don't want to become a teacher!' Anand Prakash was insistent.

'You finish your school first. We'll see later,' Kaushalya cut him short.

She sighed. She thought of how their father could guide their sons in life. She felt resigned; her sons were beyond her control. Despite her best efforts, she had been unable to instil a liking for studies in her sons. Shobhna was an exception. The issue always generated a feeling of discord within the family. Shobhna was, indeed, her mother's daughter. Their constant company and intimacy made up for everything and brought a ray of sunshine into Kaushalya's life. They shared so many things in common.

The boys, meanwhile, resented the incessant coaxing of their mother to take up higher studies; they were always restless for something mundane, something that would suit their fancy. Empty concepts and arduous routine bored them; they were unaccustomed to hard work and only wanted the simple pleasures of life. They had never known a feeling of insecurity, brought up as they had been in a traditional joint family system under the affectionate eye of their grandmother. With her passing, an intimate bond was broken and their minds went haywire. Home attracted them less and less and they wanted to venture out into the world to fulfil the flights of their imagination.

Ved Prakash had already become quite independent. Working in his spare time for the *Rashtriya Swayamsevak Sangh* he found that he came in contact with people from all walks of life and that interested and stimulated his mind. He made friends among men wherever he went; some of whom were very well-educated, having a degree in law or Masters in humanities. The freedom movement started by Gandhiji was gaining momentum and people were going out of their way to support it. Ved Prakash's active involvement brought many friends home who often stayed overnight. At times, he was also visiting other people while doing *Sangh* work. Out of many of his friends, he was particularly fond of one, Anmol Singh, who had a similar outlook and enjoyed talking about the subjects of history and politics. Kaushalya had been anxious about Ved Prakash's future and felt that she was losing him to the social movement.

Anand Prakash, meanwhile, started helping out his uncle, who ran a shop at Budin road. Kaushalya sorely resented this and protested to Ganpat Rai, 'Stop Anand Prakash if you can. This is the age to study and not mind a shop.'

'He doesn't study anyway,' replied Ganpat Rai. 'One cannot just force children if they do not want it themselves. Let him learn to work at least.'

Anand Prakash worked diligently and enjoyed his work.

He told his father, 'I wish to have a shop of my own one day. I can't be an apprentice all my life. Help me out, father!'

Ganpat Rai liked his son's spirit of entrepreneurship. By chance, a shop was lying vacant not far from their own place of work. They took the shop on rent and filled it up with all kinds of groceries. Anand Prakash was elated. He had a chance to work independently and make his own living. Hard-working and tenacious, he worked almost singlehandedly, aided by his father's inspiration.

'I want to learn English, Father,' Anand Prakash said to Ganpat Rai. 'Many of my customers are well-educated. They talk to me in English. I feel hesitant and uneasy.'

'But you don't have that kind of time, my boy, along with your work.'

'Why not? I can do both. Customers are not standing here all the time. I can study when I am free.' Ganpat Rai could tell that his son was determined.

True to his word, Anand Prakash bought the books that he needed in order to learn English. He showed them to his mother, who felt glad at her son's enthusiasm. He wanted to do well in life and take the family forward in his own way. He was doing good business and earning a reasonable profit. His diligence was paying off and he fancied himself as a responsible breadwinner of the family. An easy flow of money brought in its wake a renewed confidence in his own self and also a few annoying habits. Eating food from home every day for his afternoon meal had become old-fashioned for him and he started experimenting with street food everyday during the afternoons.

'Let's have *chole bhature* today for lunch, Uncle,' he tried to coax Arjun Dev for company.

'Why don't you join us today, my boy? We have got our food from home. It is unhealthy to eat street food in this heat. It can result in an infection of the stomach,' said Arjun Dev as he patted his nephew on the back.

Arjun Dev knew of what he spoke. Summer time in Lahore could get bad. In fact, Lahore was known to have extremes of weather, be it winter or summer.

But Anand Prakash did not heed his family and continued with his habit of eating food that was not homecooked. Soon he came down with an acute stomach infection.

He reached home that day extremely drained of all energy. He lay still, unable to move.

Kaushalya spotted him right away. 'Are you tired or unwell?'

'My stomach is upset, Ma. I feel exhausted. I don't think I have any energy left.'

His words filled her with dread. She touched his forehead and found that he was running a high fever. A doctor was summoned and he was examined thoroughly. The doctor diagnosed it as stomach infection and prescribed a few medicines. He also advised Anand Prakash to rest for a few days. He had no choice but to do as told.

Kaushalya was present to look after her son. Her constant loving care, plenty of rest, and hearty meals cooked at home, nursed her son back to health.

One day Kaushalya asked him, 'My son, do you want to continue with your studies?'

'Ma, I am fine now. And my shop has been doing so well. Let me go back and work.'

Kaushalya tried to tell him to take a few more days off but Anand Prakash was adamant. She had no choice but to let him go.

But although Anand Prakash had recovered enough to get up on his feet and go back to work, he never regained his full health. He would run a fever off and on and would often complain of an upset stomach. There were days when he was lethargic. A second doctor, also reputed, was consulted. He diagnosed the illness as typhoid and advised complete bed rest. Days passed and Anand Prakash showed no signs of improvement. He started passing blood in his stool and the doctor immediately prescribed admission to the hospital. The family grew increasingly concerned as they realized that Anand Prakash was very seriously ill.

Kaushalya and Ganpat Rai quickly set out to make arrangements for their son to be taken to the hospital. Anand Prakash, pale and only semi-conscious, could vaguely hear his parents' voices. He tried to open his eyes and in a blur saw his mother standing beside him; he could make out that her eyes were full of anxiety. Her face was calm and she tried to look brave but displayed flashes of uncertainty and inner suffering.

'Mother, I want to get better,' he whispered. 'I want to make a lot of money and enjoy life.'

'You will be fine, my dear boy! Don't worry and do not exert yourself too much. We will take you to the hospital tomorrow and you will come back home fine and healthy.' Kaushalya touched him and tried to give him comfort. Anand Prakash took her hand, kept it on his chest and fell into a sound sleep. Kaushalya felt a bit reassured.

Ganpat Rai did not waste any time in the morning and set off to town to make arrangements. Deeply alarmed, he consoled himself with the thought that his son would get the best possible medical care and he would get well. By late afternoon he was done, and he thought of dropping by his brother's shop to see if they could arrange for a boy who could look after Anand Prakash's shop. Hardly had he reached when a boy from their neighbourhood came hurrying with the message that Anand Prakash was vomiting blood and that he should hurry home.

By the time Ganpat Rai and Arjun Dev reached home, a large number of people had gathered there; loud shrieks from women filled the air. Ganpat Rai ran inside the house, horrified and fearing the worst. Neighbours led him to the courtyard where his son was. Anand Prakash lay on his cot, limp, unmoving. Kaushalya, Abhay, and Harsh Prakash surrounded him, mute and blank. Kaushalya saw Ganpat Rai and burst into uncontrollable sobs. 'Why has God been so cruel to me? I didn't do anything to deserve this. Why didn't he take me instead of my dear Anand? He was too young!' Anand Prakash was only eighteen, and had a lot of dreams and plans and had his whole life ahead of him.

There was crying all around, prayers being said, invoking the mercy of God and asking for peace for the departed soul.

Anand Prakash's siblings wailed. 'We are still there for you!' they said to Kaushalya again and again.

Darkness had descended. The grief was thick.

They all came, relatives and friends and neighbours, offering their sympathies and joining the prayers. By the latter half of the night, the immediate family was left alone with Anand Prakash. Silence embraced the house, interrupted only by Kaushalya's loud shrieks who fell unconscious many times during that dreadful night. No one dared to stop her when she would go near her son's body, hug him and kiss him on his forehead saying sweet words. Ganpat Rai sat in stony silence, holding a fixed gaze on his dear son.

They cremated Anand Prakash at noon the next day. Ganpat Rai's sisters all reached early in the morning. The rituals complete, it was time for the last journey to begin. The family and friends mourned noisily, crying and weeping, as Anand Prakash's body was lifted by Ganpat Rai, Arjun Dev, Harsh Prakash and Abhay Prakash on their shoulders. One elderly woman whispered, 'Thank God Geli Bai was not here to see such a scene.'

'Oh God! Have mercy on Kaushalya and her family!' the prayers were uttered again and again.

Kaushalya could only stare at her son as he completed his final journey. She was brokenhearted. She was, for a long, long time. She shut herself off and lost all interest in life. Nothing excited her or stimulated her mind. No one and nothing succeeded in diverting her attention to other things: all she could think about was Anand Prakash. Day after day, she altered her rituals between mechanical housework and sitting in the courtyard looking blankly into space. She did not say a word.

Subhagi came every day to see her daughter. She hoped to help Kaushalya through this crisis, the worst she had had in her young life. With the warmth and gentleness of a mother, she would try to draw Kaushalya out of her deathly silence. But Kaushalya would take no notice. Ganpat Rai, however, was affected in a rather more subtle way. He would often relapse into a kind of daze and then suddenly get up, smile in a normal way and join the crowd of mourners who visited their house regularly.

'Why have you gathered here? Don't mourn the departed soul! He must have taken birth somewhere,' he would say.

People looked at him in disbelief.

'Don't cry. Death is the eternal reality of life. Everyone has to die, sooner or later. Every fruit falls down from the tree; some fall on ripeness, some raw. Nothing unusual has happened in this house. Don't come tomorrow onwards for mourning at least. But you are all always welcome for a cup of tea,' said Ganpat Rai with a smile.

Even Subhagi was puzzled by his words.

'Oh God,' Subhagi prayed. 'Take me away before anything worse than this befalls my daughter!'

Little did she know at the time that her words would prove prophetic!

17

The nation had been experiencing turmoil for some time. Its effect was visible in all spheres of society. Politics had become a war of patience for Indian leaders. Their patriotic speeches had a great impact on the minds of the people. They were ready to sacrifice their life and comfort to follow ideologies that would take them a step further towards freedom. The society had been gearing up for a change. Gandhiji's penchant for *charkha* had greatly captivated the people's imagination. As part of the *swadeshi* movement they had taken to it with a vengeance. It had become a household object and a weapon of mass appeal as well as protest. Geli Bai had been a regular at her spinning wheel and the children had grown up with its concept and usage. Kaushalya and Shobhna would spend some time daily on it which was also a great stress-buster for them. They would spin yards and yards of cotton turning it into a thick thread which could later be exchanged for *khadi* cloth at the local *khadi bhandars*. Shobhna loved these sessions as Kaushalya would always be in a mood to discuss something or the other during this time. She related to Shobhna, one particular afternoon, as to how they had collected all the foreign cloth in the neighbourhood, placed it in the middle of the colony on a pedestal and burnt it to mark their protest against the rule. It was aptly called *videshi kapdo ki holi* (burning of the foreign cloth). Shobhna's eyes widened with wonder, 'Mother! Did it actually happen? Did you really burn the clothes?'

'Yes! We made a heap of all such *phirang* clothes and put them on fire while chanting *Vande Mataram* all the time.'

'How patriotic, Ma!'

'Yes! National sentiment reigned supreme, Shobhna. People grew out of their personal interests and united themselves for a common cause. The wave of Gandhiji's ideology rocked every nook and corner of our country.'

'Mother! Idealism does have the propensity to sway the country if led by example,' said Shobhna.

'Right you are, Shobhna! Gandhiji knows the pulse of the people and leads them by setting an example before them. People flock to have a glimpse of him and follow his dictum.'

'Ma, we also contribute in our own way. We unfurl our national flag on the top of our house on every 26th January and sing *Vijayi Vishwa Tiranga Pyara*. You also take us to the banks of the river Ravi on every Basant Panchmi where we pay our tribute at the *samadhi* of Vir Hakikat Rai who sacrificed his life for the sake of his sacred religion. It is wonderful to go to this fair riding on our bicycles and be a part of such festivities…' Shobhna beamed with pride.

'Yes, dear! These are great times of social transformation. We are blessed that we are a part of such history that is being written. We witness the most important event of this century, perhaps. The future generations will envy us, no doubt,' Kaushalya's eyes were also full of pride.

'Ma, I love to wear *khadi* cloth. Its fabric and prints are unique in their own way. While the texture of the cloth has a cooling effect in summers, it gives a cosy feeling during winters.'

'*Khadi* silk is also very fine and soft. It stands out for its quality. When your uncle Arjun Dev gets married, we will buy clothes for everybody from the *Khadi Bhandar* only. Not even a thread of foreign cloth will ever come to this house as long as I am there,' said Kaushalya.

'When will my uncle get married, Ma?'

'It shouldn't be very long, Shobhna. The girl's parents are pressing the matter almost every day. Let's see.' Their spinning session was almost over.

While Kaushalya had taken a long time to get over the tragic death of Anand Prakash and come to terms with reality, Ganpat Rai seemed dissatisfied, not only with himself but with everything else in his life. He had been greatly shaken by the death of his beloved son; he never saw himself living or enjoying life as happily as before, for all time to come. He became acutely aware of the impermanence of life, happiness and sorrow, and felt the necessity for detachment from family life as well as mundane things. He found himself more interested in the deeper issues of life and the universe; it was the insufficiency of day-to-day life that he wanted to renounce. Life, he thought, would always be full of tragedy and sorrow. Man, being a puppet in the hands of God and circumstances, would always remain immersed in ordinary life and one day, he would meet his end, even abruptly. Emotions had suddenly ceased to matter for Ganpat Rai who felt that all worldly relations were false when confronted with the mighty hand of death. Domestic life was fast turning into a mechanical routine. He toyed with the idea of renouncing the world and embracing 'Vanprastha' but the impending marriage of Arjun Dev was still to be solemnized to which he felt himself morally bound. He felt that life was passing him by and they would all become a part of history one day. He began to give more and more time to these deliberations and started shunning routine affairs to the extent possible. As it was, the warmth for Arjun Dev was gradually taking him away from Kaushalya, to whom he felt responsible and to whom he averred he should have belonged. Yet, he was never able to feel or develop a feeling of intimacy with Kaushalya in any way. She had always remained Ramchander's wife in the first instance and only later, the mother of his children. Their relationship was always built in and around the children and their loss weaned away a little segment of their ambivalent relationship from each other. Even when together, both existed in their own world of thoughts or necessities.

The summer holidays in the schools had already begun. A relaxed atmosphere prevailed in the house. Arjun Dev's marriage, to a girl named Santosh, was to be solemnized during this time. The relatives came visiting and helped with the arrangements. Kaushalya's sisters-in-law had all come home, along with their children, who made a great party. A wave of grief would pass through Kaushalya's heart whenever she would see all the children chatting or playing happily. The memory of Anand Prakash was always fresh in her heart. The visit of her sisters-in-law was always a source of great comfort to Kaushalya because they would practically take charge of the kitchen as well as the management of the house and Kaushalya would be free for other matters. She busied herself now with the preparations for the impending marriage. Lists were prepared for the purchase of various items, in which Shobhna took great interest. She was excited at the idea of going to the *Khadi Bhandars* and making purchases of clothes for herself, the bride and the other relatives. The aunts, too, were of great help. Everyone lived in harmony and went out of their way to make things easier and comfortable for each other. Basic amenities were always aplenty in the house. Sacks of wheat and gram, sufficient for the whole year, were stocked carefully in the store rooms. The huge vegetable garden at the back of the house gave them enough harvest to take care of their everyday needs. The trees not only yielded a rich crop of fruit, but also served as a playground for the children and the cattle took care of their dairy requirements.

The wedding took place with a sober tone, given the nature of the family tragedy that had just befallen them. On a bigger scale, the country had also been under the wake of a freedom struggle and any opulence shown by way of wedding events would have been inappropriate. The threat of the Second World War had been looming large, which also resulted in a steep rise in the prices of commodities for common people. Arjun Dev's shop made huge profits and soon he was able to purchase a two-canal house in Model Town, which was a good two or three miles away from Kaushalya's house.

After the wedding, Arjun Dev and Santosh shifted to their new house. But before long the bride began feeling lonely, especially when Arjun Dev kept long hours at the shop, and they decided to move back to the large family. She came from a joint family after all, and was not used to living alone. And she was in the family way, too, and so looked for some company.

For some time, peace prevailed in the household. Their home, although broken with the successive deaths of loved ones, was still home; it provided a rock-solid anchor not only for their emotions but also their innovative ideas. Slowly they picked themselves up from their grief, looked for reasons to rejoice together, went for excursions, called their relatives to visit, and had a good time. The evenings were particularly delightful when the entire family would get together at the back of the house and play hilarious games. The languorous hours would stretch long till it would be time to light the earthen lamps hanging in the rear veranda, which lent the house a gothic aura. The back garden was the hub of activity at such times, filled with cots and easy chairs and people reclining wherever they wanted. The cool breeze carried with it the aroma of the food being cooked inside the house by the aunts and other women of family. The evening meal, in such company, was never short of a feast; the fresh vegetables straight from the kitchengarden, pulses cooked on a slow fire for a long time, curd and dairy products prepared from the fresh milk available at home including sweet dishes like *kheer*, *phirni* or *halwa*, cooked aplenty and with a lot of care and love. Everyone enjoyed the sumptuous food and soaked in the cool scented air under the blissful atmosphere of the sheltering sky.

During such family gatherings, Shobhna would invariably become the butt of jokes amongst her cousins. At 17, she looked too young for her professional studies. She had already completed the first two years of her *Ayurveda* course, passing them with reasonably good grades, but the third-year course included the clinical aspect of the subject where they had to do direct examination of patients as well as learn how to conduct actual interventions like administering injections.

'Are you sure your patients will let you examine them, Shobhna?' teased Harsh Prakash. 'I hope they feel safe enough!'

'But how can they let you give them an injection?' laughed another one.

'Well, my professor asks the patients to look the other way and then teaches me quietly how to give an injection. She also teaches us how to monitor blood pressure. Patients don't take to me easily,' smiled Shobhna. A roar of laughter went up the air as all the brothers and cousins surrounded Shobhna, calling her 'Shobhna, the doctor, ha, ha, ha...'

Shobhna quickly learned the trick of ignoring them. After all, she thought, she was enjoying what she was doing. Those easygoing times ended, too, before everyone realized it. Summer vacations ended, and the relatives returned to their respective homes, their hearts full of memories of the good times they spent at Kaushalya's abode.

Shobhna lost no time in going back to her own routine of practical training, which she was undertaking at the Mool Chand hospital, located at Maclor Road. She and the rest of the students were required to oversee at least six cases of delivery and complete a few written projects. She had to stay in the hospital compulsorily for at least three weeks and complete all her work. The three-year course had been extended for another year to incorporate exhaustive practical training, without which the course would not be complete. The annual examinations were just around the corner and the political situation in the country was getting worse than ever before. Hindu-Muslim riots had become the order of the day and the political leaders were fast losing control of the chaotic situation. The extreme emotions that had gripped the psyche of the mob were rendering it nearly impossible to restore law and order. People waited for a solution in an agonising frenzy.

To Kaushalya's relief, Shobhna's annual examinations got over without any problems. Given the unpredictability of the political atmosphere, Kaushalya decided to visit and spend some time with her cousin, Prem Devi in Dhanbad, along with her children.

'They will return soon to their home in Lahore once peace is restored to some extent,' she told her children.

A month later, Prime Minister Jawaharlal Nehru declared the partition of the country on the night of 14th August, 1947. All hell broke loose as day dawned in the wee hours of 15th August, 1947.

18

Overnight the nation plunged into the throes of mania. People went hysterical as the news of the country's partition spread like wildfire. Emotions ran high in both parts of the affected nation; caution was thrown to the wind by the frenzied people. The much-coveted Lahore came under the territory of Pakistan, the unexpectedness of which threw general life out of gear for thousands of people who found themselves suddenly uprooted from a comfortable life of plenty to a life that promised nothing but struggle, poverty, and uncertainty. 'How can anyone lose everything by the stroke of a pen, that too, by way of the wily manipulations of a handful of people who happened to be at the helm of affairs at that particular moment in history?' wondered people, before giving in to a surge of emotions that would cross all limits of patience in the days to come. The anger of the moment manifested itself in many ways of carnage; the bitterness, the hurt, the deprivation drove away any feelings of decency or gentleness. People stood anchorless and watched everything burning around them, getting frantic to run away to safer alternatives and save their lives. 'Life can be started again even in a foreign land among unknown people if precious lives were saved. Family can be united again, occupations found and built with time once again,' they thought.

The city was in a state of turmoil. People ran from one place to another seeking shelter, going to their homes first and finding them occupied by strange people, with blood in their eyes and weapons in their hands. Unarmed and devoid of all their belongings, they were driven away from their land and their homes, which they had built with their sweat and love, giving them the best of their youth. Piles of possessions were left behind, to be stored only in the recesses of their memories or else burnt before their eyes. 'Would memories be enough for sustenance for a lifetime? Could they be eroded eventually, ushering in a new era of peace and happiness? Was it possible to live with the dreadful pain of having lost everything, not knowing where destiny would take them? How could they rebuild their lives without the solid foundation of their memorable past? It wasn't possible! It couldn't be done! The future generations would never know their golden past, their inherent values, the antique belongings of their grandfather and great-grandfathers. How could they sift through their memories?' Questions haunted their hearts.

People turned their backs on years of toil and hard work, tried to grow out of their nervousness and sadness, forget the enormity of the tragedy and resolved to take care of their life and children, wherever and at whatever cost. To Pakistan or India or anywhere else, they had it in them to keep going until they were dead. They fled past the human bodies, empty-handed and headed straight, looking for safer destinations where they could start all over again, leaving behind feelings of bitterness and regret. They knew they would have to live in camps initially and rough out their lives. But they were mentally prepared; unwilling to give up under any circumstances and having faith in their grit and sense of entrepreneurship. Their generation had been a hardy one and nothing could keep them down for long. They would take to life once again, much like a phoenix, emerging out of its ashes and soaring again in the sky to achieve great heights. Such was their determination and such the dreams dancing in their eyes.

Respectable people became migrants; they lost their occupations, wealth, land, cattle and everything else except some of their family members and the will to live. They looked humbly for work, scrambled to live in refugee tent-houses provided to them by the government that was itself struggling to cope with the problems of the partition. The opulent houses were suddenly replaced by shabby sheds devoid of water or electricity. They braved the heat, the wind, the rain and the cold winters with a tenacity they themselves were not aware of. They listened to each other, shared their grief and helped each other in every way they could. They lived in the refugee camps along the roads, ignoring the stench, filth and blood of their kin. They came to enjoy their hardships, took to telling tales of their golden past, amazed at the changing parameters of life, sitting before the dying embers of a bonfire in the cold weather. The rude formality of a reclusive life was forgotten in the commonplace warmth of a community life where people participated equally with a humbled pride. Their quiet eyes spoke of the memories gone by and a sense of relief that said, 'We have been saved by the grace of God. We will build up our lives once again.'

'God has been kind still!' whispered some.

'Thank God! Our lives are saved,' was the general sigh of relief as all their hopes, desires and dreams lay thwarted and broken for the time being.

Kaushalya, along with her children, had been visiting her cousin, Prem Devi in Dhanbad, when the Hindu-Muslim riots broke out in Lahore. Trains full of dead bodies of Hindus were being sent to India from Pakistan every day, erupting in extreme mutual violence. Hindus, however, were ill-equipped to meet this ordeal, having had faith in the sentiments expressed by Mahatma Gandhi that Pakistan would be made over his dead body. They were certain that Lahore would form a part of India as its capital since all big courts, hospitals, libraries, schools, colleges and other organs of administration had been functioning from there. The situation, however, took a sharp turn putting things in reverse gear and getting out of hand. The law and order situation had nose-dived, erupting in carnage on both sides. People ran away to save their lives.

All the while, Ganpat Rai, Arjun Dev, and Ved Prakash had been in Lahore along with the families of their sisters. When the violence broke out they were forced to leave their home to save their lives. While the families of Lakshmi Devi, Chetni, and Hukmi made their way to Delhi and took shelter in refugee camps, Ganpat Rai, Arjun Dev, and Ved Prakash came to Dhanbad to join Kaushalya and their family.

Prem Devi's husband, Wali Ram, was the owner of a couple of coal mines which were a source of their family's flourishing income. Money was abundant in their home and so were comforts. Besides material riches, Wali Ram and Prem Devi were blessed with a magnanimous nature and tried to help all the relatives who came looking for shelter in their luxurious home: their house became the counterpart of Kaushalya's in Lahore. They lived together, happily taking care of one another's needs without letting their worries poison the atmosphere. There was room for everyone; so was the food and even the opportunities if one was sharp enough to grab them.

Kaushalya and her family were living in comfort but it was high time they found some work and set themselves up once again in life. Kaushalya had been thinking hard and always shared her thoughts with Shobhna, who had become more of a friend to her as she grew older, rather than a daughter.

One day Shobhna asked, 'Ma, what are we aiming to do in life now that we cannot go back to our own house in Lahore? We must have something to do on our own.'

'Yes Shobhna! My head is full of ideas and I shall discuss them with your *mausi* some day.'

Kaushalya was quiet for a long time. She was thinking of her sisters-in-law and their families who would be roughing it out in the government camps trying to eke out a living for sustenance all by themselves. She wondered how they would manage, given that they were not used to living in small quarters.

She asked her daughter, 'Are you comfortable here, Shobhna?'

'Yes, Mother! Very much so! But we must do something else. Our father must find work to do. We, too, can lend a helping hand. We are educated.'

'I shall have everything talked over and see what can be done!'

They decided to settle down in Dhanbad. What was once a place for visiting had become one of settlement! Still, Kaushalya considered herself lucky that they didn't have to live in the refugee camps like other migrants and had a life that was comfortable enough for them to start anew.

Ganpat Rai and Arjun Dev had been able to bring with them a considerable amount of money safely when they left Lahore amidst the communal riots. They were able to buy a small shop in the vicinity and started trading in timber merchandise. They resolved to make it work by dint of their hard work and business acumen, involving all their sons in the venture. Prem Devi and Wali Ram, however, had other plans for Kaushalya and Shobhna. Wali Ram brought up the subject when they were all sitting together for dinner.

'I am thinking of setting up a primary school nearby. Koshi *behenji*, if you want, it is an opportunity for you and Shobhna to teach in the school and utilize your free time. The school will benefit from your experience and sense of dedication for the cause of education for women and girls. Besides, a few other women who have come here from Lahore can also teach in the school. What do you think?'

'I think it is an excellent idea, *bhai sahib*. There can't be a better proposal. I would consider it a God-sent opportunity. It would be a gainful employment for me and Shobhna.'

Kaushalya was glad at the turn of events. She had never been able to dissociate herself mentally from her love of learning. A chance was coming her way even in such strange circumstances and she would go out of her way to make it a success.

The school picked up fast. It started with the enrolment of a few students as well as teachers. Kaushalya took great pains in setting up the school, getting students and persuading them to join and taking a lot of interest in classroom teaching. Shobhna, adept in the languages of Hindi and Sanskrit, joined the staff. It was a happy sight to see the mother-daughter duo going to teach in the same school and following the same routine. They became a centre of interest even in the neighbourhood, amazing people around by their initiative and progressive thinking.

'Look at Kaushalya and her daughter Shobhna going to the school together. They look like sisters!'

'They really make a friendly and sociable pair.'

'Beautiful! Wise! Jolly!'

The activities in the school expanded along with its infrastructure and so did Kaushalya's circle of friends and relatives. Her cousin, Prem Devi, was responsible for getting Kaushalya an opportunity to settle down respectably in a new place. Ganpat Rai and the sons were also doing their best to make a decent beginning and provide the family support that was expected of them. Everyone was committed to earning a living and determined to make something of the life that lay ahead of them.

'You've got to work hard and turn small opportunities into something advantageous,' said Ganpat Rai to his sons. 'Never relent to negative thoughts. Hope is there as long as life is there and keep that in mind.'

A new opportunity, meanwhile, came Kaushalya's way. She and Shobhna had earned respect in the town for their sincerity, knowledge and amiable nature. A government-recognized school in the nearby town of Jharia offered them both, a job and premises to live in. Wali Ram encouraged them to take up the job that was a little more challenging and paying too. Besides, Jharia wasn't very far from Dhanbad and they could always travel on weekends. Arrangements were made and soon, Kaushalya and Shobhna shifted their base.

'Ma, this house is huge!' exclaimed Shobhna as soon as they reached their new house. 'And it's inside the school itself, too. How lucky!' Kaushalya could only agree. Many other teachers, most of them Bengali, also lived in the school building. They met them on their first day.

'We are all really like a big family,' said one of the teachers, Bela, who was Bengali. 'We eat together and do other things together. We love each other like comrades.'

Kaushalya and Shobhna quickly fell in place in the group, which did not surprise them one bit given that they were both highly adaptable and sociable. They were a source of inspiration to the students as well as the older teachers who were greatly impressed by Kaushalya not only for her thirst for knowledge and perseverance, but also her easygoing nature. The mother-daughter friendship that belied all traces of a generation gap between them was another area of interest that baffled the minds of the people around them. Besides teaching and managing their lives on their own, Kaushalya and Shobhna were also engaged in pursuing further studies. Shobhna had not been able to finish her internship in the *Ayurveda* course because of Partition but she still had a certificate as to the completion of the three-year course. She had already enrolled with a private college in Delhi as a long-distance student of Matric class and passed it with flying colours, getting a high first-class degree. The principal told her in a commendatory letter: 'Shobhna, you have done our private college proud! In case you decide to continue with your studies and do an FA, I can exempt your fee and also make arrangements for your stay. Do let me know.' Shobhna wrote back, 'Sir, thank you so much for the offer. Since we are settled in Dhanbad now, I can continue only as a long distance student. I shall, however, take my exams in Delhi whenever required.'

And so Shobhna passed the FA with a second division and also enrolled herself for a BA as a private candidate from Panjab University. While Shobhna was taking her BA exam, Kaushalya, too, was appearing for the 'only-English' matric exam. Both of them would attend evening classes in the college together to the utter amazement of all those present in the college, students and teachers both.

'Look at this amazing pair of mother and daughter. How brave they are and full of initiative!'

They surely were a unique example for everyone. People hadn't met or seen the likes of them ever. They were astonished. Shobhna passed her BA examination and scored a second division with English, History and Hindi as her main subjects and Punjabi as optional. Kaushalya passed her 'only-English' matric examination in her second attempt in the same year as Shobhna completed her Bachelor of Arts. When they went back to their school in Dhanbad, their colleagues looked up to them as role models.

Such was their persona and their grit, leading them to both achievement and catharsis.

19

Ganpat Rai, meanwhile, had been nursing ambivalent thoughts for a long time. The family had always thrived on his quiet strength and benign outlook, which was also ably helped by the subtle dominance of Geli Bai. Yet it had always posed a striking contrast to the vivacious personality of Kaushalya. Both were noble and right in their own way but their different natures had failed to mingle with each other in the way they do with other couples. What had bound them together through the years was the commonality of interest and love for their children; until that suffered a severe shock upon the untimely death of their beloved Anand Prakash. Not too long before that, Geli Bai's sudden demise had left their marriage bereft of a common umbrella under which they had taken shelter. Their long separation during the chaotic days of Partition and its aftermath had worsened the cracks in their marriage, even becoming visible to those around them.

For Ganpat Rai, it might have been the death of Anand Prakash that dealt the most severe blow to their marriage. He admitted that he had never been the same person again after they lost Anand Prakash. He suffered from bouts of disinterest in life and often expressed his desire to renounce his worldly ambitions and take to the path of spiritualism. Whenever he voiced such thoughts, Kaushalya would always resent it.

She would say, 'You should not give way to such thoughts. All our children are still unsettled and we have to rebuild our lives from scratch. Can't you see the difference in our living standards from the days of Lahore?'

'Everyone will follow one's destiny,' Ganpat Rai would reply, his tone resigned. 'Everything is in the hands of God. He will take care of everyone and everything.'

'But one has worldly responsibilities too. Since one has to live in society, we all have to fulfil our duties. You are the head of the family now, are you not?'

'Koshi, in our case, it is you who has always acted like the head of the family. You've always had your own ideas and you have lived your life on your own terms. Whenever there was any dissent, you chose to listen to your own mind. What is your problem now?'

'If I have followed my own interests, so have you. Have you not shown more interest in the life of your brother Arjun Dev than in the lives of your own sons? Home has hardly ever attracted you; it was either work or Arjun Dev, even after his own marriage!' Kaushalya seethed.

'Let me be honest with you. The death of Anand Prakash has forced me to look at inevitable reality as never before. "Grihastha ashram" no longer beckons me with its temptations. I want to renounce it and move on to the "Vanprastha ashram".' Ganpat Rai sounded certain of his decision.

'And what happens to me and the children?'

'God will take care of all of us!'

The conversation came to an abrupt end. It had become impossible to discuss the matter further. They had both violated the sacred bond of marriage that had tied them together, albeit loosely, until now.

Ganpat Rai became an outsider in the family. He shut himself out of all family affairs. He fixed for himself a simple, daily routine. He would get up at the crack of dawn and go for a long walk in the nearby forest, taking along with him a *potli* of fruits and dry grains. Books and religious texts became his constant companions, the study of which he would find greatly invigorating and spiritually satisfying. He spent the entire day meditating about the mysteries of the universe, trying his best to dissociate himself from the relationships that bound him to his family. His world of thoughts encompassed human beings irrespective of family, caste, or creed. He was particularly influenced by the tenets and teachings of *The Gita*, the analysis of which endeared him to many people. Soon he acquired disciples, some of whom belonged to rich Marwari families who had an *ashram* built for him in Dhanbad where they then held regular spiritual discourses. Ganpat Rai immersed himself totally in the study of *The Gita* and other Hindu scriptures and lived the life of an ascetic.

Word soon spread about Ganpat Rai's renunciation of his family in favour of spiritual pursuits at a time when the family was struggling to find a foothold in Dhanbad in the wake of Partition. All sympathies fell on Kaushalya who, once again, lost a male figure in her family. Her relatives were very strongly against Ganpat Rai's decision, especially because even as he dissociated himself from Kaushalya and their children, he maintained close ties with his brother, Arjun Dev.

One aunt said it best when she remarked, 'He should either sever all worldly ties and take "*sanyas*" or fulfil his duties towards his own family first instead of his brother's family!'

As far as Kaushalya was concerned, though, she had made peace with her life. While Ganpat Rai continued living in Dhanbad, Kaushalya and Shobhna moved to Jharia where both of them were doing well, teaching in a highly reputed school. They came back to Dhanbad on the weekends, meeting the relatives and participating in Ganpat Rai's spiritual activities too. There were religious discourses in the evenings and Ganpat Rai insisted that these begin with a religious *bhajan* (hymn) by Shobhna. Her bhajan *'insan ban ke rehna'* (live like a good human being) was a great favourite with everyone and became a prologue for the evening discourse, ending with Ganpat Rai's religious monologue. Kaushalya, too, would actively participate without feeling the least bit of remorse over the strange happenings in her family. Her relationship with Ganpat Rai had undergone a subtle change; they had never been intimate as husband and wife, to begin with; nor had they ever been friends. And yet their family life had always flourished. The facade was carefully maintained for society to see. But now their relationship and its complexities were out in the open. The relationship, having seen many ups and downs, had finally hinged onto that of a *'guru'* and *'bhakt'* (devotee) or even equal participants in their spiritual journey, if at all it could be called so. Both had found their routes in things that interested them. They had made a compromise with life and reached an understanding not to interfere in each other's lives.

Kaushalya accepted the situation without ill feelings. She had never been the kind to be cowed down by adverse circumstances. She had been blessed with tremendous resilience and versatility of character. Having her children around her, she continued making the most of her life. Jharia, with the activities of the school where they were teaching, offered a diversion as well as a solace of its own kind. School life was congenial and exciting. Various functions were organized on festivals, farewells and other important days of the year that required celebration. Hindi and Sanskrit components of the school functions were prepared by Shobhna and Kaushalya, respectively, which were highly appreciated by the school staff. They were an integral part of the school's cultural life and they enjoyed it.

Kaushalya also excelled in the writing and singing of *bhajans*. Whenever the school lost a teacher who either got transferred or had retired, Kaushalya would compose an appropriate *bhajan* and bid farewell to the colleague by singing in her mellifluous voice. She always managed to make her audience cry, or at least feel emotional over the farewell. Shobhna and Kaushalya made a great pair and earned respect and affection from the members of the staff for their knowledge and sociable behaviour. Nothing could escape their attention and nothing could deter them from partaking in any activity. Their enthusiasm crossed all barriers of age, language or place and gave a new dimension to the traditional mother–daughter relationship. They represented the soul of the school in their togetherness, spirit of adventure and tolerance.

One day, the school principal informed Kaushalya and Shobhna that a girls' guide camp was being organized at Ranchi.

'In what connection?' asked Kaushalya. She was eager to participate.

'It is being organized at Ranchi and our foreign minister, Smt. Lakshmi Menon, is expected to be the chief guest.'

'We would both like to go and take part in it,' Kaushalya said.

'Are you sure, Kaushalya*ji*?'

'Yes, absolutely!'

The Girls' Guide Camp came through within a fortnight and the participating young girls benefited greatly from the activities, especially with the able and enjoyable presence of Kaushalya and Shobhna. Kaushalya's sheer energy and ability to communicate with the young girls was amazing and she was adored by the girls and the other teachers, too.

The camp ended with a cultural show in which the foreign minister was the chief guest. The performance, featuring a group dance where Kaushalya and Shobhna were the main participants, was a huge success.

Kaushalya was happy. She uttered a prayer thanking God for giving her these little consolations in life, amidst all the tragedy and sadness that had befallen her family life. Shobhna had always been special to her ever since she was born. The presence of sons, too, instilled in her a feeling of strange security and satisfaction. The woes and travails of an incomplete family life were quietly forgotten in the contentment of the moment. Kaushalya had come to terms with her life.

Shobhna, meanwhile, had applied for a BEd in a college affiliated to Patna University, at the behest of her mother. When the letter for admission came, Kaushalya encouraged her to pursue higher studies.

'Shobhna, you must avail of this opportunity. It is a godsend.'

'But you will be alone, Ma!' Shobhna wanted to go, but was concerned about her mother and she felt torn.

'Don't worry about me, my dear,' Kaushalya continued. 'I am well settled in this school. All the teachers are my friends and your brothers are also there to take care of me.'

Shobhna felt reassured. 'Will you come and drop me there, Ma?'

'Of course, without any doubt!'

Thus preparations were made for Shobhan's journey to Patna.

The Women's College of Training was situated on the banks of the Ganges. It had a spacious building and offered a scenic view. Shobhna loved the college that lay solitary with the sacred river on one side, and an expanse of land stretched on the other side, with a mix of wild growth and carefully planted vegetation. She was allotted a room in the hostel which was to be shared by three girls. The room happened to be at the end of the corridor, next to the washroom, where girls would meet up while waiting for their turn. Though it annoyed her in the beginning, it gave Shobhna an opportunity to know girls who had come from diverse backgrounds. It helped her through the homesickness and the longing for her mother's company. For the first time in her life she was on her own. It excited her: she was going to see and live life according to her own perspective. Before long, Shobhna was at home in her new surroundings and with the initial hiccups over, it was time to face the rigorous schedule of studies. The medium of instruction happened to be English for all the subjects, including Hindi or Sanskrit. The other subjects included psychology, history of education, and teaching methodology.

The novelty of the subjects left Shobhna quite overwhelmed. While she enjoyed Hindi and Sanskrit, she did not even comprehend the other subjects. She felt discouraged and out of place and wanted to tell her father. She wrote a letter to Ganpat Rai:

Father! I wonder whether I will be able to continue my studies here. Everything is taught in English. I don't understand much in the classroom. I want to come back to Jharia to join my school along with Ma.

Ganpat Rai wrote back:

Don't get disheartened, this is only the beginning. Give yourself some time and you will begin to understand your course gradually. Don't worry much about the results also. Take it as an experience that you are visiting a new place and having a picnic with your friends. I am sure everything will fall in place slowly.

Her father's words boosted Shobhna's morale. She took it in the spirit it was meant to be taken. Things started improving with time. Meeting new friends also helped. When it came to the teaching of subjects in the classroom as a part of training, Shobhna chose the subjects of Hindi and Sanskrit as she was confident with her expertise. When it came to evaluation, she scored the highest marks in teaching methodology. Eventually she passed her BEd examination, getting a high second division and a horde of lifelong friends.

Kaushalya was elated with her daughter's achievements. When Shobhna came back to her old school, she was given a rousing welcome by the staff, led by their Principal. She felt like the star of the school.

The weekend after her homecoming, they went to Dhanbad to meet her father. Filled with pride, she told him that she had completed her BEd with good marks!

Ganpat Rai couldn't be happier. 'I am proud of you. May God bless you!'

Shobhna knew she had done her family proud.

20

For a long time now, Shobhna had been the anchor of Kaushalya's life. Shobhna had saved her spirit during the turbulent years of her middle age when she braved not only her uneasy relationship with her husband but also the apathy of her sons. Kaushalya and Shobhna enjoyed an ideal companionship and had grown together in intimacy. But now it was Kaushalya's turn to think about Shobhna's life in the same way her mother thought of her own, many years ago. It was time for Shobhna to have a little nest of her own.

The thought would invariably flit across Kaushalya's mind whenever she looked at Shobhna's beautiful face and her graceful movements. The brown-eyed beauty breathed in the essence of life in its purest form—she was shy in a romantic way; sensitive, humane, and strangely mystical. And yet so immensely talented and educated! She had a lineage to be proud of and an education that put her in a different league altogether, much above the rest of the young women her age. What was more admirable about her daughter was that she took pride in her learning and therefore had the education to reinforce her pride. Kaushalya was not only her mother but her great friend, admirer and companion. Their intimacy transcended the material world and included their world of ideas. They both were different from the rest and often felt so. Shobhna was a mirror image of her mother. She had inherited from Kaushalya her lust for life and passion for learning as well as a fondness for travel. A fierce independence of mind marked their personalities which often prompted them to take the untrodden path when it came to taking decisions pertaining to life.

Her brothers, on the other hand, followed their own instincts and cared little about the legacy they were supposed to enhance or rather their own interests or career. They were unable to come to terms with their lost esteem or make determined efforts to regain their past glory. They also resented the mother and daughter's secret dominance over the household affairs and in everything else. The young men felt indifferent and cut away from the family despite seeking financial support from them. They enjoyed themselves in the company of their own friends, some of whom they often brought home. Shobhna's elder brother, Ved Prakash, was particularly fond of Anmol, who had also been his companion during the pre-Partition days when they were members of the *Sangh* and had regularly attended their *'shakha'* sessions.

Anmol had been a regular visitor at their home since then and was clearly a favourite of them all. Kaushalya too approved of him on account of his fondness for books as well as his literary sensibilities. He had a natural talent for witty remarks and an uncanny sense of humour that made him the centre of attraction wherever he went. He was based in Calcutta, barely four hours' away from Dhanbad, and visited them often. Slowly, the intimacy with the family came to concentrate on three persons: Ved Prakash, Kaushalya, and Shobhna. Ved Prakash was a friend while Kaushalya was like a mother. And then there was Shobhna, to whom he felt attracted. But Shobhna was bent on being aloof. She always hesitated to appear before him or be around when he came. Kaushalya, however, loved talking to the boy. They always found subjects of common interest, most of them pertaining to books or current issues. Their heated discussions about these perked up the youthful atmosphere in the house and made it more interesting. Consequently, an exchange of favourite books followed that resulted in increased frequency of his visits. Such occasions came to be eagerly awaited by all of them and soon, the weekend was no longer complete without him.

One Saturday morning Shobhna was busy cleaning up the house, getting rid of obsolete knick-knacks and rearranging their modest setup when she heard footsteps coming towards their doorway. She checked to see and spotted Anmol opening the heavy gate. He hesitated a little as he saw Shobhna, and then proceeded shyly as he said to her, 'Holiday mood, I suppose!'

'Once in a while, yes!'

'You don't seem to like it much.'

'I am more of an outdoor bird. Staying inside the house doesn't interest me much.'

'Just like your mother, I suppose.'

The conversation was interrupted by Kaushalya's voice. 'Aha! It is Anmol, my boy. Why don't you come in? You will have a long life. I was just remembering you the other day.'

She invited Anmol to take a seat as she went about preparing food. She then asked Shobhna to help her hurry things up.

'Would you like to eat or drink anything before the meal, Anmol?' asked Kaushalya.

'No, thank you.'

'Besides books, what is it that keeps you busy these days, Anmol?'

'Oh, a lot! Something or the other always keeps happening in the *Sangh*.'

'They do insist upon a regimented life and a whole lot of discipline, don't they?'

'Yes, they do. It is an organization based on certain principles.'

'They leave no time for one's personal life. Do they?'

Kaushalya was in a mood to talk while Anmol's eyes were glued to Shobhna, who was helping her mother cook. He watched her every move. It was the first time he was seeing Kaushalya and Shobhna actually working together side by side on one task and Anmol was impressed by their fluid teamwork. He also realized how different the atmosphere in this house was from that of any other household he had seen so far. Here, women possessed a strong character and made decisions for the household. They were doers. They went about following their own instincts and dreams and challenged the domain of men with their quiet strength and amiable behaviour. They were interesting women, full of life, bright ideas and energy. It was a new world to him that offered him a different perspective of looking at life. Anmol was fascinated; struck by its peculiar novelty. He wanted to know them more, interact on a different plane, live nearer even.

His thoughts were broken by Kaushalya's question, 'How about your family, dear? Tell us a little about your life.'

'Well, I have not been as lucky as the children of this household. I wish I too had an indulgent mother like you. I lost both my parents when I was an infant. I don't even remember their faces. I have been most unfortunate in this regard.' Kaushalya and Shobhna heard his sigh.

'Who brought you up?' Kaushalya asked.

'At first it was my paternal grandfather. He was a landlord and owned almost half of the village! He was very fond of me. At times, I still recollect his kind face with a long, white beard.'

'How about your mother's family?'

'My maternal grandfather was also there for some time but I don't remember much of him except the stories about both my grandfathers getting along well with each other and their concern about my future.'

'What happened then?'

'I jostled between the two households for some time and was made to feel loved and cared for till my maternal grandfather passed away which greatly cut short the frequency of my visits to their place. My *nani* tried to keep the link alive as long as she was there which was not for long either.'

'Would you like to take a glass of milk or some tea perhaps?' asked Kaushalya.

'Maybe a cup of tea. Talking to you about my personal life has had the effect of a catharsis on my nerves,' replied Anmol.

'Shobhna, could you prepare some tea for us?' said Kaushalya, as she took a small chair to sit across Anmol. She found his life story as well as his willingness to share interesting. She wanted to know more. The young man had appealed to her mind and heart both. Kaushalya looked at him and noticed an agitated, hurt look in his eyes.

'So, Anmol, you were brought up virtually by your paternal grandfather...'

'For a couple of years more or so, as far as I can remember. Things were comfortable as long as he was there. All my needs were taken care of and I did not want for anything. My mother had owned a lot of gold jewellery and I still recall that some of our well-wishers had advised my grandfather to put them securely in the bank.'

'Did he do that?'

'He was a robust, well-built man who was immensely proud of his strength. He would put aside all such suggestions by saying "I am not going to die so soon. I will live up till hundred years. Nobody can dare mess with little Anmol's future."'

Meanwhile, Shobhna prepared tea and *pakoras* as she listened to her mother and Anmol's conversation. She would occasionally cast a glance at the young boy. He was tall and thin but his eyes were quick and bore an impatient look. His regular features, interrupted only by a pointed nose, gave him a gentle look; he was almost handsome, she could say. Shobhna was used to the ordinariness of her brothers' minds and the commonality of their existence. A new fresh male opinion expressed with literary sensibilities was like a breath of fresh air in a household which had been bereft of a strong male influence. Shobhna was as mesmerized as she was bewildered.

She suddenly became aware of his intense gaze that seemed to be soaking her in. She resented it and made sure to keep aloof. Her work was done and she placed a plate of *pakoras* and two tea cups on a tray. Anmol for the first time addressed Shobhna directly,

'Won't you sit down and have tea with us?'

'I have got some work still left in the other rooms.' Shobhna excused herself and turned to go.

'Shobhna, take a chair and relax for a while,' said Kaushalya while getting another cup from the shelf. Shobhna, tired by now and taking her mother's advice, opted to have a cup of tea while Kaushalya continued with her conversation with Anmol.

'Did your grandfather live a long life? Which area did your village fall into?'

'We came from a small village called Granthgarh on the periphery of what is now the Indo-Pak border. My grandfather owned a lot of land and commanded respect. At some point of time, the village suffered a plague of an unknown disease and many people lost their lives. My grandfather was one of them. With him I lost all my hopes and the only person who ever showered love and affection on this unfortunate boy. I became an orphan in the true sense after my grandfather died.'

Kaushalya looked at Anmol with sympathy. She offered him the plate of *pakoras* while Shobhna looked up at him but said nothing, although she was indeed touched by his sad story and wanted to make amends for her initial indifference.

It was in this atmosphere of mutual bonding with Kaushalya that Shobhna started taking notice of Anmol, or rather stopped being indifferent to him. He was already good friends with Ved Prakash and the other brothers, too. Kaushalya's friendly nature and an eagerness to converse with him gave him an air of subtle intimacy with the family. It was certain that he would visit them on weekends, if not at least once during the week.

Shobhna rarely talked to him on her own accord. Though she had stopped being antagonistic to him or his visits, she kept a reasonable distance from him and busied herself with her household tasks whenever he was around. Anmol too, sensing her discomfiture, tried to avoid direct communication with her as far as possible. The mutual hesitation only heightened the spells of silence that crept up naturally between them, leading to in due course of time, an eagerness to catch a glimpse of each other or indulge in some communication or talk about whatever would suit the situation.

One evening, as Shobhna was relaxing in the front courtyard, Anmol suddenly emerged from the road. As he opened the gate and walked inside both of them looked up and met each other's gaze. Anmol, gathering his wits, said with a smile, 'You don't mind my coming in, do you?'

'Oh, no! Why should I? My mother and brothers would be very happy to see you, I am sure.'

'What about you?'

'Why should it concern me?' said Shobhna, a little too agitatedly, she realized. She got up from her chair and started walking towards the house.

'Why do you always avoid me?

'What?' Shobhna was taken aback by his remark. 'You are sadly mistaken.'

Shobhna smiled shyly and led him inside the house while calling her mother and shrinking away from his intense gaze which had started troubling her.

The initial embarrassment over, it was time for fascination to rule over the young minds, under the benign, maternal eye of Kaushalya.

21

That there was mutual affection between Shobhna and Anmol, it was too early to conclude. Young and sensitive as they both were, it was not unnatural for their fancy to take a long ride where everything would seem romantic and out of this world. Shobhna's literary sensibilities had flourished under her mother's intense longing for knowledge and their compatibility had led to an appreciation of anything aesthetic.

Anmol's thirst for knowledge, however, was guided by more mundane reasons. After the death of his grandparents, he was brought up by his mother's widowed sister who had a son of her own. After he completed his school education in his village, the family's financial circumstances had forced him to look for a job in a factory which he had undertaken with a lot of reluctance. Not one to give up his education under any circumstances and bow down to pressure, the young Anmol continued to study in the evenings and successfully passed the examinations of *'Ratna'*, *'Bhushan'* and *'Prabhakar'* degrees in the Hindi language. This enabled him to change his job from a manual hand to a school teacher in a recognized institution. His patriotic leanings had led him to join the *Rashtriya Swayamsevak Sangh* in the evenings where he loved to interact with middle-class intellectuals who exposed him to their deep national sentiments. The organization instilled in him the qualities of discipline, moral values, and integrity of character. He came in contact with people from diverse backgrounds and immense abilities which were united by the national cause and patriotic sentiments. His deeply impressionable nature and thought process underwent a subtle change where he wanted to contribute his share towards society and the country. It was here that he had come in contact with Ved Prakash and developed a friendship with him.

A desire for attaining recognition in society and a resolve to make something of his life prompted him to continue with his studies. Anmol subsequently passed the intermediate and the Bachelor's degree in English and was greatly in demand for those native learners of English who wanted to hone their skills in the language.

That was what had led him to Kaushalya's house through Ved Prakash. It was here that he met a maternal figure who matched not only his sensibilities but also an indomitable spirit for the acquisition of knowledge. Both shared a passion for learning and were ready to go a long way in getting it at whatever cost.

Ved Prakash was instrumental in getting him home. He had suggested the availability of an English teacher and introduced Anmol to Kaushalya. His visits became frequent as he started finding an affectionate anchor in Kaushalya; a person who was as equally fond of him as he was of her. Anmol had never known motherly love. He fell under Kaushalya's spell. His yearning for a home and the need for genuine intimacy drew nourishment from the mind and heart of Kaushalya. The house would suddenly come to life when the two were together and engaged in animated conversation. Gradually, he became a member of Kaushalya's extended family, who loved his open-heartedness, his willingness to partake in all activities and his simple and frank nature. Discussion on books and issues of national importance added spice to an otherwise listless family life that also looked forward to an enlightened, strong male opinion. Anmol offered a much-wanted different approach to life and views. Kaushalya was fascinated by his personality and willing to share her thoughts with him.

Meanwhile, Anmol had been pursuing his Master's degree in History, a subject he had been incredibly fond of, as a private candidate. He loved the subject for its sequence of events as well as its impact on the present events that had a propensity to draw lessons for the future. The country was undergoing a period of transformation and slow consolidation. It was the making of history in its most naked and vibrant form which provided fodder for thought for people like Kaushalya and Anmol. It was amazing how two people with differences in age, background and upbringing could share such similar thoughts and interests! Their relationship was less that of an elder and younger one; rather it rested more on friendship and equality. But for the difference in age, they could have been companions in life with the same destination in view. Kaushalya held him in high esteem; he was more educated than her own sons, more assertive with firm views, had a deep sense of right and wrong and offered his opinion with an objectivity that showed his strength of character. While Shobhna was docile and offered Kaushalya no resistance on any account, Anmol expressed his views fearlessly. That was probably why Kaushalya liked Anmol. The liking had been mutual.

It was almost a certainty that Anmol would visit them on the weekends. The weekdays were busy for everyone and the leisure time was scarce. When Anmol came that Saturday evening, the boys were out of the house and Kaushalya and Shobhna were taking a short walk in their garden. Suddenly, an excited comment went up the air, 'Shobhna, come and look at these early flowers!'

'Yes, Ma, what is it?'

'Remember the seeds we got from Jharia! Bela, that Bengali teacher, gave us these to experiment with. How well have these come up! They will bloom fully in a couple of days.'

'Well, Ma, I forget the name of these deep-maroon, velvety flowers,' said Kaushalya. Her mind was clearly somewhere else.

'But aren't they beautiful?'

Kaushalya was as excited as a child. A walk in the small garden was an endless delight for her. She revelled in its quaint beauty, soaking in the fresh air in the mornings and enjoying the myriad colours of nature during dusk. She certainly knew each and every blade of grass and the blooming buds. The poet in her always took precedence over her other roles concerning day-to-day things.

'It is a lovely little garden!' exclaimed Anmol, joining them from the other side. 'And what a calm atmosphere!' Shobhna looked up at him and realized that he had been looking at her closely. Feeling conscious for the first time ever since she had met him, a feeling of subdued happiness came over her. Unmindful of her mother's presence, she felt as if she were alone with him in the garden. She hesitated to look at him again; rather she looked at the sun setting on the other side, leaving in its trail a dim glow of light spread evenly over the objects of nature. She saw Anmol and her mother engaged in conversation; perhaps admiring the beauty of nature and getting along so well. She felt for a minute as if she did not fit in and a feeling of pain gripped her heart. She looked at Anmol closely for the first time; saw that he was tall and well-built but thin and had strong, broad shoulders. His black eyes bore a painful look, making him appear all the more handsome. A feeling of loneliness prevailed upon his personality. Shobhna felt a tinge of sorrow for this unfortunate boy whom destiny had placed across their path. Shobhna felt she must keep her reserve and must not give him any wrong notions about her feelings. Her mother could take care of him for the time being.

Taking a turn towards the house, she hurried inside, fretting over small and insignificant issues. She felt her heart was slipping away from her and she needed to exercise some restraint. Her hurried going away from the scene had not gone unnoticed by Anmol. He watched her from the corner of his eye and saw her face from a distance. It seemed clouded momentarily with ambivalent feelings which Shobhna was trying desperately to hide. She looked a little afraid; rather troubled. But she looked innocent and beautiful, as always, thought Anmol to himself.

'What is the matter?' asked Kaushalya, noticing his sudden disinterest.

'Nothing at all! I thought it was getting dark. We better go inside.'

'Yes, why not? Perhaps Shobhna can give us a cup of tea.'

They walked past the little grassy patch of land, crossing a few shrubs on the way and heading towards the interior of the house. Anmol was conscious of the uneasy feelings rising up in his heart. He wanted to talk to Shobhna and yet he could not get across to her. He was as unsure of her as of his own feelings towards her. She appealed to his heart but his mind got its stimulus from Kaushalya. If he wanted to get closer to Shobhna, it had to be through her mother. He saw the need of getting into the good books of Kaushalya if he ever hoped to expect the reciprocity of sentiments from Shobhna or her family.

When they walked in, Shobhna was already in the kitchen making tea. She had never been fond of cooking, just like her mother, and entered the kitchen only when Kaushalya was occupied elsewhere. Ever since she could remember, she had seen her mother's obsession with books or her concern with issues related to women in society. For Kaushalya, household work had always been a responsibility which she would rather get rid of, if there were a way. Shobhna thought likewise.

'Would you help me, Anmol, with my English lessons?' asked Kaushalya.

'What do you need them for, Kaushalya*ji*?' Anmol was surprised.

'Am I past the age of learning?'

'I really didn't mean that. It is never really too late. I, myself, fall in that category.'

'Not knowing or understanding English can be a great impediment in life. It restricts your reading of classics and exposure to some of the great thinkers of the world. Even Raja Ram Mohan Roy saw the necessity of Indian people learning English if they ever hoped to take on the mighty British Empire.'

Anmol was amazed at the ease with which the words came out of Kaushalya's lips. The veracity of the statement could not be denied or countered. 'This certainly is no ordinary woman,' thought Anmol.

'Besides, an educated woman is the strongest pillar of the family. She is in a much better position to teach her own children as well as guide others who might need her help. She can keep pace with the changing times and adjust accordingly.' Kaushalya was in no mood to stop.

They were all sitting in the ante-room facing the kitchen. It was a long, low room with dim lights in the corners and a colourful *Khadi* drugget spread in the middle. A couple of easy chairs lay carelessly around. Pictures of Mahatma Gandhi and Swami Dayanand adorned the rear wall while the side one had a small niche in the corner which could be used as a fireplace in the winters. A vase with a small bouquet of seasonal flowers was kept there as a makeshift arrangement. The nearness of the kitchen gave it a warm, cosy look. The room was ideal for lazing around and for leisurely talk.

Anmol knew he had touched Kaushalya's sentiments the wrong way and he must continue with the subject.

'I must appreciate your will to learn, Kaushalyaji. I was wondering how you found time to manage so many things. Managing two households, looking after children, teaching and then studying also on top of it, your plate seems more than full already.'

'Well, where there is a will, there is a way!'

'Certainly, no doubt! I would love to be of any use to you and your family. You can tell me when to begin.'

There was a knock at the door and Shobhna got up to open it. She was glad to see family friends who had come visiting them. Their weekends were almost always busy because it was the only time that Kaushalya and Shobhna were home. The atmosphere suddenly became warm and happy as Kaushalya hugged all of them affectionately. The house reverberated with their vibrant laughter and the conversation rested on a humorous note and trivial talk.

It was time for Anmol to leave. He did so with a promise to see them the following week. He always found Kaushalya very cordial. She made him feel at home and helped him unburden his inhibitions. He felt strangely welcome and wanted by her. It was as if he were an object of pride for her which she liked to flaunt before people. She always took keen interest in all his activities, especially his evening studies. She loved to talk books with him. What her own sons lacked, she found it fulfilled through Anmol! He might as well have been a son.

'Who was he?' Kaushalya came out of her reverie as her friend Vidya asked casually.

'A friend of Ved Prakash. I also want him to teach me English.'

'Kaushalya, you never think of anything else, do you?'

Vidya, her closest friend, could take liberty with her remarks.

'Well, how else do I keep my mind occupied, tell me? One needs an anchor in life. Books have been and are my sole companions. I have never known anyone else. My books know me the way no one else does. They have seen me through turbulent periods of my life. I owe them a debt. They've kept me sane and happy. I wish my sons could understand that. Men in this family have always been occupied with the world outside. The inmates or the interiors of my home have never interested or fascinated them.'

'Take it easy, Kaushalya. You have seen good times also. God has still been very kind. We all must thank him!'

'Vidya, the world at large would never understand what it takes to live with people who live only by their own ideals without taking into account the sentiments of their other half. It is their own family that bears the brunt of their lofty ideas while the benefits are reaped by those who have had no contribution whatsoever in the lives of those they are taking so much advantage of.' Kaushalya heaved a deep sigh.

'The world functions the way it is, Kaushalya,' said Vidya. 'We are all fulfilling our roles. There is a crunch in everybody's life. You are not the only one.'

'That may be the only solace. Besides, I have my children to look up to.'

'Shobhna looks as beautiful as ever, Kaushalya! I wonder how long you can keep her with you.'

As Kaushalya looked up at her friend with a deep, painful look, Vidya could see the welling up of unexpected tears in her eyes.

22

Kaushalya worked very hard with her lessons. She never wavered in her resolve. She would be up the whole day with housework but would soon be dissatisfied. She would crave for a diversion by the time it was evening. Anmol's visits during this time brought a glimmer of hope to a mind that was tired of trivialities.

'Don't you like being at home, Kaushalya*ji*?' asked Anmol one day, sensing her bitterness.

'I love being at home but there has to be more to life for a woman of substance!'

'And what might that be?'

'A chance of being an equal partner in marriage and looking at life together! Learning, for instance, shouldn't be the domain of men only. We must have an equal opportunity and be allowed to do whatever we want in life.'

'Wouldn't that upset the balance of society as a whole?' Anmol tried to put it mildly.

'Why should it? That is a very chauvinistic statement, Anmol.'

'That's not what I mean. Who would manage homes and raise children, if women don't?'

'Menfolk can always lend a helping hand instead of spending all their time away from home.'

Anmol thought it best to let the subject go. He knew he was dealing with a woman of substance. He tried to concentrate more on whatever Kaushalya wanted to know. She was indeed a fast learner and could already read and write English much better than many others. He marvelled at her determination and mental ability even at such a stage in life. She could give all her children and relatives put together a run for their money when it came to the articulation of ideas or sharing of responsibilities.

When Anmol came to the house the next day, he found Shobhna lazing around with a book. She was absorbed in it and failed to notice him. He stood still for a moment and watched her in silence. Her reclining pose with her head bent intently on the book made her look beautiful and vulnerable at the same time.

'Hello!' he said at last. 'What is it that keeps you so engrossed?'

'Oh!' Shobhna was a bit startled. She looked up the same instant and met his eyes. 'Nothing much really. It is just a book of poems which I had got from the library.'

She put the book down and noticed that her hand was trembling. She got up and looked around for her mother. His dark eyes blazed at her and made her soul shiver.

'What are you looking for?'

'My mother! She must be around somewhere.'

'Sit down for a while and talk to me.'

'I'll go and call my brothers.'

'Let them come on their own. Do you mind talking to me?'

'Oh, no, not at all!'

They sat opposite each other, feeling a little awkward and conscious in each other's company. Though silent, both could feel subdued warmth inundating their souls with strength and brightness. A glow came over their faces as they looked at each other admiring secretly at the intensity of their feelings.

'You know, Shobhna,' said Anmol, clearly overwhelmed, 'I like to teach English to your mother a lot better when you are also around. I draw my strength and happiness from both of you. Kaushalya*ji*, no doubt, is a great woman. I have yet to see such will power and strength of character. You both are a foil to each other and yet complement.'

'Oh my God! I really don't understand such lofty ideas.' Shobhna's eyes sparkled with mischief. 'Your words and ideas are meant more for my mother. She draws sustenance from your thoughts. I can see she admires you a lot.'

'What about you?'

'What about me?' Shobhna pretended not to understand his implicit meaning.

A silence fell between them and Shobhna turned her face towards the door. They could hear voices coming near and there was a knock.

Anmol got to his feet to open the door. Shobhna saw his silhouette and a deep feeling came over her. She thought she cared for him in an unusual way. She had become aware of his deeply set sense of loneliness and his desperate efforts to overcome it when in their company. His soul longed for companionship.

'Good to see you, Anmol!' Kaushalya exclaimed as soon as she saw him. She set down a bag full of goods. She was panting a little but was pleased to see the young man. 'How long have you been here? I hope I didn't keep you waiting too long!'

'No! Not much, Kaushalyaji. I chatted with Shobhna in the meanwhile.'

'So, how are things? Somehow, I couldn't do my English homework this time.'

'I might have to go to Rohtak to pursue my BEd studies. The admission has come through!'

Kaushalya looked long at him before asking casually, 'And so, are you happy?'

'I don't have many alternatives. One must make an effort to improve one's position in life.'

'Oh, indeed! Everyone has a right to do so in life. When do you leave?'

'In about a month's time.'

'I hope to see you during weekends before you leave?'

'It is a pleasure for me to come here and see you both.'

The evening was drawing to a close and their conversation veered more towards trivial talk but with a certain degree of reserve on all sides. No one dared talk of impending plans.

Distance, time, and space, however, could not slow down their enthusiasm or efforts to remain in touch. Communication between Anmol and Kaushalya continued regularly in the form of letters. Both exchanged notes and had a lot to say to each other. Thinking individuals as both were with firm minds of their own, their command over language made their exchange of words witty, interesting and thoughtful. Letters were becoming increasingly frequent and so were their ties of mutual affection. No subject escaped their attention and none could pass without sound observation or comments. Kaushalya, a born romantic, and with words at her command had found a match in Anmol; somebody who could at once be a friend as well as a rival. Family matters were also being discussed in these letters and advice sought with an open mind. Occasional references to Shobhna and her life also found space in this exchange of words. She became a common link; a prized possession of one and an aspiration for another. Neither wanted to let go of one's share and compromise. Both waited for the other to take the lead and drop a hint. It became a war of will and patience between the two strong individuals with one nucleus between them. The trio of Kaushalya, Anmol, and Shobhna waited with bated breath for events to unfold themselves. All believed in destiny and wanted it to lead them wherever destined. The peculiarity of the situation fascinated all around them and the delicate thread of mutual respect tied them together.

Anmol finished his degree, completed his training and got a job in Delhi in a government-aided private school. He earned a regular salary and felt settled professionally for the first time in his life. His own immediate family being in Calcutta, he got an opportunity to think seriously about his own life. He was in the prime of his life; his uncomfortable past lay behind him; he had made a reasonable, respectable beginning in his career and it was time for him to settle down. His distant relatives had often come to him with proposals of marriage. Somehow, these had not materialized for one reason or the other. And then Anmol had come in close contact with Kaushalya and her family. A new family setup and perspective had opened before him where a woman with novel inclinations gave a certain character and soul to the family. He saw the role of an educated woman in raising a family and giving it the right direction. His emotional dependence on Kaushalya had brought an element of positivity in his life and he did not want to let go of it so easily. Besides, he was struck by the beauty and good nature of Shobhna, not to talk of her education or qualifications. The only note of concern he saw was the extraordinary emotional bond that existed between the mother and the daughter and Kaushalya's extreme dependence on Shobhna for everything. Their interdependence could delay or prove difficult in Shobhna's adjustment to a new phase of her life. And then, the matriarchal influence would always remain and guide their family life, too.

Anmol had been toying with these ideas for a long time. A sort of dilemma had always marred his enthusiasm. He had hesitated to make the first move or even let his fondness become apparent in any way to Kaushalya. He wanted to think hard and carefully weigh his options. Though in Delhi, he was bound to remain in touch with Kaushalya or even meet them once in a while. Ganpat Rai's sisters had all settled in Delhi after the Partition which ensured Kaushalya's occasional visits to Delhi along with Shobhna. The letters had kept them informed of each other's movements and plans.

Anmol had been busy at his work for a few months when a letter from Kaushalya brought tidings that she was planning to visit her relatives in Delhi along with Shobhna. Her own sons had always preferred to lead their own lives bothering or interfering little with her or their sister. Well, it had suited them all! It had become an accepted fact of their family since long ago.

Anmol was happy at the prospect of meeting them both which, of course, did not take long to materialize.

Kaushalya, an extrovert by nature, had always loved meeting people; relatives, friends and acquaintances. Her visits were carefully planned with a lot of time at her disposal to accommodate all her programmes. She had kept a few evenings free to meet Anmol and have a long chat with him. She had come prepared to take his mind about many things as also to give her own. And she hoped for the best.

'Nice to see you again, Kaushalya*ji*,' Anmol's heart warmed up to her as he gave her a tight hug and glanced affectionately at Shobhna.

'It seems ages ago since I saw you last in Dhanbad. I have been missing you and your English lessons,' said Kaushalya with a smile.

'Me, too! Where would I find such informality and affection? The more I see you, the less, I feel, I know you. I really wish we had been staying nearby to be able to meet more often.'

'How much I wish that too! Tell me about your job, school and the new friends you might have made. Tell me everything about your life here, Anmol.'

The two chatted like long-lost friends, probing deeper and deeper about each other's mind and inclinations till Kaushalya said suddenly, 'Don't you think about marriage, Anmol? I think it is high time you get married and settle down. What are you waiting for?'

Anmol fell silent for a few moments before exclaiming with a loud laugh, 'Only if I get someone like you, Kaushalyaji... someone so noble, full of life and beautiful too!'

'And if you get one...' Kaushalya looked close and hard at him.

'Then I will marry her straight and will not even blink,' Anmol tried to laugh it off.

'But I am serious!'

'I am serious, too, Kaushalyaji.'

'Do you promise?'

'With all my heart!'

'I can offer you myself for a mother-in-law and propose Shobhna's hand in marriage to you, if you so wish!'

'I would indeed be blessed and cannot hope for a better union. But I need time to think,' Anmol's eyes had acquired a solemn look.

'What do you have to think about? Have you not been thinking long enough?' Kaushalya gave him a meaningful look.

'I have to prepare my relatives for this alliance. As for myself, I couldn't have got a better family.'

'And the girl?'

'I am the happiest man on earth today!'

'Really, Anmol?'

'Without any doubt, Kaushalyaji,' said he and bent down to touch her feet.

23

Kaushalya returned home, excited and happy as a lark and eager to share her news with the members of her family including close relatives. Shobhna's consent, she had taken for granted already. She was not sure of the response from her own immediate family, nor did she care much. She knew her daughter well enough and was convinced that she had made the right choice for Shobhna. Many proposals of marriage for Shobhna's hand had come her way but Kaushalya had found them lacking in something or the other. Where the families were good and well settled, the boys were not educated enough to make a good match. An educated boy like Anmol did not have a settled family background but he had influential relatives to look up, if at all the situation warranted. Besides, he was a decent boy with a strong character and a sociable nature. He would make a good husband and keep Shobhna happy under all circumstances.

Kaushalya first broached the subject with Ganpat Rai before bringing it to the notice of her sons. She was met with initial surprise even leading to mixed feelings about the match. Anmol, felt Ganpat Rai, was a little older for Shobhna and would always be the dominating influence. Kaushalya, well versed in Hindu scriptures as she was, cited from these that a husband should be or could be even twice the age of the bride for the marriage to be happy and everlasting. Shobhna's brothers, too, did not seem enthusiastic about the match. But Kaushalya was determined and would not listen to any argument. Her mind was made up; no argument against the match appealed to her. She chose to go further in this matter on her own. She had full faith in her own judgment and the adaptable nature of Shobhna, which she thought would rather complement Anmol's nature in its own way.

The good tidings were gradually brought to the notice of the relatives who were not very surprised. Sensing the frequency of Anmol's visits to Kaushalya's house, many had seen it coming; it was only a matter of time. They could vouch for Kaushalya's fondness for the boy and their instant camaraderie. Shobhna's husband, they surmised, had to get along well with Kaushalya too, as she was emotionally dependent on her daughter. Shobhna was and had always been the strongest bond in Kaushalya's life. Their mutual dependence was beyond anybody's comprehension. Shobhna's husband would have to accept this fact and respect its sacredness.

Months passed and still there was no sign of confirmation of the news from Anmol. Busy though he was in his new job and needed time to settle down, he could at least inform Kaushalya about the progress of his talks with his own relatives. The inordinate delay and prolonged silence on this front greatly annoyed Kaushalya. She was miffed at being taken so casually or informally. She couldn't take the suspense any longer and decided to write to Anmol asking about his final intentions.

Kaushalya felt that Anmol was behaving too big for his shoes, keeping the fate of a girl like Shobhna hanging in the air with his lack of decision. After all, what was his own status or credentials except his qualifications and a determination to study to further his prospects in life? He would stand to gain everything from this alliance; an established family status, an extremely good and educated girl and relations to fall back upon. What was he waiting for? As far as Shobhna was concerned, there was no dearth of boys.

Now she wondered whether she had made the right choice. Should she have consulted her husband and sons before making this offer to Anmol? In the deepest recesses of her heart, Kaushalya felt hurt and insulted. The continued delay had angered her more and more with each passing day. She couldn't bear it any more and decided to pen a strongly worded letter:

> *Dear Anmol, I am sure you must be happy in your new job. I can already see the influence of the Delhi culture growing upon you which makes a person indifferent to the needs and sentiments of others. Perhaps you can guess what I am driving at! Wasn't it obligatory on your part to take my offer seriously and intimate your intentions, whatever they might be? It hurts my pride to be waiting for your answer or may be your dwindling mind. Please let me know your intentions by return of post! Yours sincerely, Kaushalya.*

The letter had a magical effect. That weekend, Anmol showed up in Dhanbad. Kaushalya was overjoyed, her anger dissipated. And Shobhna was happy too. But attending to Anmol was still Kaushalya's prerogative. Both had a lot to update each other about.

'What's brewing in your mind lately?' Kaushalya asked Anmol as soon as they were left alone.

'Oh, my mind is perfectly in order,' laughed Anmol. 'And it is going in the right direction. Right decisions, too, take some time, especially if they need the concurrence of elders.' Anmol wanted to drive home his point in a subtle manner.

'What is the hindrance?' asked Kaushalya.

'My *bibi* has her own reservations and the other relations, their own choices and suggestions.' His *'bibi'* was his mother's sister, the one who had brought him up.

'I understand. But what is your decision?'

'My decision remains as firm as ever. I will never reconsider it. I just need time to convince my relatives.'

'What exactly are their reservations, Anmol?'

'Oh, don't bother about these, Kaushalya*ji*. They are the usual sorts. I know very well how to handle them.'

'There has to be a time frame. One can't wait for very long in these matters. A girl's youth and marriage proposals have a short time-span.'

'I know, Kaushalya*ji*. Have faith in me?'

'All right then. Keep me informed. I have taken a great risk in my judgment.'

'God willing, everything will turn in our favour.'

They ended their conversation and Anmol took his leave. He gave Kaushalya a hug.

Anmol's visit renewed their faith in each other. His heart was filled with tender feelings for this extraordinary woman who had stepped up to be the head of the family as a result of the peculiar circumstances of her family life. He marvelled at her grit, energy, enthusiasm and never-give-up attitude that had seen her through the worst phases of her life.

'Shobhna, too, must have inherited some of the qualities of her mother,' thought Anmol. 'But she has a more docile temperament, no doubt!'

Life fell back into a routine for all of them and time passed by fast enough before disturbing thoughts took hold of Kaushalya's mind once again.

Anmol, meanwhile, was trying to juggle his time and energy between his job in Delhi and his relatives in Calcutta. The long time span between his visits made his task all the more difficult. The formalities involved in coordinating such relations always took a backseat on account of the lack of initiative on the part of his own relations and the hassles of time and distance from Kaushalya's family. Things had to suit everybody before the relationship could be taken to the next level. And somebody had to take things in his or her own hands for talks to move forward. Anmol's *Bibiji* did not seem to be in a hurry about the whole thing. Rather, it was she who kept putting off these formalities on one account or the other. It was difficult to guess if she was possessive of Anmol or not comfortable about this relationship. Her suggestions for other marriage proposals were also deferring the ongoing talks with Kaushalya's family. Sensing her discomfiture regarding this alliance, Anmol turned to other women of the family for help. Kaushalya's frequent letters expressing her discontent only added to his sense of urgency.

Amar Kumari Verma, wife of Rai Bahadur Verma and Principal of FC College, Lahore, was a distant maternal aunt of Anmol. A prominent educationist, she had always encouraged Anmol in his studies even when he faced great odds in his life. Anmol decided to seek her advice and if need be, the intervention of other elderly relatives to press his *bibi* for a favourable response. Meetings and deliberations followed for many months before a date for the engagement was finally fixed and communicated to Kaushalya and the members of her family.

It was a great day for Kaushalya when she received the news. She felt a breeze of happiness flowing through her veins that percolated to every nook and corner of her home. She saw to it that arrangements and formalities were all in order and the guests were treated with all the respect that they deserved.

Finally, Anmol and Shobhna were engaged to be married in due course in the presence of relatives from both the sides who blessed them wholeheartedly. Anmol's close relatives had travelled all the way to Dhanbad where the ceremony took place in the home of Kaushalya's cousin, Prem Devi, who had helped Kaushalya with the arrangements. Kaushalya's tears flowed as Shobhna was presented the engagement ring along with a beautiful, georgette saree of magenta colour with a border of zari work on all the sides. Almost all of Anmol's relatives gave her beautiful presents in the form of small trinkets of gold or sarees. And so did Kaushalya's relations. Shobhna was showered with love and blessings from both sides. It was a moment of pride for Anmol too. He had become part of an illustrious family who took pleasure in being educated more than anything else in the world. He acquired a sense of belonging to that age of tradition, something that had eluded him in his early days of childhood and youth. Life gave a ray of faint hope of promise to come. There were stars in his eyes and his imagination blazed with thoughts of Shobhna.

'Shobhna!' thought he. 'That beautiful girl with the face of an angel and the spirit of Kaushalya. The daughter was a mirror image of her mother!' Anmol was elated.

It was an intense, novel experience for Shobhna, too. She felt herself bound, morally and emotionally. That carefree feeling of being on one's own or the right to make one's own choice and living life on one's own terms had vanished. She felt herself overcome with new emotions. She dreamed of having a home of her own where she could be the nucleus of the family, where life would stem from her and bring offshoots to the fore. Where she would be the root of the life that would result in generations to come! She would be the starting point of a new family line. Shobhna was lost in a reverie and a pat from Anmol brought her back to reality.

'Dreaming already!'

'No, not at all.' Shobhna's tone was demure.

'Kaushalya*ji*, can I now take her out for a meal before I return to Delhi?' asked Anmol, addressing Kaushalya. Kaushalya, caught unaware, deliberated for a moment before answering, 'Yes, why not? Ved Prakash can go along too! You'll all have a lot to talk about. Whenever you want, Anmol! I have no problem.'

Anmol returned to Delhi in a couple of days with a promise to return as early as possible. There would always be a reason for his increased frequency of visits to Dhanbad or Jharia wherever his love interest would be.

The evening was coming to a close as Shobhna and Kaushalya sat opposite each other, feeling relaxed and sipping tea along with a plateful of biscuits. The two were ruminating, lost deep in a world of their own. Their minds were occupied with plans for the future, albeit in different directions. A faint feeling of insecurity had crept in Kaushalya's mind and heart, who felt her life sustenance being drawn away from her slowly but firmly. She could not imagine her life without Shobhna.

'How will I live away from her?' thought Kaushalya a little depressed. 'My home will be dull without my dear daughter.' Ever since Shobhna had been born Kaushalya had not let her out of her sight. She had been her constant companion in the journey of life, through the good and the bad. Shobhna filled a great void in her life; she had made her living purposeful and easy. Her home would lose her sheen without her.

Yet she was happy for her daughter, indeed very happy. She thought Anmol was a good man who doted on Shobhna. He would keep her happy and take good care of her. Besides, he was her choice first, and she was certain of the match. Kaushalya knew that Anmol would be a great help to her, too, given their equation with each other. She need not worry about Shobhna on any account. Anmol's lack of emotional dependence on his own immediate family would also draw him close to their family.

Shobhna, on the other hand, was busy making a nest of her own dreams. She was unaware of her mother's conflicting, emotional thoughts. Kaushalya had been very good with hiding them from her.

At the moment, all Shobhna could think of was how she was going to be the queen of Anmol's life and home. She looked bright, and felt that way, too. The silence of the moment made her look towards Kaushalya. She had a fleeting sensation of her mother being taken away from her. She wanted to hold onto her, to keep her close to her heart always. She felt almost sorry for her; this frail woman who had faced the ups and downs of her life with tremendous strength and energy.

She thought of how her mother would cope without her. Her brothers did not know their mother in the same, intimate way that she did.

'What is it?' Kaushalya asked her daughter, seeing her pensive mood. 'What are you thinking about?'

'How will you live alone, Ma?'

'Don't worry about me, dear.'

'Why not? Who else will?'

'You see, my mother lived through this and so did her mother and so had hers. It is the law of life. We end up being alone sometimes and we need to go alone.'

'Oh, Ma!' Shobhna sobbed uncontrollably and put her head in her mother's lap. 'How will I live without you?' Shobhna realized that it was not her mother that she needed to worry about but herself.

'May God give you all the happiness in your married life that I never ever received! May Anmol substitute me in every way! I am sure he will love you, dearly. May God bless you, sweetheart!' Kaushalya wept bitterly for the first time in her life. She cried for the dearest daughter she was about to lose.

24

But Shobhna did not get married that month, or the next. The marriage kept getting postponed for one reason or the other. Kaushalya was flustered, although she knew that there was a right time for everything. The stars have their own rhythm. Destiny takes you through strange, dark alleys before bringing you to the final destination. Anmol and Shobhna had to undergo their share of uncertainties before they were to be finally pronounced man and wife. Through the agonizing wait, Kaushalya was their link and greatest support. Things might have simply fallen apart without her support and steadfastness.

Alas, the hurdles were huge. Distance and lack of time accentuated the indifferent attitude of Anmol's immediate family. Nobody seemed to be in a rush. Anmol's job in a Delhi school left him with little time to look after his own marriage arrangements. Except for Kaushalya, the close families on both sides were clearly not in a hurry to make the marriage happen.

The response of Kaushalya's own family was not, in any way, very encouraging. They had all agreed to the proposal because Kaushalya had set her heart on it. Ved Prakash, though a friend of Anmol's from their *Sangh* days, still had his own reservations. The other brothers, too, did not find the family of Anmol to be a suitable match to their own status. Shobhna's father, Ganpat Rai, and uncle, Arjun Dev, had really little to say or do while fixing the match. It had been the women's domain. And it continued that way, making the situation weary. Kaushalya, sensing the uneasy lull before the actual event, decided to write a letter to Anmol to suggest that they soon confirm the date of the marriage. As for her own preparations for the marriage, she was almost ready, having gotten Shobhna's clothes and ornaments in order. She decided to undertake a trip to Delhi to finalize the minute details along with Anmol. She appreciated the heart-to-heart talk she had with her future son-in-law, who himself did not seem to be taking the matter forward at the speed she wished for. Kaushalya and Shobhna boarded the train for Delhi at Dhanbad Railway junction, without waiting for Anmol's reply. Finding Kaushalya at his doorstep one fine morning, Anmol was utterly amazed at her audacity.

An informal talk, however, put all his inhibitions at rest but it became clear to Kaushalya that he had yet to prepare his relations for a quick wedding ceremony in the near future. Kaushalya was annoyed, 'What is he waiting for?'

'Anmol, let us fix the wedding date and act accordingly,' she said.

'Oh yes, Kaushalyaji. It is my priority too.'

'What is stopping you, then?'

'I have to consult my relations about the date. It has to suit everybody. Give me some time?'

'Time is running out fast. We are not getting any younger, Anmol.'

'I know it, Kaushalyaji,' said Anmol, 'A little more patience on your side.'

Kaushalya came back to the relatives she was staying with in Delhi. Everybody was keen to know the details of the meeting, which annoyed her a great deal, putting her on the defensive. She felt extremely lonely and longed for a shoulder to lean on so that her worries could be laid to rest. Their short stay in Delhi did give

Anmol and Shobhna a couple of opportunities to meet each other in private and get to know each other better. Of course, Kaushalya always lurked around and kept a watchful eye. Their meetings were always pleasant, ending on a happy note and bringing about a renewal of sentiments. To walk aimlessly through the streets of Delhi, stopping for a cup of tea or coffee at roadside kiosks or watching a popular movie together during the days of the courtship had its own charm and did wonders for the feelings of the betrothed. Anmol and Shobhna discovered that left to themselves and away from the monotony of routine life, they had a lot to say to each other! They thoroughly enjoyed their moments of privacy. Both longed to be with each other and yet could not bring themselves to discuss the subject of matrimony. A whole lot of issues lay before them that needed immediate attention. While one felt shy to discuss the issues openly, the other could not give specific answers due to the uncertainties involved on account of the decision resting with others.

Soon it was time for Kaushalya to return. The mother and daughter came back without anything specific in view. Anmol had promised to speed up the process. And that is what the talks had yielded. While Kaushalya's mind was in a muddle given the societal norms, Shobhna's heart danced. She had found Anmol totally besotted with her. His eagerness to please her in every way spoke volumes about the nature of the feelings he nurtured for her. She sported no doubts about his intentions and tried to understand his constraints. She knew it was only a matter of time before they would be ready to make a home of their own. She knew his circumstances at home had resulted in this inordinate delay and Anmol could not be entirely faulted. But she understood her mother's point of view, too. Kaushalya had become weary of waiting; being in limbo did not appeal to her at all. She was accountable to her own family. Anmol certainly owed an explanation at least to Kaushalya. She had taken a great risk with him and ignored the advice of her own near and dear ones. Kaushalya had an urge to talk to Shobhna about the whole thing with an open heart. Finding her occupied with her own thoughts one day, Kaushalya seized the opportunity.

'How much does Anmol love you, Shobhna?'

The question struck Shobhna like lightning. Recovering quickly from the shock of the blunt statement, Shobhna gulped hard before making a faint reply, 'Oh! Very much, Mother.'

'Did he say so?'

'Yes.'

'In as many words?'

'More or less.'

'Was he very vocal about it? What did he say?'

'Oh, Ma, don't ask me how exactly he said it. You know Anmol much more than I do, don't you?' answered Shobhna. Kaushalya knew Anmol had a great tenderness for Shobhna. Being passionate by temperament, he would never fail her. He wanted to belong to Shobhna and also to the family that had intrigued him by dint of its peculiarities.

'A man is always fascinated by odds,' thought Kaushalya to herself. 'And his mind always possessed by women unpossessed.'

Kaushalya knew that it was only if the marriage took place soon, that everything would end up well. Anmol should not keep her daughter waiting like this, for whatever reasons he might have.

Kaushalya couldn't restrain herself. 'Did Anmol touch you, Shobhna?'

'Ma! What has come over you?' Shobhna tried to look away.

'Answer my question, darling!'

'Well, he held my hand while we were roaming about in the streets and also when watching a movie,' Shobhna whispered.

'Did he say he would marry you soon while kissing you on your forehead?'

'Yes, Ma, and let that be the end of it! I will answer no more.'

Kaushalya heaved a sigh of relief with a smile on her face. All the uncertainties simmering within her heart had vanished. She became her calm self and prepared to undergo the usual rut once again. Somewhere, deep in her heart, she was reassured about the nearness of the event. She prayed to God to hasten the approach of the right time that would give her immense joy and prove her right in many ways.

It still did take a good one year for the marriage to take place. But when it did take place, it was quite grand as far as Kaushalya was concerned. She had measured up all her resources and made elaborate arrangements. Her parental relatives were of great help. Her cousin, Prem Devi, and her husband Wali Ram, who owned a big bungalow and had accommodated almost all the relatives during the days of Partition opened their abode to accommodate the *barat* that arrived from Calcutta. Generous and benevolent by nature, they had left no stone unturned in welcoming the guests and making them feel at home. Kaushalya was their favourite sister and they would not let her feel the absence of her own parents or brothers in any way. The *barat* was treated like royal guests; their needs and likes catered to, their whims and fancies carried out with utmost respect. They were Kaushalya's guests and they were dear to them all.

The marriage ceremony was arranged to take place in the premises of the big school where Kaushalya and Shobhna taught. It had come as a special request from the principal who extended this facility to them as a goodwill gesture. There was a lot of excitement in the air. Teachers and students of the school volunteered to assist with the decorations and help in welcoming the guests. After all, their favourite colleague was getting married! They wanted to make the experience memorable for a lifetime for the guests who had come all the way to take away their beautiful Shobhna. Emotions were brimming in everybody's heart and they had to make an effort to keep them in balance. Everybody dressed their best. Kaushalya had put on the most beautiful saree in her wardrobe; a piece she had brought along with her in her trousseau. Though old, it was exquisite in design and embroidery and radiant in colour. She looked truly the bride's mother and could have easily given the bride competition with her beauty. She stood at the entrance of the *pandal* surrounded by her sons to welcome the guests who had started pouring in early. Ved Prakash, dressed in an immaculate white *dhoti-kurta* looked very handsome. Harsh Prakash, Abhay and Vijay Prakash had come dressed in long-sleeved shirts and trousers. Well-built in stature as they all were, they looked very striking.

All of them were wearing red turbans, part of their dress code as brothers of the bride. Though happy, all of them looked a little lost, as if trying to come to terms with the reality of Shobhna's marriage and her imminent *bidai* from the parental home.

The *barat* arrived at the right time, looking regal in demeanour and resplendent in attire. The ritual of *'milni'* of relatives from both the sides took place at the entrance of the *pandal*, after which the poetic *'sehra'* was read out loud. The atmosphere reverberated with loud applause from the guests. The initial ceremonies over, the *barat* proceeded to enter the *pandal* where relatives of the girl got up from their seats in respect and busied themselves with attending to the needs of the guests. Sweets, snacks, soft drinks, milk and lassi appeared in abundance; soft notes of the *shahnai* were audible to everyone in the background and the atmosphere was one of extreme happiness and affection.

Anmol, looking majestic as a bridegroom, was led towards the *vedi* where the ceremonies of *jaimala* and *pheras* were to take place.

The *vedi*, erected straight as a square structure with bamboos, was decorated with rows of white flowers and red roses. A *purohit* was there, busy with his preparations and organizing various religious ornaments. The night was cool; the stars were twinkling in the sky, the scented flowers exuded a fresh aroma, the wedding premises were decorated tastefully with lights. The sound of people's voices was full of excitement and laughter. The setting was almost perfect for a union of the lovers. Almost, but for one major flaw: Shobhna's father, Ganpat Rai, was nowhere to be seen. He had left for Hardwar the night before, following an altercation with Kaushalya who had wanted him to play a more active role in their daughter's wedding. Ganpat Rai was reluctant, referring to his embracing the Vanprastha. This led to an argument and, right at the wedding, his absence. Undeterred as Kaushalya had always been, she did not allow her husband's absence to dampen the spirit of the occasion.

The food was laid for the guests on the other side of the *pandal* while the marriage ceremony would take place in the set up. The close relatives had all started gathering around the *vedi* where the garlands would be exchanged, to be followed by *pheras* amidst chanting of the *Vedic* mantras.

Shobhna was led towards the *vedi*. She looked ravishing. She was dressed in a red bridal ensemble, looking demure, surrounded by a bunch of friends, cousins, colleagues, and students. She looked like a princess. Everyone around jostled to have a close view of the bride who, till then, was an integral part of their lives but stood now on the threshold of a new beginning. Her head covered with an embellished *dupatta*, her arms and neck full of elegant ornaments, her eyes downcast and blushing, Shobhna was the perfect picture of an Indian bride whose beauty outshone that of every other woman present there.

With the *jaimala* and exchange of flower garlands, the bride and the groom completed their first step of belonging to each other. They were made to sit on the *vedi* for the *pheras* and the completion of the sacred vows. The ritual started strictly according to the *Aryasamaj 'Vidhi'* as Kaushalya had instructed the *purohit*, and the chanting of religious mantras from the *Vedas*. It took less than one hour for the ceremony to be completed along with the seven *pheras* where the groom took his vows to take care of the bride till the last breath of his life. Flower petals were showered on the newly married couple as they rose to touch the feet of the elders, starting from their mother Kaushalya and uncle Arjun Dev who had performed the ceremony of *kanyadan* in the absence of her father.

It was time for the *doli* to depart in the wee hours of the morning. As the time for *bidai* came, Kaushalya's heart sank. It was not easy for her to part with Shobhna whom she had loved the most in her life ever since she was born. As Anmol and Shobhna bowed to touch her feet and Anmol took a step forward taking Shobhna along on his arm and took their leave, Kaushalya felt faint. Her head swam with all kinds of emotions and she looked around for a shoulder to lean on, maybe even cry her heart out. She watched her daughter walk away, and before anyone could catch her, she fell on the floor, unconscious.

Her sons were the first to run to her side. The guests gathered, worried about the mother of the bride. Harsh Prakash picked her up and, with the help of his brothers, brought her to her room.

As she regained consciousness, her first words were about her darling Shobhna. 'Has Shobhna really gone from my house? When will I see her again?'

Relatives sat around her, trying to console her and help her come to terms with the situation. Her lost look and blank expression brought tears to everybody's eyes.

Kaushalya had lost her moorings once again and along with it, the will to live. A fundamental part of her had gone along with Shobhna to her new abode.

She prayed, 'When I think of my own married life, I hope God will be more bountiful to Shobhna!'

25

The distance from Dhanbad to Calcutta was covered in about four hours by train. The *baratis*, anxious to get back home, waited patiently for the train to come to a halt. Shobhna and Anmol, however, had been immersed in their own feelings, trying to keep their emotions in check. While Anmol looked forward to his future life with Shobhna with a sense of pride, she was having a nostalgic journey down memory lane. She thought of her privileged upbringing, surrounded by a large family of five brothers and other relatives, mostly staying together in an affectionate atmosphere. The credit for her education she owed mostly to the liberated and progressive outlook of her mother, Kaushalya Devi, who had acted as the family's backbone. Though influenced by the strong women of the household in the formative years of her life, first her grandmother Geli Bai and then her mother Kaushalya Devi, Shobhna had also inherited a few traits of her father which made her a little more gentle, persuasive and less assertive. She remembered her childhood as the pampered sister of her brothers and cousins; the special affection of her parents for being the only daughter; the pride of her entire clan when she became the first girl in the family to complete her graduation and above all, she remembered the ever-smiling, vibrant face of her mother Kaushalya Devi who was always happiest when with her. It was as if she had finished reading a chapter in a book and waited to start a new one, afresh.

A part of her life had been left behind but she could take the memories and keep them safely entrenched in her heart and go back to them whenever she wanted, for solace or remembrance. Happy memories, when used as a foundation for building a future life always had a greater propensity for happiness, mutual understanding and complete trust in each other. Shobhna sat in her seat, composed, lost in thought and utterly oblivious of the excited voices of her new relatives.

Anmol, mindful of the approaching station and the halting speed of the train became busy in getting all his relatives and their luggage together asking them to be ready to disembark.

Everyone made sure to take care of Shobhna first.

Anmol then brought Shobhna to her new home—the home of his younger brother, Satya Prakash, who had lived with his mother since Anmol shifted to Delhi. They lived in a house in a narrow street in the midst of a busy town where different sounds were always audible. Calcutta had been and was always in the throes of excitement; people were fond of music, *paan*, travelling in trains and engaging in intellectual discussions. Roadside pubs and kiosks were always thriving with people who loved to eat fish, drink innumerable cups of tea or coffee and indulge in leisurely talk while bursting into loud laughter. It presented a stark contrast to the calm and peaceful life of Dhanbad and Jharia. The spirit of Calcutta matched the excitement that prevailed in the hearts of Anmol and Shobhna. A new life awaited them, with hope, promises and even struggles, they reckoned.

Though located in a narrow street, the house looked rather presentable to Shobhna. It was an old structure and housed many families at different levels. Anmol and his family lived on the first floor. When Anmol knocked, his *bibi* opened the door and brought a *thali* of *puja* to welcome the new bride and the guests who had come along. Being frail and a little unwell, she had stayed at home to look after the arrangements and make preparations for receiving the newly-weds. The *grih-pravesh* ritual over, Shobhna touched the feet of her mother-in-law and entered the house while being welcomed with a shower of flower petals by the relatives who also uttered blessings of '*dudho nahayo, puto falo* (May God give you prosperity and sons!')

Life in Calcutta remained hectic and eventful for Anmol and Shobhna as long as they were there, which was not more than a fortnight as Anmol's special leave from work was limited. Anmol took pride in introducing Shobhna to all his relations who called them over to their homes for a meal as a welcome gesture. Anmol's distant maternal uncle, Rai Bahadur Sh. Verma and his wife, Amar Kumari Verma, always had a special soft spot in their hearts for Anmol. They threw a party for the couple and formally welcomed her by showering her with blessings and gifts. Shobhna was overwhelmed. She felt blessed for being part of Anmol's family. She reciprocated their gesture by touching their feet, her head covered by the *pallu* of her *saree*. She quietly resolved to fulfil her marriage vows.

Day after day was spent amidst a lot of activity, excitement and sightseeing. Shobhna's *devar* Satya Prakash, took it upon himself to show her around the city. He would be ready with his plan for the day every morning and would coax Anmol to accompany them if he so wished. By the time their stay ended, Shobhna had a fairly good idea of Calcutta, its historical significance and rich cultural heritage. She was charmed by its hustle and bustle, its omnipresent noise, the rushing speed, the vehicles that raced on the roads, and the ability of its people to keep pace with everything while yet finding time to sit and talk, mostly about intellectual and philosophical issues. The novel experience opened a new perspective for Shobhna to assimilate, and she chose to see everything from her own outlook for the first time in her life, her mother Kaushalya Devi having always been the guiding spirit till the day of her marriage.

Shobhna felt liberated, having left her pre-marriage phase behind, though still tied with the unbreakable bond of relationships and blood ties. The thought of her mother, without any emotional anchor to hang on to, filled her eyes with tears. Her heart ached for her mother's loneliness. Her mood was soon lifted by the affectionate and caring attitude of Anmol and his family who never allowed her a moment of distress in any way. Her own new status of a bride and the elder daughter-in-law of the family entrusted her with the task of keeping everybody together and happy.

For once, *Bibi* too looked happy. Shobhna had instantly won her over with her gentleness and affection. She liked the girl and her behaviour. The fact that Shobhna came from a large family and knew very well the manner of living together in harmony in a joint family only helped the whole circle of relationships. Bibi's heart was touched as she gradually opened herself before her *bari-bahu*.

Anmol was overjoyed, watching his new bride. He felt himself lucky that he had found and married a girl like Shobhna. He surmised that God had taken pity on him and his woes and was compensating him for the miseries he had endured in his childhood. 'Life may yet prove to be good to me!'

Days flew by before the euphoria of marriage had even shown signs of slowing down. Anmol had to return to Delhi to rejoin his school. He also had to find a suitable place to rent for Shobhna and himself. A lot of issues were already occupying his mind and he had to take quick decisions.

A new chapter in his life had started. He had to act quickly, firmly and appropriately. Moments of leave taking had crept nearby making everybody sad and teary-eyed. They had decided to go back to Dhanbad where Shobhna would stay for about a month or so, until Anmol was able to make arrangements for their new home in Delhi.

On the train to Dhanbad they quietly savoured each other's company. Taking her hand in his, Anmol said, 'How will I stay without you all these days, dear!'

'The same way as we have lived till now. It is just a question of some more time,' Shobhna replied, looking at him with affectionate and mischievous eyes.

They both knew their brief stay in Dhanbad was going to be hectic. They were received eagerly at the station by Kaushalya and her sons; they had all missed their sister like never before. Shobhna's joining another household had finally dawned on all of them and they had sorely missed her. Their home became dull in her absence. Kaushalya Devi too, seemed to have lost her zest for life in Shobhna's absence. It was only the news of Shobhna's arrival that pushed her out of her cocoon. She was eager to receive Shobhna and Anmol in their home for the first time after their marriage.

The train's arrival had put the platform in a tizzy. People ran from one end to another looking for their loved ones. The vendors were all around, constantly shouting to sell their wares. The *coolies*, looking conspicuous in their flaming red dresses and wearing shining golden badges on their arms, looked expectantly at the arriving passengers.

Kaushalya was the first to spot Shobhna who stood at one of the train doors looking as eagerly through people as Kaushalya did. Attired in a deep pink, silk *Salwar-Kameej*, which made her typical Indian beauty stand out, she looked happy and content. Anmol stood behind her, looking strong, obviously keeping a watchful eye on his bride. The mother and the daughter ran towards each other, ending up wrapped in a tight embrace as tears ran down their faces. They met like long-lost friends: keen to talk to each other and be left alone. They were ready to enjoy talking to each other, share stories and unburden their hearts. The two soulmates were together again. Her brothers, too, were overwhelmed. They hugged Anmol with respect and affection, picked up their luggage and ushered them to the gate that would take them out of the platform and lead them home.

A couple of days alone were all Anmol could spend in his bride's family in Dhanbad. Kaushalya's relatives vied with each other to call the new couple to their homes and bless them. Kaushalya's cousin, Prem Devi, to whom she was extremely close, decided to throw a party to welcome the newly married couple.

It was a scene of pure jubilation as the relatives came together, focusing all their interest on Shobhna and Anmol. To them the couple looked perfectly matched and made for each other. They showered the newly-weds with compliments, good wishes and presents.

Kaushalya felt proud of her son-in-law; he looked dashing and had impeccable social skills. Shobhna and he made a good pair. They were extremely fond of each other. Kaushalya hoped and prayed for their eternal, happy married life. Sharing in their joy, she resolved to come out of her shell and begin life anew, without the companionship of her dear Shobhna. She prayed to God for strength as she imagined herself treading the uneven journey of life, all by herself. She knew that such is what God had ordained for her, and she could no longer complain.

Anmol arrived in Delhi in time to rejoin his school. He was faced with numerous issues. He had to find a small place to live in before he could ask Shobhna to join him. He had been sharing a room with a couple of other men near his school before he got married. The circumstances now warranted a decent room in a decent locality where he could bring Shobhna and start a home with her. He would spend all his free time looking for accommodation and sorting out his plans. He toured the adjoining areas on a bicycle. His colleagues helped him, too, suggesting options and joining him in his search.

Delhi post-Partition was more a city of cycles for common people. There were bicycles everywhere on the roads, hundreds of them; a number of scooters but fewer cars. The common mode of transport was the public buses but these were generally crowded.

The city, being the capital, was the cultural and intellectual hub of the nation. It had a soul and a spirit that fascinated all. People here were ready to struggle and make good use of the opportunities that came their way. In a place like Delhi, one only needed to have determination. One could work one's way up in life by sheer dint of perseverance and searching out the right opportunities at the right time. And if one happened to be educated, too, then it certainly made things easier.

By its nature and character Delhi offered a stark contrast to the small towns. While life was easier in smaller places in terms of movement and social relationships, distance within the city of Delhi could take its toll on such things, making life a bit cumbersome and more complicated.

Thus, he thought, Shobhna would have to make some adjustments to her lifestyle when she joined him. He pictured her privileged upbringing of the pre-Partition phase and her comfortable stay even in Dhanbad. He placed his trust on his love for Shobhna. That, he knew, was what he had in abundance for her.

Anmol eventually found a one-room set in Gole market area that was in the centre of the city. Though a little far from his work place, it suited his meagre means. The affectionate tone of the landlady also impressed him. 'Come in, young boy,' she had said when he first came to see the apartment. 'Let me show you to your room. I understand you have recently got married. When are you getting your bride here?' She found an easy listener in Anmol who answered all her questions patiently.

The room was of medium size with a small kitchenette and a veranda in front. Like the rest of the house, it looked towards the street that faced a common park abutting the main road. Anmol could see a few neighbourhood children playing, their mothers or caregivers watching them closely.

Overall Anmol found the apartment to be a good deal. Shobhna would have good company while he was in school. Connaught Place was only a stone's throw away, and he and Shobhna could go there when they needed some entertainment.

Anmol liked what he saw. Though it was nothing in comparison with what Shobhna was accustomed to in Dhanbad or Jharia, this was the best he could offer her at the moment. Eventually, he believed, they would prosper and be able to live more decently.

He spent the next couple of days buying a few necessities like a double bed, a few pieces of cane furniture, and some linen. He deferred buying the kitchen items for when Shobhna would be around.

Satisfied with his arrangements, Anmol posted a letter to Kaushalya Devi asking her to send Shobhna to Delhi as soon as possible.

The train that brought his beloved to Delhi arrived in the late afternoon on a Sunday. As he waited for Shobhna's arrival, Anmol's heart pounded with anxiety and desperation. He could not wait to see his wife again and take her to their new home.

The train came and Anmol shushed his heart. He quickly found Shobhna, who was collecting her luggage from the compartment. A month's separation had made the lovers long for each other. They stood hand in hand and looked deep into each other's eyes, as if that alone could make up for lost time. The huge crowd and the hustle-bustle as people ran about and shouted at each other brought them back to the present. They picked up their luggage, walked out of the compartment, and hailed a cab to take them to their home.

They walked past a row of houses before Anmol stopped in front of one. He looked at her as if to say, 'This is it!' He opened the lock of the room with a key and ushered her in.

'Whose house is this?' asked Shobhna, utterly amazed.

'Your house, my dear. This is our love nest!' Anmol tried to avoid her eyes.

'My home! You're making me stay here?' Shobhna was in such disbelief that tears began streaming down her face.

'Shobhna, let me explain!'

'How did you have the heart to bring me here? Don't you know anything?'

That was all Shobhna would say before running to the room and slumping down on the bed. She quickly dozed off, shock and fatigue mastering her completely. Anmol did not dare disturb her.

26

When she woke up, Shobhna looked at the clock and realized she had slept for nearly two hours. She also saw that Anmol had taken off her shoes and her other accessories, and had covered her with a sheet. She found Anmol sitting on a chair near the window, looking out dreamily and smoking. Hearing the ruffling of the sheets, he turned to her and smiled, 'Oh my beautiful bride! Awake at last! How are you feeling now? Refreshed after the long journey and in a better mood, I am sure.'

Shobhna sat up, stretched her arms and yawned, 'I feel much better now. And yes, I am sorry for my outburst. I was completely taken aback and shocked beyond words. It was so unexpected, exactly the opposite of what I had been dreaming.'

'I understand perfectly, my dear.' Anmol came to her and sat on the edge of the bed. He tried to take her in his arms as he kissed her on her beautiful neck. 'It is only the beginning, Shobhna. I was in a hurry to get you here. This was the quickest arrangement I could make in such short a time. Now that you are here with me, we will look for better alternatives, something that will make you happier. Now, are you hungry or not?'

'I am starving. I haven't eaten much on the train since yesterday. By the way, I don't see any food around.'

'Why don't you freshen up, change your clothes and come out to have a bite somewhere in Connaught Place? Let's hurry up. It is getting late for dinner.'

Shobhna put on a bright orange saree with an embroidered black blouse, put her hair up in a tight bun, wore a few ornaments that her mother had given her, and smeared a little vermillion on her forehead. Anmol watched his ravishing bride, his heart full of pride and happiness, then took her hands and walked her out of the home and came out on the main road. They stopped a cab and asked to be taken to Connaught Place.

They got off at the centre of CP and took a walk around. Anmol pointed out to Shobhna landmarks, famous eating joints and cinema houses as well. Anmol spotted United Coffee House, which he liked, and decided to take Shobhna there for their first dinner date. Shobhna instantly loved the place, its ambience enhanced largely by the elegant furniture and decor. She was impressed with the little details, how the tables were laid, the cutlery placed neatly and with a small vase of flowers at the centre. Wooden lamps let out a dim light, contrasting well with the large chandelier hanging in the middle of the room. Most of the tables were occupied; the guests looked well-dressed, maybe even wealthy, thought Shobhna. She was mesmerized by the romantic atmosphere, much like a dreamland where soft music played in the background. She savoured and breathed in every moment in that place with her husband, thinking how she grew up not seeing any such intimacy in a married relationship in her household. She belonged to an almost-broken, mismatched home where the husband and the wife were used to leading their own lives. She never saw her own parents in an intimate relationship. She had never even seen them talk affectionately to each other.

It was like a whole new world was opening before her eyes: a new perspective, a new approach to a relationship. Marriage, she now saw, was not the end of a relationship; rather it was a beginning where the two individuals could meet normally, talk to each other, and enjoy life together. Such outings could only enhance the element of romance in a marriage and rekindle it from time to time if necessary. Shobhna was overwhelmed. She looked at Anmol with lovelorn eyes and felt guilty for her earlier behaviour, throwing a childish tantrum about their small apartment. Anmol did not notice her gaze, though, as he was busy poring over the menu card.

'My dear young lady, what would you like to have for your dinner, some South Indian cuisine or our very own Punjabi food?'

'What would you like?'

'No, it is your prerogative tonight, my love.'

'I think we can have our own food today.'

'Very well, my dear.'

While Anmol ordered the food, Shobhna looked around her and saw many couples, young and old, interacting with each other, immersed in their own small world of a table while allowing others to have their own space. No one glared at any other person or disturbed anyone in any way. She saw large families, too. The old, the middle-aged and the children, all generations combined, sharing a big table. It was an unthinkable scene where she came from. There was an extremely young couple at another table, looking totally smitten with each other. They did not look married; perhaps it was their period of courtship or they were simply friends or lovers maybe. Delhi had the time, place and occupation for everyone; it embraced humanity unhesitatingly and without discrimination.

Shobhna liked the novelty of it all.

'What a place Delhi is! It has a look and character far removed from that of small towns. Life seems very different here. It gives a very liberating feeling. Ah, the fresh breeze....'

Anmol could see her eyes shimmering with delight.

'Shobhna, if this is your first reaction, God knows what you will say after a few days or maybe months!'

'I will say what I really feel like. You will always know what lies in my heart. I would never be untruthful to you.'

'Let us make a promise today. We will never be unfaithful to each other or lie about anything under any circumstances ever. We will respect each other's feelings and not hurt our sentiments. The foundation of a good married life is always based on trust, understanding and cooperation, don't you agree? We must respect the sanctity of the institution of marriage.'

'I will do my best. God will give me the strength to come up to your expectations.'

The waiter came with the food, steaming hot and looking appetizing. Shobhna's pangs of hunger sharpened. The food was served in dainty little brass bowls with a plateful of fresh salad in the middle. As they helped themselves to rice, *dal* and vegetables to start with, the *tawa chapatti* and *nan* were served fresh to them, straight from the *tandoor*. They ate bit by bit, enjoying each morsel and communicating with their eyes mostly, and a few words only wherever necessary. Time stood still for them as they enjoyed their first solitary meeting since their wedding. It was the first mutual flush of happiness writ large on their faces intoxicating them. Feeling satiated with their sumptuous dinner, Anmol and Shobhna roamed the streets, hand in hand, talking and laughing till they found themselves standing outside the Regal cinema house. The time was just right for the late night show and Anmol decided to give his wife another treat. He bought tickets for the current movie, called *'Duniya'*, which he had heard so much about.

It was midnight when they left the cinema. In the cab, Shobhna thought of the night they had just had and the happiness engulfing her. She made a vow to accept things as they came, to adjust if necessary.

They made their way to their room quietly, taking care not to make a noise lest they awaken their neighbours.

Touching the bed in the dim light of the bulb hanging above, they sat on it for sometime looking around for their things till Shobhna got up and looked for a change of clothes.

'Do I help you unpack?' Anmol offered. 'You have not had time to take out your things.'

'No, you don't need to,' she replied. 'I will do all that tomorrow when I'll have plenty of time. I will just need a change right now.'

'Then hurry up, it's already very late!' Anmol teased and let her be.

They lay down on the bed and soon fell into a deep sleep in each other's arms. They woke up late that Sunday morning. They were not in a hurry to get up. They lazed around in bed till the rays of the morning sun acquired a reasonably bright tone and the local life came alive. They could hear the newspaper-*wallah* making his rounds, the vendors who hawked their bread and eggs, fruits and vegetables, and milk, too. Shobhna paid special attention to the chirping of birds nearby, the distant call of a love bird, probably for its mate or even the flutter of a wing in the front *veranda*. Being used to life in a small city, she was more receptive to the sounds of nature, however faint or distant, and responded more to them while finding mundane noises quite annoying. Anmol simply watched her. He stroked her hair gently and said, 'This is Delhi, my dear. The pace of life is rather quick here. It'll grow on you soon, you'll see and you'll even miss it if you go away.'

'Well, I like it already!' Shobhna got up and walked to the front window, drawing the curtains open to get a clear view of the morning scenery.

'Would you like some tea? We do have a kettle?' Shobhna smiled lovingly at her husband, who was still sprawled on the bed.

'Have patience, my dear. And don't forget that you are on your honeymoon. If you were living in a big family, you wouldn't have been allowed to work in the kitchen for three months, at least! That's how we welcome a new bride! So here you are not going to cook for fifteen days at least.'

'I feel like a queen already!' She smiled.

'You are a queen. You are the queen of my heart!' Anmol pulled her to him and showered her with kisses on her cheeks.

'The window is open. People might see.'

'Let them see! Everyone knows we are newly married.'

'Come on, there is still some decorum in public life...'

'This room is our own. Personal. People have no business to peep into our private life.'

'So, what is the programme for the day?'

'Whatever you want? I am at your disposal, my fair lady.'

They sat on the bed for a long time, chatting, talking of days spent in Dhanbad and even going down the memory lane of Lahore. The pre-Partition days seemed like a golden era or a sweet dream that had come to an abrupt end, bringing in its wake this sordid reality.

'Those days were really wonderful!' Shobhna's eyes moistened once more. 'I wish we knew at that time that they were short-lived. They seemed eternal, with peace and happiness all around.'

He felt her melancholy and decided to change the subject. 'Shobhna, my dear, aren't you hungry?'

'A little bit.'

'Then let us get ready fast and go and get a bite somewhere.' He got up from the bed, certain that he didn't want Shobhna to have her moment of sadness. Shobhna got up as well and got ready. Anmol's love-talk had perked up her spirits and she was as chirpy as an early bird in the morning. She took out a pink saree with *'mukeish'* work, which her *bua*, Lakshmi Devi, had gifted her, with a matching blouse and accessories. She made a long plait of her hair and ended it with a pink *paranda*. She looked as fresh and exuberant as the first ray of the morning sun. Anmol was bewitched by her beauty, her innocent face, and felt a tinge of sadness that he could not afford to keep her in a better house that was more suited to her upbringing.

They spent the entire day roaming about the streets of Delhi and eating wherever they liked. Anmol had planned to show her the important landmarks of Delhi. They started at India Gate and Jantar Mantar, the day being a holiday and full of people. For their afternoon meal, they went to the Madras Hotel which was known for its excellent South Indian food. The narrow entrance of the staircase for the hotel itself reeked of an irresistible pungent South Indian aroma.

Anmol and Shobhna ordered a *masala dosa* and a plate of *vada* each and finished with delicious filter coffee. The late afternoon, almost on the verge of early evening, was the right time to go towards India Gate where people would gather in the front lawns to have a picnic or eat ice cream bought from the vendors who always plied the area for big business. A small boat ride was also a popular feature in the artificial ponds of water created there.

'It is a beautiful place!' exclaimed Shobhna. 'People look so happy here!'

'It is rather busy on the weekends when people are free from work.'

Like others, Anmol and Shobhna relished some ice cream and went on a boat ride. They then walked along the pavements, hand in hand, talking, laughing and enjoying in a way they never had before. With love in their hearts and dreams in their eyes, they thought of their future life ahead: it seemed full of hope and promise.

Anmol was convinced that with Shobhna by his side, he could conquer the world. Once again he uttered a prayer of thanks to God for giving him a bountiful present in life in the form of Shobhna.

The honeymooning couple were oblivious to the world around them. All that mattered to them was their togetherness, away from the prying eyes of relatives and friends. The periodical winter break in Anmol's school came as a windfall to their holidaying mood. This was the best time for them to get to know each other. This was also their first brush with romance, the likes of which they had never experienced before. They were completely under the spell of love and passion and could not tolerate a minute of separation from each other.

One morning as they lazed in bed, Anmol said to Shobhna, 'We belong to each other!'

'We do, my love!' said Shobhna. They kissed passionately.

Shobhna felt she could bear anything for Anmol; she would struggle along with him or suffer for him or walk with him hand in hand, whatever would give him pleasure and contentment. She would never desert him; so great was her love for him. Her eyes blazed with a great tenderness for him as she looked at him and saw that Anmol, too, was watching her affectionately.

'What are you thinking about?'

'I was thinking why you did not come in my life earlier. Shobhna, I love you. I love you very much, sweetheart.'

She put her head on his chest and could feel his heart throbbing.

As they hugged each other, a great feeling of satiation came over them and they felt quenched to their very core.

27

For the first week or so, Shobhna and Anmol were interested in nothing else except eating and sleeping. They experienced a great feeling of contentment as they got up late in the mornings and lazed around in bed, talking of the simple pleasures of life. There was no hurry or rush for anything and they liked to be on their own. The day was spent in discovering the city and eating meals at different places or watching a movie every second day. By late evening they would be tired out with excitement and they would sleep in their spacious bed for about ten hours at a stretch, waking up dreamily in the morning. Lying next to each other in the privacy of their small room, they realized that they did not miss anyone at all. All their life, they had been surrounded by people; shouldered their responsibilities and cared for family and others. Living on one's own could also be very peaceful; rather a wonderful relief at times!

When winter break ended, Anmol went back to his teaching. Left alone, Shobhna discovered that she did not feel lonely at all. Rather, she felt completely at ease, occupying herself in things that gave her pleasure. She was away from her mother, brothers and other relatives for the first time in her life and she loved it. She had never felt the secret domination of her mother, Kaushalya Devi, till she felt the fresh breeze of freedom. Shobhna discovered the luxury of absolute leisure and independence. Surprisingly, she felt happy to be away from her past life which though comfortable, had been full of complexities. She did not even miss her teaching career or books, which had been an integral part of her life. For the time being, she was happy being on her own. Her love-nest, though small and ordinary, had a charm of its own. It was her domain with the promise of great companionship with Anmol, something that she missed in her parental home. There was no one here to disturb their solitude or moments of romance. She had all the time in the world or the luxury of idle physical leisure. And she was ecstatic.

She thought that at the end of the day a woman wanted a husband, a home, and children. She also wanted to love, totally surrender herself and be loved with the same passion in return. She felt that it was not too much to ask these things from God. These were the natural corollaries of the institution of marriage. A woman's life depended heavily on how lucky she was in marriage and her compatibility with her partner. That only can lead to happiness. Even the poorest woman on earth can be as lucky in this gamble called marriage as a rich woman.

She thought of Anmol, how gentle a lover he was and how truly he loved her. He needed a companion with whom he could talk intimately. He took care of all her needs and feelings too. What more could she want in life? The best thing about Anmol was that he didn't consider women as a weakness. He certainly wanted them as companions in his life. Perhaps, thought Shobhna, that was what education did to a man.

'We will have a good life together,' Shobhna smiled to herself. This was a phase of life she had never seen before. Life seemed so beautiful.

At that moment Shobhna's thoughts suddenly turned to her mother. Her eyes welled up in tears as she thought of her with pity.

Shobhna was happier than she had ever been, except perhaps

for those moments she had spent with her mother in complete intimacy. Lost in her thoughts, she failed to notice that Anmol was back and was watching her with a smile. He went to her and held out his hand, 'Come my love, we'll have our lunch outside.'

'When will I have the privilege of making food for you with my own hands?'

'Don't be in a hurry! This time of life will never come again. Let's enjoy.'

'It's like being in heaven. No worries of any kind!' Shobhna's eyes rested on him lovingly.

'Don't come to a conclusion so soon, dear. Life is full of struggles in this city. Such moments are rare and therefore, precious.' He clutched her hands as he kissed her passionately.

A week passed before Anmol took Shobhna to the market to get items for their humble kitchen. Shobhna was enthusiastic at the mere idea of having a kitchen of her own where she could cook for Anmol. Anmol, too, was very happy. Ever since he had lost his mother in his infancy, he couldn't remember having anyone cook specially for him. Having a loving home with a life partner of one's own choice was altogether new feeling for him, a practice which was not very common, since matchmaking was largely handled by the elders during their time. For Shobhna, too, Anmol was the first man who had come in her life. They matched each other's eagerness, feelings and excitement. Anmol watched her closely as she set up her things in the kitchenette adjoining their room.

'Would you like a hot cup of tea?' she asked.

'I would love some, my dear.'

Anmol followed her into the kitchen and helped her put the water on the stove while she set the teapot on a tray along with cups and saucers and a tea cosy. As the water came to a boil, she put a spoonful of loose tea leaves in the kettle and poured boiling hot water into it and covered it with the tea cosy. As the water brewed, she boiled the milk and put some sugar in the cups. She carried the tray into their room with Anmol following her with a plateful of biscuits.

'Excellent tea!' remarked Anmol, sipping from his cup and offering a biscuit to Shobhna.

'From now onwards, I will call you my *Annapurna*,' he said.

'Why so?'

'The first role of a *grih-lakshmi* is that of an *Annapurna*. She brings food and prosperity along with her.'

'I shall always keep that in mind and try to do my best.'

'May God help us as we start our new life together!'

They drank their tea at leisure, eating biscuits and stretching out on their bed long after their tea had finished.

And so, Shobhna, the queen of her little house with a loving husband by her side, set out in earnest to make a small home and start a family. While Anmol kept himself busy with his school work, Shobhna took it upon herself to shoulder the responsibilities of the home. Both shared their notes in the late afternoons when Anmol got back from school and they would go for a round of the Connaught Place after having their meal. They would catch up with stories about their day, buy small knick-knacks and enjoy the hustle-bustle of the city life in the evenings. They would occasionally visit the Buddha Garden or Talkatora Garden for a long walk depending on their time and convenience, often eating out or watching a movie, depending on their mood.

Days turned to weeks, and weeks to months, and the season was due for a change. The cold winter was losing its sheen, giving way to the first warm rays of the sun.

One evening, Shobhna stood by the window of her room looking at the front garden, trying to soak in the various subtle smells of the flowers and looking at the fading, beautiful dusk.

The sky looked radiant with the diminishing rays of the sun. The squeaking sound of the birds for their mates made the atmosphere dreamy and romantic. While she was so absorbed in her thoughts, she did not hear the door open as Anmol came in and stood beside her. He patted her on her shoulder, 'Dreaming still, my dear!'

Shobhna turned coyly toward him, blushing deeply but not saying anything.

'What is the matter, Shobhna?'

She put her head on his shoulder, 'You are going to become a father!'

'What?' Anmol shouted. 'Did you just say I was going to become a father?'

Shobhna nodded, smiling contentedly.

'Hurrah!' Anmol let out a roar. He couldn't hide his happiness. He picked her up in his arms, his eyes dancing with joy.

'Shobhna, you have come as a fresh breeze in my life. For the first time I am going to have somebody who can be absolutely mine, besides you. My name will flourish even after I am no more.' Anmol was overjoyed.

And Shobhna and Anmol found a new purpose in life. They knew that all their waking moments would now be spent in taking care of each other and planning for the baby. Shobhna duly informed her mother and Anmol's relatives about the good news. Kaushalya naturally was bubbling with excitement at the prospect of becoming a grandmother. She was already making elaborate plans of visiting and staying with Shobhna closer to her due date. She looked forward to happier times once again, this time with her grandchildren on her lap, reading to them and telling them tales.

Shobhna was getting heavier each day. Soon she found it difficult to cope with the domestic chores. Anmol had been taking her for regular check-ups at the nearby health centre. He had also booked a private room in Safdarjung Hospital where a distant cousin of his happened to be a leading physician. He had engaged a part-time help to assist Shobhna with the household work. All activities had become geared towards Shobhna's confinement which was getting nearer day by day. Her mother, Kaushalya Devi, arrived almost a month before the due date, taking a three-month leave from her school.

Their humble home was filled with both anxiety and excitement. Kaushalya was together with her daughter for a long span for the first time after her marriage. The togetherness with her greatly lifted her spirits, filling a void in her life that had crept in since Shobhna's marriage.

There really was nothing like staying with one's daughter, she thought wistfully one day. While sons are also part of one's flesh and blood, a mother can really communicate emotionally only with a daughter. Suddenly she wished she had another daughter to take care of her in her old age. She prayed for a granddaughter.

Shobhna was then lying on the bed, looking at her mother and trying to read her thoughts. She got up suddenly and sat up, her face and lips clenched with a sudden pang of pain.

'Mother, I think the time has come to go to the hospital.'

'Yes, I think so, Shobhna. I'll tell Anmol to hurry up with the arrangements.'

Shobhna stayed in the bed, closed her eyes, calmed herself through the first labour pains and waited for Anmol. When Anmol entered the room running, she tried to smile at him and put up a brave face.

'We are leaving for the hospital right away, Shobhna. You will be in safe hands. May God help us!'

Kaushalya and Anmol helped her walk towards the waiting cab. Kaushalya had earlier packed a bag full of necessities for Shobhna's labour.

Two hours after Shobhna was taken to the hospital, the doctor came out to tell Anmol and Kaushalya that her labour was going to take some time. They would have to wait. Shobhna grappled with the pains by herself, assisted by the doctor and the nurses. Kaushalya and Anmol whiled away their anxiety with small talk.

'The first baby usually takes a long time to come out,' Kaushalya said to Anmol. 'It is a hard struggle for the woman.'

'Shobhna is a brave girl,' Anmol replied. 'I am sure she will endure it well.' He got up and paced the veranda, looking at his watch constantly.

'Is the woman conscious all the while, *Maji*?'

'Oh, yes! She has to be. How will she push the baby out otherwise? Though things are different in a caesarean delivery. But Shobhna is going to have a normal procedure which might take longer. It is healthier and more satisfying no doubt, but painful.'

'I hope the child is born soon,' said Anmol. 'Shobhna will be in deep pain. I hope everything goes well.'

It turned out to be a long wait. The child wasn't born until six hours later, leaving Shobhna completely worn out by pain and exhaustion. She didn't have an ounce of energy left in her to even open her eyes and see the beautiful little girl that she had given birth to. She was vaguely aware of the shrill cry of a baby and a feeling of sudden relief coming upon her instantly.

'Take a look at your lovely baby girl!' said the nurse to her as she cradled the little bundle of joy in her arms to show to Shobhna.

Shobhna bent quickly to give her baby a kiss, getting only a quick glimpse of her before relapsing into a kind of stupor. The nurse picked up the baby and put her in the cradle next to Shobhna's bed. The doctor came out of the labour room half an hour later and informed Anmol and Kaushalya Devi about the normal birth of a baby girl.

'God bless you, dear!' shouted Kaushalya Devi in joy. She hugged the doctor and gave her a fifty rupee note. 'I have become a grandmother!'

'You certainly don't look like one, *Maji*,' the doctor smiled back.

Anmol was jubilant and eager to see Shobhna as soon as possible. 'When can I see my wife and child?'

'Just in a while. We are going to bring her to the private ward in about an hour.'

They waited for that time and when it came, it was pure joy. Shobhna saw Anmol whose eyes were fixed on her, full of joy and pride.

She smiled at him.

'You look weak, dear! You should rest. Thank you for giving me my most beautiful gift. She is as precious to me as you are.' Anmol didn't hide his emotions.

Shobhna's eyes bore a soft look; she clutched Anmol's hand and forgot all the pains and aches needling what seemed like every nook of her body. She lay watching him while Kaushalya had the infant in her lap, showering her with kisses, singing her a sweet lullaby.

Kaushalya's wish had been fulfilled for a second time: the first time, when she asked to bear a daughter and now, having her first granddaughter. The baby looked just like Shobhna. 'Oh my adorable little doll!' Kaushalya whispered to the baby, delirious with joy.

Anmol looked at Shobhna, Kaushalya, and his daughter, girls and women of three generations, all tied to him inextricably. He saw and perceived happiness in its purest form, the delicate thread of relationships as its progenitor and source. The essence of life did stem from these, he thought, only known to those who have experienced it personally. 'Oh God! I can't thank you enough!' he uttered in prayer.

He watched the ecstatic face of Kaushalya Devi and the weak but blissful face of Shobhna who glowed with a new mother's pride. He looked at the innocent and angelic face of his newborn daughter, peacefully asleep and the centre of her family's lives.

These were the three generations of women, two of them already proving time and again their beauty as well as strength, and the third one, newly born, with her whole life ahead of her. What a spectacle! Anmol said another prayer, asking God to bless these women for their strength of character, femininity and the courage of their convictions.

In their mighty presence Anmol felt subdued.

28

Shobhna and her baby girl gained strength as days passed. They had almost everyone wrapped around their fingers to take care of them. The doctor monitored their condition regularly, the nurses were caring and kind and Anmol was always at hand to look after the arrangements under the affectionate eye of Kaushalya Devi. The mother and the baby thrived on the care and nourishment and recovered fast.

Three days later, Anmol brought his wife and daughter home. Kaushalya Devi received them at the door and ushered them inside while chanting the sacred *mantras* and rituals attendant to the birth of a child. Kaushalya performed a special *havan* for the new baby, showering her with rose petals and blessings.

The fortnight saw a flood of visitors at their house. The birth of the first grandchild for both the families was an event of great celebration. Visitors, relatives, friends and greetings poured in from all sides with gifts, love and blessings galore! The baby girl was the apple of everybody's eyes. She was so beautiful; fair-complexioned with a crop of dense black hair that had a tendency to curl naturally; big, black eyes; and a temper to match. A little plump for her age, she looked like a baby doll whose cheek dimples deepened when she smiled or threw a fit. Each day enhanced or changed a new feature on her lovely face and people saw in her the likeness of both Shobhna and Kaushalya Devi. She was sleeping a little less each day; had ceased to cry as much and spent each waking moment either responding to little sounds or sights around her or being cuddled by her mother or grandmother. A cute, small cradle was bought for her with rows of bright beads strung on all corners; these amused her. The little girl smiled whenever anyone picked her up or sang her a lullaby. The whole house or the life at home revolved around her and her waking schedule. Anmol had rejoined his school and every day awaited the closing bell and ran home. Shobhna was recovering fast under the caring, watchful eye of her mother. She could attend to her daughter and her needs as dexterously as an elderly person would have by now. It was better because Kaushalya's leave from school, too, was coming to an end and she would have to go back to Dhanbad soon.

Kaushalya Devi wanted to perform the *'namkaran sanskar'* ceremony of her granddaughter by organizing a *havan* and calling her relatives who lived in Delhi. A day was fixed in consultation with each other and the guests were invited to grace the occasion. Kaushalya had a list of traditional names ready to choose from and give the little one a beautiful and meaningful name. A *purohit* was called from the nearby *Arya Samaj* who would assist Kaushalya Devi with the necessary rituals. When the moment came for choosing a name, Kaushalya Devi promptly produced the piece of paper on which she had written about a dozen names. Anmol and Shobhna were asked to select a name by the *purohit* and other people.

Anmol pondered the choices, consulted Shobhna, looked at Kaushalya Devi and said, '*Maji*, as an elder of the family present here, let it be your prerogative. I would love it if you name your granddaughter. Shobhna, too, wants this.'

Kaushalya Devi was touched and felt proud of the son-in-law she herself had chosen for Shobhna. She deliberated for a moment and then said, 'How about Nayantara? She is really the star of everybody's eyes. Literally and figuratively! This suits the little one the best!'

'It is a beautiful name!' said Shobhna.

'I like it, *Maji*. There can't be a better name for her,' exclaimed Anmol.

The guests liked the name, too, and found it thoughtful and meaningful. They showered the infant with their blessings.

The simple ceremony was followed by a sumptuous meal which the guests enjoyed. At the end of the day when the family was left by itself, Kaushalya Devi gathered the presents so that Shobhna could open them. They were delighted at the lovely frocks, baby-sets, towels, sheets, trinkets of silver jewellery, all showered with love for their little girl.

Shobhna and Anmol were happy. Kaushalya also managed to forget her worries about the future of her sons. 'God has certainly reserved some blissful, happy moments in my life too,' she thought as she looked again and again at the cherubic, innocent face of the little one, now, Nayantara darling.

'My dynasty is on its path of preservation!' she exclaimed.

On the last day of her third month of visit, Kaushalya Devi boarded the train for Dhanbad. Though her heart was still in Delhi along with Shobhna and her family, she couldn't have stayed even for a single day more as the school had already sent her a couple of telegrams requesting her to join as soon as possible. During her stay with Shobhna, she had hardly known a relaxed moment but the happiness had taken the tiredness away. Anmol and Shobhna, along with the little one, had come to see her off at the station. As the signal turned down and the loud siren went off loudly, Kaushalya Devi cuddled her granddaughter, kissed her repeatedly and then embraced Shobhna and Anmol who bent down to touch her feet. Anmol helped her get on the train, taking her quickly to her seat and putting her luggage in place. They waved goodbye to her as she watched from the window when the train started leaving the platform. Anmol and Shobhna turned back and came out of the railway junction to go back home.

Kaushalya Devi's thoughts raced along with the moving train as she sat reclined on her seat. Her mind went back to the times when Shobhna was born, to the time when she was a little school girl to when she was a grown up, beautiful young lady. She gave way to remembering until she fell asleep dreamlessly for a number of hours. She woke up to the sudden halt of the train and heard the loud voices of the vendors who boarded trains at every station with their eatables and *kullars* of tea. Kaushalya bought a cup of tea and opened her *'potli'* of food that Shobhna had cooked and packed with care. A good nap had taken away her exhaustion and the food from home rejuvenated her spirits. She ate slowly and sipped her tea. She looked around and watched other passengers who were travelling in the same bogey.

She thought of her life, how it had been an eventful journey, where her relationships were like destinations and she had to give and take, before she could move on to the next junction. Joy and sorrow were intricately woven in her life and she had grown because of it. She looked at her fellow passengers, at the fast fading view and objects from the moving train, she looked at the dim twinkling lights outside whenever the train passed by a village or a city or any platform. Was she dreaming or was she wide awake? The images were blurry, even her thoughts. She continued to be in this kind of haze for some time before she fell asleep; the tide of life around her slowed down a little, bringing silence and darkness.

She woke up the next morning feeling better not just in body but also mentally and emotionally. She looked forward to her routine: going back to school, teaching young children, taking care of her sons and helping them if they needed her.

Kaushalya was received at the Dhanbad Railway Station in the evening by her sons. She was glad to see them all; she felt wanted and cared for once again. She saw herself duty-bound to them, most of all, and she owed them her attention. They were the ones who would stay with her always until she turned them away or they went on their own accord after they got married. Either possibility seemed remote at the moment as she had a home of her own and she helped them with money, too.

As for Shobhna and Anmol, they were extremely happy, engrossed in their own little world. It seemed as if time had ceased to matter in their routine. Day would dawn with an agenda for both of them: Anmol with his school activities and Shobhna with her responsibilities at keeping home. Little Nayantara would keep her busy all day as her world started widening with growing consciousness of her surroundings. She responded actively to sights, sounds and images around her and Shobhna had to keep a watchful vigil over her all the time. She loved being with her little daughter, listening to her childish talk and catering to her silly pranks.

'Motherhood, indeed, is a blessing!' thought Shobhna with a contented look. 'No pleasure in the world can be greater. God, the progenitor, understood this and created women specifically for this purpose. The world over centuries has survived and grown because of the woman, the mother,' Shobhna's mind went again to her own mother, Kaushalya Devi. 'Maybe some day I can understand her fully and the justification of her many decisions. Only a mother can understand the predicament of another mother.'

Days became months and months became two years. Seasons followed and gave way to another. Each season had its own beauty, whether it was the ripeness or the blossoms of spring or the rain-washed beauty of the monsoons or the elongated, dizzy days of summer or the warmth of the sun rays during winter. Nayantara grew up each day, becoming more chirpy and beautiful and bringing immeasurable pleasure in the lives of Shobhna and Anmol. They were totally devoted to her, never letting her out of their sight. Besides each other, Shobhna and Anmol had found another common interest. Their little world revolved in and around Nayantara whose comfort and priorities became their prime concern. They were deep into their routine when Shobhna found out that she was in the family way again.

On the first of October, when Nayantara had just turned two years old, Shobhna and Anmol were blessed with a baby boy. The baby came into this world two weeks early, and so Kaushalya had not arrived yet. But Shobhna did well in the delivery, experiencing bearable pain. The baby was beautiful and slender, with a mop of jet black hair on his head and long, dark eyelashes. His features looked chiselled even at this stage; his hands, feet and toes were all in perfect shape. He was unusually calm even when he was hungry and opened his cherry mouth and tugged at Shobhna for a touch. When sleeping, he was a picture to look at with thick eyelashes, bushy eyebrows and round cheeks. Anmol loved him so much that Shobhna felt wonderful having brought happiness in his life once again. Little Nayantara, too, was very happy. Jealous at first for having suddenly lost attention to a newcomer, she sulked for a day till the baby was placed in her lap and said that she would love him as her little brother.

'He has come to play with you, darling,' Anmol had told Nayantara while hugging her warmly and showering her with kisses. And Nayantara had taken an instant liking for her little brother. She adored him, especially when he started taking little baby steps and learned to walk. They chased each other the whole day and never left each other's company. Shobhna would have a tough time keeping household things out of their reach. They loved to fiddle with everything that caught their fancy. No number of toys was enough for them and they clamoured to go out in the park the moment they saw their father return from school. Anmol and Shobhna felt blessed; they were eager to fulfil their children's smallest wishes.

In the evenings, Shobhna and Anmol took the children to the nearby garden where they had plenty of space to run around and feel delighted in the sight of trees and flowers. They would chase each other or play ball or try to catch butterflies and tire themselves out with activity and excitement. Anmol and Shobhna, too, made sure to do something like play badminton. Familiar with every part of the small garden, Nayantara and her little brother had found a perfect spot to hide from their parents whenever they got into a mood. Not finding them around for more than five minutes, Shobhna and Anmol would sternly call out, 'Where are you both, darlings? Come out of your hiding this instant!'

There would be a low chuckle and Shobhna and Anmol would feel relieved that the tots were nearby. They would coax them out of their hiding place with chocolates and the two would then crawl out, bursting into peals of laughter and clapping.

'Isn't it time to buy chocolates, children? It's getting late. Look at the sun going down to the other side.'

'Papa, why does the sun live so far?' Nayantara asked. 'Why can't we catch it? It looks just like a ball.'

'Let's go home now, darling. Tomorrow, I will tell you the story of the sun, the moon and the earth.'

'What about our chocolates?'

'Yes, we will go to the market first!'

They reached home half an hour later, and it didn't take long for the children to fall asleep after a quick meal. Anmol and Shobhna, before going to bed, discussed their plans for the next day.

The four of them represented a typical middle-class family in the yet nascent independent India.

29

Shobhna couldn't believe this was the same apartment that they had moved in not too long ago; she had made it into a home completely their own, comfortable and cosy. It lacked space, though, especially for the children to run around. She resolved to take up the matter with Anmol sometime when they got some rest from their hectic lives. There were days when she got weary of the monotony, too. The children, of course, provided not only her but Anmol also a ray of hope.

One day as the children played in the garden, Shobhna said to Anmol, 'Do you think it is a good idea for me to take up a job?'

'Take up a job?' Anmol was surprised. 'But why? Where is the need?'

'We can always do with some additional income. We could perhaps move to a better apartment too. The children are growing up fast, they need more space.'

'I don't see the need. We don't lack anything. The children would suffer if both of us worked,' Anmol decided.

'We could always get somebody to help. I have always worked along with my mother; it won't be difficult for me. I am a qualified teacher with a professional degree. I can get a job in a nearby school.' Shobhna was decided, too.

'Then who would look after the children and help them with their schoolwork?'

'I could call my mother and she could stay with us.'

'Have you already discussed this with your mother?'

'Oh, no, not at all! She has no idea about it at all!'

'Shobhna, there is no substitute for a mother for the children.'

'My mother also worked and we all grew up fine, did we not?'

'Maybe that is why your brothers haven't done so well in life. Have you ever thought about that? Maybe that was the sore point between your mother and father. Besides, your grandmother was always there to look after the house and the children.'

Shobhna was stung. She knew he did not mean to hurt her but still he was blunt. It was not as if he had not been aware of the whole thing; he had known about all this first-hand since Ved Prakash had been his first link with the family. Ever since he had come in contact with her mother, Kaushalya Devi, she thought he had genuinely respected her for her thirst for knowledge. Wasn't it their common love for books that had brought them together?

'The blame can't belong to one party alone. Men should also take into account the likes and dislikes of their wives. The responsibilities, though divided, must be borne equally.' Shobhna's hurt was palpable.

'Shobhna, I can see your eagerness to work and that too, for the betterment of the family's finances. I appreciate that. But even if your mother agrees to come and stay with us, our society does not take very kindly to women who choose to stay with their sons-in-law.'

'Since when have you started bothering so much about society? You have always taken cudgels with this society whenever you didn't agree with it. Besides, we will be there to take care of everything.'

'I don't see the need for your persistence.'

'I do not want to waste my education and training. First, my father did not want me to study so much and now, you do not want me to work. You men are all the same, educated or uneducated.' Shobhna wiped her tears.

'Dear!' Anmol took her hands in his. 'You will not be wasting your education. You will be putting it to best use when you teach your own children. Their personality will flower the best when you are with them all the time.'

'Look at our hand-to-mouth existence. Expenses are growing each day. Eventually we will be forced to compromise with facilities or opportunities that we offer to our children. I do not want that to happen. Our struggle has just begun and being educated, I thought I could help you raise the status of our family.'

'But Shobhna, certain things are best left to men. Women alone make the best homemakers and mothers.'

Shobhna was dumbstruck. She was face to face with a different Anmol; she had not seen or even imagined this facet of Anmol's personality. She had always believed in his progressive mind, his liberated ideas and his frank nature. She had failed to see his rootedness in traditions, his belief in the demarcation of gender roles and his propensity to hold on to whatever he believed was right. Anmol, she thought, was genuinely caring, honest, sincere, immensely hard-working and had a remarkable strength of character but he hated to yield to anyone or lose an argument. Anmol was headstrong. He would never give up easily once he was convinced that he was right.

Shobhna felt defeated. She could not drive home her point any further. She had tried hard to make Anmol see her point of view but had failed. She was dismayed. The children meanwhile, done with their playing and running around had crept near them, sensing that their parents were involved in some serious discussion.

'Mummy, we are hungry. Let's go back!' demanded Nayantara. Taking the opportunity to wriggle out of their argument, Anmol picked up Nayantara and told Shobhna, 'Let us hurry up now. We will think about it later.' Shobhna picked up her little son, whom they had named Abhinav, and followed Anmol. The difference of opinion gradually died down in the pace of their routine. No altercation or long discussion followed since their last exchange of words in the garden. Both Shobhna and Anmol were mature enough not to let their differences of opinion ruin the harmony in their house, especially when it came to the interests of the children. Mornings were the busiest when it was almost an ordeal for all of them to get ready for school. Anmol left early since his school was at a distance and it had fallen on Shobhna to walk the children to the nearby municipal school after giving them a hurried breakfast. It would be almost school time when Shobhna would finally push them out of the house carrying a lunch box, most days containing sandwiches.

'Come on, children, fast!' she would invariably need to shout.

It would always be a little before seven in the morning when the road would be busy with many neighbourhood children going to the same school.

Their school was a two-storey, ordinary building that stood at a little distance from the main road. It was rectangular in shape with a wide, shady veranda running all around where the children could be allowed to sit during assembly or lunch break if it was raining outside. The school had a fairly spacious ground at the back that was used for the morning exercises and sports for various classes at different timings. Once in school, Nayantara and Abhinav loved its activities despite a strict, regimented, disciplined schedule. They were both good in their studies and were liked by their teachers, some of whom even favoured them over the other children. Nayantara, who was ten years old, had a special flair for reading and writing. She had a razor-sharp memory and needed to read anything only once before reproducing it exactly. The teachers were amazed at her ability for retention of her reading material at such a young age. Her fondness for books reminded Shobhna of her own mother. Clearly, Nayantara had inherited her *nani's* genes as far as books were concerned.

Abhinav, on the other hand, was more fond of playing games. He was more of an extrovert and enjoyed sports much more than his books. Even at home, he had to be coaxed hard to pick up his books and finish his homework. When it came to comprehension, he was far above the rest of his classmates. He needed less time to grasp his lessons; he was rather innovative in temperament and had a great way with tools and mechanical tasks. His teachers were fond of him for different reasons; they loved his friendly behaviour, his energy, full-throated laughter and his great fondness for the game of cricket.

Nayantara and Abhinav were the stars of their school and their teachers were as proud of them as Anmol and Shobhna were. The teachers often compared the duo, who rather complemented each other's nature and personality when together or participating in school activities. They always brought home a prize or two.

Shobhna often felt a tinge of sadness whenever she would go to their school for parent-teacher meetings. Though the teachers were qualified and dedicated and the children excelled at everything in their school, she at times wished that they had the resources to put them in a better school where they could be exposed to a better method of learning as well as different streams of ideas that would shape their personalities in a more open environment. She made hushed references of this to Anmol whenever she got the chance.

'Perhaps we could put them in a public school in a couple of years from now,' she said to Anmol one day as Nayantara came home with a trophy in a school function.

'Why? What is wrong with their school?' Anmol was obviously peeved.

'There is always a better alternative, don't you think? And room for improvement, too. The children are growing up fast and there is no harm if they are given wider opportunities and exposed to a different section of society.'

'It is also always good to be rooted in your own traditions and realise one's limits.'

'Well, as it is, they have got all their *sanskars* from us. Their value system is indeed in its right place. They can only benefit from a larger perspective. Besides, I do feel that we need a bigger home. Their needs are growing and soon they'll start being uncomfortable here.'

'Shobhna, we must make do with whatever we can afford right now. You know very well how we stand with our finances.'

'That is why I wish we raise the status of our family, like the one we had in Lahore.'

'I wish I could match up to your expectations.' Anmol let go a deep sigh.

'You neither do anything extra yourself, nor let me do anything besides looking after home and family.'

'Isn't that your primary contribution to our family?'

'But women are capable—I am capable—of much more. I can be an equal bearer of your responsibilities, too.'

'We'll see when there comes a time that I need your help in earning money.'

That is how their discussions ended every time Shobhna tried to talk about their home affairs. Though still in love and still compatible with each other, they would voice their opinions to each other honestly even if they did not come to a common conclusion. Even if Shobhna was not working, Anmol could see the streak of independence in her which he attributed to the genes and influence of her mother, Kaushalya Devi. She was a woman of strength and a breadwinner too, who had succeeded in overstepping her shoes as compared to other women of her generation. These women were made of a different mettle, he thought, who dreamed of a life and career outside their home. Anmol believed otherwise; for him, a woman's place was in the home. Even if he was tempted to allow Shobhna to work and earn extra income for the family, he had too big a male ego to admit that he needed his wife's help to run his household. Yes, it was *his* household. Besides, he would not let a third influence enter the portals of his house that could prove to be a threat and disturb the peace of his otherwise happy home. His children must be brought up personally by him and his wife. This is what he had missed himself during his own childhood and he was determined never to let his children experience the same.

He resolved that he would compensate for the physical hardships with his love and affection. Shobhna was indeed his better half in this respect. He wished he could provide his family with more luxury, but he also reckoned that his children would benefit from their ordinary upbringing, bereft of luxuries. After all, it is in diversity that an individual acquires the best education in life.

Save for their financial difficulties, life was otherwise pleasant for Shobhna's family of four. Avid reading, a passion that Kaushalya and Shobhna shared, had given Nayantara and Abhinav an excellent vocabulary at their young age. Now 14 and 12, the two had grown into intelligent and academically sound young individuals who were interested in everything around them. While Nayantara wanted to take up English literature in Delhi's most reputed college, Abhinav was showing an inclination for the sciences and dreamt of becoming a medical doctor. Aesthetically inclined as Nayantara was, like her grandmother Kaushalya Devi, she had a way with words and could create magic with them. She wanted to take up the teaching profession and join a university eventually. At the same time journalism also fascinated her. Abhinav, meanwhile, had made a decision. In his own words, he wanted 'to serve humanity' and becoming a doctor would help him do just that.

It helped that his father gave him full support. 'Medicine still remains the noblest profession in the world,' Anmol would tell his son. 'Perhaps this is the only field that leaves one with the feeling of utmost satisfaction if one wants to work for a good cause. But son, you have to come in the merit-list on your own.'

'Don't worry, Papa! I will work so hard that I will deserve it in my own right. And after I become a doctor, I will join the Army and serve my country.'

Anmol's heart sank. It was the first time he was hearing about another dream, that of being a soldier and, naturally, being far away. He felt ambivalent: his heart filled with pride but he felt a shiver down his spine.

'Papa, I will become a professor and wear my mother's sarees,' Nayantara was telling him at the same time, momentarily erasing the fear that he felt. 'That way, we will not have to spend more money and we will share everything, including my earnings. You will see, I will also raise the status of my family one day.' Nayantara's eyes gleamed with pride.

Anmol looked at Shobhna, whose eyes had begun to moisten with tears, not of sadness but of a happy sense of achievement. They both knew that they had done well in raising their children, that despite the various middle-class hardships they had to face, these had not been in vain. Nayantara and Abhinav had grit, energy, and sincerity of purpose as well as a streak of self-reliance; some of the virtues that a person needed to make a mark in life.

She remembered her mother Kaushalya, and her relentless fight against the age-old darkness of mind that could only be vitiated by education.

Shobhna wished Kaushalya was there with her now, to hear her say how proud she was of her. She watched Nayantara, who always reminded her of her mother. 'This is how I keep you in my heart,' Shobhna whispered to her mother who wasn't there. She rushed to the kitchen and kept Anmol from seeing her tears.

30

'Do you think you will be able to do justice to your English Honours course if you are admitted to this college?' the interviewer asked Nayantara. She was at Lady Shri Ram College, sitting in the office of the head of the English department for an admission interview.

'Yes, Ma'am!' Nayantara replied with utmost confidence. 'You can be sure that I will put my heart and soul into it.'

'Are you certain?' asked another member of the panel, 'Even though you have completed your schooling in a Hindi medium school?'

'Yes, Ma'am! I am certain. Ma'am, I compete with others on the basis of marks and merit. I can work as hard as any of my counterparts, maybe harder. It is not only the students of elite schools who have merit and the determination. I am hard-working and highly focused.'

The members of the interview panel nodded softly at each other; Nayantara could see that most of them were smiling. That could only be good news, she thought to herself. The panel was indeed impressed by her confidence and her solid views. They thought she could withstand pressure, hold her head high and think out of the box, and would do their institution proud.

'All right, Nayantara. That will do,' said a third interviewer. 'We will put up the list of the successful candidates on the notice board in a day or two.'

Nayantara bade them goodbye and came out of the room. As she walked past the queue of aspiring candidates, she noticed how markedly different they appeared: in their clothes, their mannerisms; their aura of affluence. They spoke English with an accent, batted their eyelashes and strutted about the corridor as if they owned the college. Nayantara, for a moment, felt daunted in their presence as they cast an indifferent glance at her and turned their faces. She remembered her father's words, 'Don't be taken in by the outward show of others, darling. The world is full of such people. They can give you a feeling of inferiority but at the end of the day, a person with genuine qualities of head and heart is the one who wins. Never feel that you are less than anyone else. Children of middle-class families excel because they have grit, they have that fierce longing for great achievements. Single-minded devotion and constant perseverance is what is needed to succeed. The elite can sometimes be bogged down by their complacency.'

Nayantara felt reassured. There came in her heart an instant feeling of pride for her roots. She was the offspring of educated parents who had sacrificed their own ambitions and comforts to bring them up in the best way they knew how. She thought of the beautiful but slightly worn-out face of her mother who had given up her own ambitions for the sake of providing the best help at home to her children. She remembered her day-to-day struggle with the household chores in the midst of financial limitations. She had put up with adverse circumstances with a lot of courage and a positive mindset, thus setting before them an example of an indomitable spirit. She thought of the visits of her grandmother, Kaushalya Devi, who whenever she had come visiting them always taught her the importance of real education.

'Books are always your best friend, Nayantara dear,' Kaushalya Devi would say, 'And at every age. They are always there whenever you want them. They never desert you. They are your biggest asset and an invaluable treasure.'

'What do these girls know about life?' thought Nayantara with a sneer. 'I am going to excel above them all! I have the genes of my grandmother and my mother, after all.'

When she reached home, she was welcomed by her father and mother who she knew were waiting eagerly for her. But Abhinav was the first one to ask, 'How was your interview? Did you make it?'

'Well, I answered almost all their questions,' smiled Nayantara. 'They seemed positive, to me at least. The merit list will be declared in a couple of days.'

'Come, eat something,' said Shobhna lovingly. 'You must be tired and hungry, dear.'

Nayantara looked at the anxious but deeply affectionate faces of her parents and vowed to make them proud.

Her mother seemed to have read her thoughts. She smiled at her and said, 'Your journey has just begun, my dear.'

The list of successful candidates for the stream of English Honours was put up on the college notice board the evening of the following Saturday. Nayantara was in the top ten candidates. She rushed home to share the news with her parents.

Shobhna felt instantly nostalgic and told Nayantara, 'Though I am also a graduate and have had teacher-training, you will be the first girl in our family to go to a regular college and that too, the most reputed one. Your grandmother will be ecstatic!'

'I would always like to see a book in your hand, Nayantara,' said Anmol to his daughter. 'You have to reach the top slot of your profession, whichever one you may choose.'

'Papa, I will try to never fail you and mother. And yes, my grandmother, Kaushalya Devi, most of all! She still stands strong as an oak tree of our dynasty. When can I see her again?'

'Let the news of your admission reach her. Despite being quite old, she wouldn't be able to restrain herself for long,' laughed Anmol, looking at Shobhna.

With Nayantara firmly set on the path of her career, all eyes naturally turned to Abhinav who stood a class apart from her sister in everything. He suddenly found himself in the epicentre of the family and wondered whether he was prepared for such a position.

Indeed, Nayantara and Abhinav were two different individuals. It was amazing as to how the same parentage as well as environment had instilled the same values in them while they grew up with opposite temperaments. While Nayantara was the more talkative of the two and loved to discuss other people's failings, referring to them as characters in works of fiction, Abhinav was more tolerant of the faults of others. He had inherited the calm and meek nature of his mother and always made sure to listen first before venturing his opinion politely and with compassion. Despite dissimilarities in character, the brother and the sister shared almost every thought with each other. They were great friends; they shared many ideas, even tastes and respected each other's likes and dislikes. Their relationship was a matter of great pride for their parents.

And so Abhinav found himself being asked about his plans for his future. What he knew for sure was that he loved the game of cricket much more than his books. He was the captain of his school's cricket team, in fact; and even in the neighbourhood, especially among the children, people knew him as a talented player.

Anmol asked his son, 'Abhinav, if your heart is set on following the medical stream, you need to work harder and defer your sports for a while.'

'I don't neglect my studies, Papa. Playing cricket helps me concentrate more and teaches me discipline,' replied Abhinav. He sounded nonchalant.

'My young boy, these are more or less clichés. It is better not to divert your attention at the moment. You have your whole life ahead of you to follow these pursuits. Your cricket must take a backseat for now.'

Shobhna interrupted with her own sentiment. 'Maybe you can regulate your hours of study and still take an hour or two for cricket.'

'Shobhna, please,' Anmol was annoyed. 'Can you let me have an honest conversation with my son? Just the two of us?'

'I will try my best, Papa!' said Abhinav, wanting to end the topic at that.

Nayantara felt like voicing her opinion, too. 'Papa, I feel you are being a little harsh to Abhinav at times. His mind is set towards his goal. I know it.'

Anmol would hear nothing of it. 'Nayantara, can you just concentrate on your own studies, please.' They ended the conversation with all of them knowing that it would be talked about again very soon.

The onset of the new year increased the pace of work in their household. It also meant that the examinations were coming nearer. Both Nayantara and Abhinav had set their targets and strictly adhered to their work schedule. Studying through late nights and getting up early in the mornings to cover the vast syllabus, they were a source of inspiration to each other, especially during moments of doubts and frustration. The time was crucial, particularly for Abhinav, who had to appear for the medical entrance examination along with his usual annual exams. Throughout it all, they were each other's closest friends. They were set to take the plunge.

Before they realized it their exams were over. It was a warm, sunny day and they lay stretched out on the grass in the nearby park, savouring the unique feeling of finishing all their examinations. A classmate of Abhinav suddenly came to them running. 'Abhinav!' he shouted. 'The medical entrance test results are out! Are you aware of it?'

'By Jove! No! How would I know? Have you seen them?' cried Abhinav, jumping up. Nayantara quickly got up, too.

'Then, let's go and see it together.'

'Yes! Let me call my father. We'll go together.'

It took them half an hour to reach the school. By then a huge crowd of students and their parents had already gathered. They took turns in front of the notice board, looking for their names on the long white sheets tacked to the board; those lists decided their future. Abhinav, excited and nervous both, did not find his name on the first two sheets of paper. Dismayed, his eyes went up and down the third list; he still could not spot his name.

It was Anmol who saw it on the last list. He jumped with joy and hugged his son, who was ecstatic. Abhinav swapped congratulatory notes with his friends who were all savouring their success.

It was a happy moment and Anmol could not wait to get home and share the news with the family. 'Let's go home, son. Your mother and sister must be waiting.'

Shobhna and Nayantara were indeed eagerly awaiting the news. As soon as they came, Shobhna took one look at the faces of her son and husband and immediately knew that Abhinav had made it. Nayantara ran to his brother and hugged him. 'Hurrah! We have done it. Abhinav is going to be a doctor!'

Anmol put his arms around Shobhna and looked at her lovingly, his eyes telling her that their sacrifices had not been in vain and God had rewarded them with their children's success. Who knows, Anmol thought of telling Shobhna, the pre-Partition phase of affluence might yet return to her own family, too. They only needed to wait.

Shobhna rested her head on Anmol's chest, her eyes shining with joy. She was deeply aware of the flood of emotions inside Anmol's own heart.

And they used all those emotions to tide them over the difficult and costly admission process for Abhinav's medical college. Anmol, who had always been a careful planner, had made sure to use his limited resources in a way that he could take care of all such exigencies without asking for help from any of his friends or relatives.

'Time and tide will one day have to turn in favour of me and my family,' thought Anmol. He was feeling somewhat overwhelmed but kept faith. He believed that there would have to be some kind of poetic justice in store for his family in the near future. The middle classes, though tenacious of life, must have their own share of happiness as they deserve it by dint of their own merit and strength.

Upon hearing the news, Kaushalya Devi boarded the first train to Delhi. Though aged, she was mentally agile and still retained the same lust for life. A readiness to respond to new situations and surroundings had made life still worth living for her. Her sons, meanwhile, had also got married and had families of their own. She had kept herself busy with her teaching job and with the lives of her grandchildren, too, whenever possible. Shobhna had been dearest to her heart and her children were now well set on their professions to make a mark in life and head towards the path of glory. She was content. 'Life has not been bad at all,' she thought. 'It has been eventful, full of unexpected happenings, and God has always given me the strength to bear all trials and be thankful for blessings as well.'

It took only a couple of minutes for Nayantara and Abhinav to spot their *nani* and run to her. They embraced her and touched her feet.

'May God bless you both, my dearest children! You have given me some of the best moments of my life. You are dearer to me than even Shobhna and Anmol,' said Kaushalya Devi, smiling at Shobhna who was not very far from her and touched her gently.

'Shobhna, my grandson is going to be a doctor and Nayantara, a professor. I couldn't have dreamed better! God has been merciful in granting me my wish. Look, children, there is no substitute to education in life,' continued Kaushalya. 'An educated mother is the backbone of a middle-class family. She creates an enlightened environment in the family for her children, much the same way that God has created this universe and brought light in our lives. You owe your success to your mother first and then to your father who has been a pillar of strength for the family.'

'*Nani*, maybe you can save some of your lecture for home also?' teased Nayantara lovingly with a glint in her eye.

'It is not difficult for my *nani* to cook up another lecture at home, Nayantara,' followed Abhinav, mischievously. 'Sermonizing comes naturally to her! Have you forgotten, she is the head mistress of her school in Dhanbad! And she has also taught our mother.'

'And your father also in my own way,' laughed Kaushalya Devi. 'Once a teacher, always a teacher!'

'Oh God! *Nani*! God save us!'

The train was wheeling out of the platform at a slow speed. Anmol and Shobhna picked up their mother's luggage and followed Kaushalya Devi, who was busy chatting with her grandchildren while holding each one of them by her hands. It was time to go home now!

31

It had been close to five years since Nayantara and Abhinav had first taken their baby steps in their professional lives. The years had flown by, marked by an extremely busy work schedule and the demands of the cut-throat competition in their market-oriented careers. They kept themselves abreast of all the latest developments in their respective fields, giving them an edge against their peers. Inspired by the struggle of their parents as well as the innate desire of their *nani* to see her grandchildren excel, Nayantara and Abhinav worked hard and were never scared to go that extra mile in order to push their career prospects forward. Nayantara was about to finish her post-graduation in English from the University of Delhi. She had also completed a course in Journalism and Mass Communication from a private institute, passing it with flying colours. She had appeared for the annual examination in her post-graduation and was awaiting the results. She had already started applying for jobs. She had come across a couple of slots for management trainees in reputed private firms and had appeared for interviews for those positions. She had also applied for ad-hoc vacancies as lecturer in various local colleges and stood a good chance at getting selected.

It was Nayantara's dream, however, to get a teaching assignment in her own college, which at one time had questioned her ability with language skills on account of her being from a Hindi-medium school. She had maintained a good academic record ever since she had gained admission in the prestigious college. She had been in the good books of all her teachers; they had appreciated her sincerity, consistency, and hard work.

'Oh God! Please help me and reward my hard work,' prayed Nayantara. She hoped to land in the top five successful candidates so she could get accepted to teach in her own college.

Abhinav, too, had not lagged behind in his studies. He had to spend long hours in his medical college. He was often required to stay overnight whenever they were put on practical assignments. He still had a year more to go before he could start with his mandatory internship.

For both Nayantara and Abhinav, their first line of support had always been their parents. After all, Anmol and Shobhna's lives revolved around them. They were sure that their efforts would be rewarded soon. As they witnessed their children grow up as good human beings, and on top of that doing well in their professions, their hearts filled with pride and joy. It was only a question of time now when Nayantara, their eldest, would be all set for a career in teaching, the stronghold of their family, following in the footsteps of both her mother and *nani*; maybe even going many steps further.

Come the summer vacations and Nayantara's results were announced. She did extremely well, securing a first division overall. She was ahead of almost her entire class, finishing among the top three candidates in her college and among the top ten in the whole University. She ran back home and burst into tears as she told her parents of the results.

'May God bless you, my child!' said Anmol as he hugged her.

'Let God decide your career and destiny now,' Shobhna said, choking with emotions. 'And that of your groom, too.'

'Mother, please, no talk about marriage for a long time,' said Nayantara, embracing Shobhna. 'Right now I have to go and meet my teachers in the college. Let me find out the possibilities of a placement in my own college.' Nayantara's eyes shone with excitement.

'Yes, my dear, do so, by all means,' said Shobhna. 'I have to write a letter to your *nani*. She has not been keeping too well for the past few months and has been worrying about your results also.'

'Oh God! What has happened to my *nani*, Ma?' Why didn't you tell me?'

'She had forbidden me to tell you. You were very busy with your studies.'

'But what has happened to her?'

'Nothing in particular as such. She is suffering from old-age problems, a number of them, in fact.'

'Ma, why don't you bring her here? Abhinav can show her to a renowned specialist in his hospital.'

'Only if she is in a position to travel. Let me see! Anyway, don't worry too much. Take care of your career first. Your good news will cheer her up like nothing else.'

'Yes, Ma!'

A God-sent opportunity did come Nayantara's way. She had gone to meet the head of her department in the college and was greeted with much appreciation. 'You have done our college proud, Nayantara. And so have Rukhsana and Rita. We have slots for three teaching positions in the coming session. One of our teachers is getting married and going abroad while the other one is taking maternity leave. The third one has applied for a long study leave which might come through. If you apply for any one of these posts, we might select you on the basis of your marks and rank.'

'Yes, Ma'am! I will do so immediately,' stuttered Nayantara. She couldn't believe her ears.

'Then fulfil all the formalities, Nayantara. I wish you all the luck.'

Was Nayantara's destiny sealed with these words? The formalities took barely a month to be completed and she was selected as lecturer in her own college against a leave vacancy for two years. She was only twenty-one years old. Anmol and Shobhna were extremely happy and contented. And so was Abhinav. His sister had always been a source of inspiration. She was a go-getter; she would set a target for herself and then just slog towards it till she had it within her reach. He admired her zeal and the sense of urgency with which she pined for her goals.

The family sat together over a cup of tea and delicious snacks that Shobhna had prepared while Nayantara talked non-stop, describing all the little details and anecdotes of her student days in the college. All the four sat together until dinner, everyone full of life and warmth, their faces glowing with extreme happiness. No one wanted to get up.

Nayantara's heart was full, as if all her feelings and longings had suddenly burst forth like a torrent from heaven. It was a big day in her life and her family wanted her to enjoy it bit by bit, letting her soak in the first flush of success and achievement. The evening had deepened by now and the sky looked a deep ashen colour with the emergence of a faint glimmer of tiny stars. Anmol looked at Shobhna and smiled. The brightness of her face was shining through the wrinkles that had started appearing near her eyes but her skin retained its freshness. Feeling nostalgic, he took her hands into his and said, 'Let's all dine out tonight. Let's celebrate and raise a toast to your mother. She deserves it as much.'

'There we are, Papa!' Nayantara exclaimed.

'Hurrah!' echoed Abhinav.

When the college opened for the new session, Nayantara was

a bit nervous. After all, it was so much different being a student and enjoying a life filled with books and studies. Being a teacher brought with it a whole load of responsibilities. As a student, she remembered, she could leave out any particular author or critic if she did not like them; but a teacher could not afford such choices.

On her first day, Nayantara rose early and dressed with care. She wanted to look simple but elegant, with a bit of modernity blended with old-fashion. She was aware of the need to make a good impression on her students.

She called out to Shobhna, 'Ma, please help me choose a saree from your wardrobe, a simple cotton one?'

'Choose any one, my dear!'

'But help me?'

Shobhna considered her closet and picked one from Bengal, in traditional pink with a white border.

'Here, the colour suits you well.'

'Will it not look too bright for my first day?'

'Not at all, Naina! It is fabulous. The colour is pale pink, just right for the day. Pair it with a white blouse.'

'You're my angel, Ma. Pray for me! I am so nervous!'

'Don't you worry, my dear! You will come out a winner in this too.'

As Nayantara reached the college and made her way through the gate, she felt a thrill run down her spine. It seemed like everything around her was the same: the building, the lawns, corridors, classrooms, the trees and seasonal flowers. Only she had changed, she thought, in her position and maturity. Students looked at her keenly, curiously. She thought she was dressed immaculately; she noticed the admiring glances of those around her. There were juniors who recognized her and were happily surprised that she was back as a teacher.

'Nayantara, why didn't you tell us the good news before?' said one of the juniors.

'Well, a teacher is only a step ahead of a student. The line of demarcation is indeed thin between the two. And the distance is covered in a matter of a day only. Next year, it could be you in the same position.'

Nayantara walked to her classroom confidently. She greeted her students with a smile and responded to their curious gaze with an equally compassionate eye. They quickly felt at ease as she asked them to introduce one another. They then discussed the syllabus and the teaching schedule.

It all happened so fast for Nayantara that when the bell rang to signal the end the session, she couldn't believe she had survived the first day!

She would repeat her routine day after day, until she felt completely at home in her job as a college teacher. A couple of months later, she came home one day to find her mother in a very gloomy mood. She knew instantly that something was wrong, as her mother, who was usually calm, was behaving in a restless manner.

'What is it, Ma?' Nayantara asked Shobhna. 'What is troubling you? Is something wrong?'

'Your *nani* is really unwell and I might have to go to Dhanbad,' Shobhna replied. 'Will you be able to manage the house and everything else?'

'Can I come along, Mother?'

'But somebody has to be here to look after the house. It can only be you.'

Nayantara considered and decided to obey her mother. 'When are you leaving, Ma? Will you bring her here if she can travel?'

'Let me go and see her and then I will decide.'

Shobhna left by the morning train the next day. Dhanbad

was a good twenty-four hours away. Anmol and Abhinav had gone to drop her off and Nayantara had stayed home, the day being a holiday.

Around noon time, there was a loud knock on the door and Nayantara heard the voice of the postman. 'Is there anyone home? There is a telegram…'

Nayantara opened the door in a hurry, took the telegram and opened it with trembling hands. It said: 'Mother passed away today morning. Come soon! Abhay Prakash.'

Nayantara felt faint, gave a loud shriek and ran towards her father; her face streaming with tears while she sobbed uncontrollably: 'Father! My *nani* is no more. Mother doesn't know it and she has gone all alone. How will she take it?' Anmol and Abhinav stood motionless for a few moments, letting the shock sink in before they mustered enough courage to think or act accordingly.

All the three sat on the bed in silence. The children thought of their last meeting with *Nani*, her kind face shining and bearing an enlightened look, her keen but curious gaze, her vibrant nature and her entire persona oozing out a rare charm and beauty. They would never forget the stories and anecdotes she would relate to them when they were small and would visit Dhanbad during their summer vacations. She had been an icon of progressive thinking for her entire family and clan.

'Oh, Papa! She was so special, so extraordinary. How will Ma bear her loss? I wish we could all be together with her. Only if we had known! Everything happened so suddenly,' cried out Nayantara again and again. Anmol, though restrained, was lost in his own thoughts. His mind was in a maze…of golden moments spent with Shobhna and her mother before he got married. He remembered how he had been introduced to Kaushalya Devi through Ved Prakash; how he had started visiting them during the weekends; how Kaushalya Devi had asked him to help her learn English which had led to their regular meetings and then she had liked him and chosen him for Shobhna. Her infectious laughter and sparkling eyes haunted him again and again as he accepted the reality of her death. A fleeting remorse escaped his mouth, 'I couldn't even thank her enough for giving me such a lovely jewel as Shobhna! I wish she would come back just once so that I could lay bare my heartfelt feelings before her. Oh Ma! Why did you have to leave us so suddenly? You filled the void of a mother in my life and now you leave one that will never be fulfilled!' Anmol found himself unable to control his feelings.

Utter silence prevailed at her home in Dhanbad when Shobhna reached there after her long journey. She was surprised that no one had come to receive her at the railway station and had presumed that they had not received the information about her arrival. When she entered her home, she saw that her father and brothers were all sitting on the ground in the front courtyard. A few people were also sitting casually but she could tell that the mood was too sombre. What is this? She thought. Were they mourning? A feeling of disbelief overpowered Shobhna as she ran towards her father. 'Where is my mother!' she cried bitterly. 'She can't go without meeting me. What happened? Why didn't you call me sooner?' Shobhna was angry and sad and wailed her heart out.

'Control yourself, Shobhna!' said her father. 'Everyone has to go one day. This is the law of nature. We must accept it fully.'

'I am not a saint like you, Father! Nor do I want to be one. My mother craved for your affection and companionship all her life and she never got it. Her going away may not have affected you but I have lost my mother and so have my brothers. She cared for us in a way nobody else did. She did not even give us a chance to repay our debt to her.' Shobhna's grief and regret flowed without end.

'Tell me about her last moments,' Shobhna told her brothers.

'She remembered you again and again,' said Harsh Prakash. 'Her eyes were glued to the door till her last breath. She was unable to speak but her eyes said it all. Her gaze was fixed in one direction only.'

The youngest, Vijay Prakash, said, 'She was gradually losing consciousness but she held on. She waited and waited until she could not wait anymore.'

Arjun Dev, Shobhna's paternal uncle, muttered to no one in particular, 'With her has gone the last of her family tree.'

The tributes came from all around Shobhna.

'Hers was truly an extraordinary life.'

'She was a pillar of strength for her family.'

'She was remarkable for her strength of character!'

'She was made of solid mettle. Tragedies in her life could never kill her indomitable spirit!'

'God broke the mould when he made her!'

'Women like her are rarely seen these days. She was great indeed!'

Shobhna sat meek and mute, listening to these outpourings of grief for her mother's passing. She, too, had seen a lot in life but had always felt secure and undaunted with her mother around. The affectionate face of Kaushalya Devi flashed before her mind's eye again and again; their inseparable friendship of her school days, their carefree interaction and their dependence on each other; everything had come to an abrupt end suddenly. 'Oh, Ma! Why did you have to go so soon? Dhanbad and home will never be the same without you. What will I come here for? I can't imagine my life without you. Abhinav and Nayantara were so fond of you. What will I tell them?' Shobhna cried uncontrollably.

'Tell them that an era has come to an end with the death of their *nani*. She was a great Indian woman… A true follower of Swami Dayanand Saraswati!' Ganpat Rai broke his reserve for once as everyone looked at him in utter amazement.

'Oh! Father! We still have you,' Harsh Prakash said as the siblings gathered around him, embracing him in their entangled arms.

Shobhna was shocked to see a lone tear trickling down her father's face!

32

Life slowly began to mend for Shobhna and her family after she came back from Dhanbad. She took a long time to come out of her grief. She carried out all her household activities in routine and without zest. It was clear that the whole family suffered immensely, facing their most tragic and unsettling time. Shobhna felt disoriented, anchorless; and suddenly grown up. Such peculiar silence in the house had an unnerving effect on Nayantara and Abhinav in particular. When they came home, they would find their mother sitting alone, looking blankly in front of her. They would make small talk to draw her out of her cocoon and try to persuade her to take her old interest in life but it was all in vain. Shobhna remained immersed in her grief and responded very little. Mundane activities failed to kindle her old spark.

One day Abhinav came home early from his college and went straight to his bed. Shobhna followed her son and, feeling anxious, asked, 'What's the matter, Abhinav? Are you alright?'

'I have a pain in my stomach, mother. I have taken some medicine, don't worry,' replied Abhinav.

'Rest for a while. Your father will also be back soon. Let me give you one of my home remedies.'

'Oh, Ma! I will be just fine in a few hours!'

The next couple of hours stretched into the evening and Abhinav's pain, instead of going away, only increased in intensity.

He had become delirious. Anmol decided to take him to a private doctor, who was also a good friend. The doctor diagnosed acute appendicitis; Abhinav needed urgent surgery.

Shobhna and Anmol were disturbed. Tears fell down Shobhna's cheeks as she looked at Anmol with fearful eyes and touched him with trembling hands.

'Don't worry, Shobhna,' said Anmol caressing her. 'We will get the best treatment for our son.'

'What about the expenses?'

'That is for me to worry about. You take care of Abhinav. You should start getting ready now.'

Abhinav's operation went successfully on the same night in one of the best nursing homes of their locality. The recommendation had come from their doctor friend who put in a word to the surgeon to take only the direct costs involved and not his professional fees. Nayantara and Shobhna watched over Abhinav while Anmol organized their needs. Shobhna, fully back in her element, did not leave Abhinav's side.

Abhinav was cleared by his surgeon for discharge after a week and prescribed bed rest for another two. He was told to take extra care and not to exert too much pressure on his body. He was not supposed to do any heavy lifting, for example. Shobhna took full charge of her son when he came home and was given a very affectionate welcome by Nayantara and his father. The family felt complete once more, bonded in perfect intimacy.

One day, Anmol remarked to Nayantara, 'The incident had one good effect. It brought your mother out of her self-imposed silence. She has grown out of her grief for the loss of her mother.'

Nayantara nodded. 'I believe my brother's malady proved to be a catharsis for her.' She looked at Abhinav who had seemingly overheard them.

'I would give my life to see my mother happy and well!' said Abhinav, trying to sit up on the bed. 'Papa, I have to appear for a practical test in my college in a day or two.'

'How can you go in this condition? You can get exemption on medical grounds.'

'I don't want to do that. I will take all the necessary precautions. We can talk to our teachers who will let me sit and make things easier. I can certainly appear for my practical exams.'

And so Abhinav did have his way. His earnestness and courage were much appreciated by his teachers, who went out of their way to make him comfortable and allowed him to take his examination. Anmol and Shobhna could be nothing but proud of their son.

Shobhna said, 'If only my mother were alive, she would have been proud of him too.' It was the first time she had spoken about Kaushalya Devi since her death.

'Mother, her benevolent eye must be watching us from heaven even now,' said Nayantara. 'She must be smiling, seeing us happy and well-knit. Her blessings will always remain with us. My *nani*'s relentless efforts to make something of her family and relatives have not gone in vain. She must be heaving a breath of contentment for sure.'

The house returned to normalcy, though not without a brush with a feeling of mortality. Shobhna's interest in her home and children was renewed with a new fervour. Nayantara was set on her academic career and could always work towards furthering her prospects by taking up research, thought Shobhna. It was only a matter of time before they would need to look for a suitable groom for her if she herself did not choose one. As for Abhinav, he would be completing his medical degree in a couple of years before doing his internship.

One evening, Shobhna was so engrossed in her thoughts that she did not notice that Abhinav was back home from his college and was beckoning to her excitedly, 'Mother!'

Shobhna turned to her son.

'There was a blood donation camp in our college today,' Abhinav continued, almost out of breath. 'I donated my blood for a good cause. Look at my certificate!'

'That's a good thing you did, son,' Shobhna said as she read the certificate.

Just then Anmol opened the door and came in. 'What's going on with you two?' he asked happily.

'Abhinav has donated blood in his college. There was a camp,' said Shobhna. 'Our son has grown up, hasn't he?'

Anmol didn't share their enthusiasm and said, 'But Abhinav! You are not so strong as yet. You could have easily avoided it or done it at another time. You will get weak.'

'Papa, a normal healthy man's body takes only twenty-four hours to compensate for the loss of this much blood.'

'I would advise you to restrain yourself from doing these things in the future.'

'But Papa, if everyone thinks the same way, there would be no blood left in the Blood Bank. I'm doing my share. I think it's a good cause.' Abhinav was bent on defending his action.

'Don't you argue with me, boy. And you will remember what I said.' Anmol was clearly upset.

Abhinav restrained himself. 'Yes, Papa!'

Abinav's medical course was drawing to a close and his final examinations were coming to an end. Soon, they would all be interning for the practical part of their training. The family would be able to relax more, indulge in chit-chat and have fun together.

One day as Shobhna returned from a lecture session at the *Arya Samaj* she wanted to share her learnings with her family.

'Did you know that plants, too, are very receptive to music?' she began. 'They have feelings much like us human beings.'

'Well, our money plant is kept near the radio,' said Nayantara. 'It must be familiar with the old Hindi songs and by now fond of them.'

'Not really!' laughed Abhinav. 'Our money plant must be well versed in national affairs. It certainly knows what is happening around. It listens to the news the whole day!' Abhinav winked at Nayantara while looking affectionately towards his father who loved to listen to news whether in Hindi or English.

'Abhinav, you really don't let go of any chance to crack a joke!' Anmol said as they all burst out laughing.

And so the days passed at a leisurely pace. Struggle and torment seemed to have been left behind in the past at least for the time being, thought Anmol and Shobhna, with a feeling of satisfaction as they recalled their stressful life in the past.

When Abhinav went back, he began his internship, doing practical training at the hospital that exposed them first-hand to patients. The morning round under the guidance of the senior doctor was a learning experience that could never be acquired through books alone. The classroom teaching had to be supplemented with the practical experience. Their hours were unusually long and sometimes totalled thirty-six hours at a stretch. In other words, the internship meant slogging. They disliked it at times when the pressure of work and the hospital smell overpowered their tired limbs and they craved for rest and distance. It hung on their necks like an albatross; they wanted to fling it away sometimes but it was a necessary rigour they were expected to undergo in order to go to the next step.

Perhaps it was the fatigue but Abhinav's sore throat became chronic and did not go away even after a few months. Not wanting to self-medicate, he sought the advice of an ENT specialist at his hospital, who recommended the removal of his tonsils through surgery. Abhinav made a decision to undergo the surgery without letting his parents know the exact facts; he didn't want them to worry too much. The long hours of stay at the hospital, as it is would make the whole procedure simpler from the logistics point of view.

He told them the news casually one evening over dinner.

'Papa, I am thinking of getting my tonsil glands removed tomorrow morning in the hospital. They have been troubling me a little too much for the past six months or so.'

'Tonsil glands removed? You mean you're getting an operation?' asked Anmol.

'It's a mild one. I'll be surrounded and treated by the doctors. There is nothing to worry.'

'We will be there by your side, okay? Say no more.'

But Abhinav was insistent. 'Oh no, Papa! There is no need absolutely. It will only upset our routine. Mother will also get worried unnecessarily. It will be over in twenty minutes! All my seniors and friends are doctors and there is no cause for worry at all. I'll be in safe hands. I'll be home day after tomorrow in the evening at my usual time.'

Anmol and Shobhna left it at that and decided to give their son the decision. The next day he underwent the surgical procedure and, like he told his parents, was back home the next evening. Some friends had come along with him. As they all relaxed over food and chit-chat, Anmol was shocked to hear from one of Abhinav's friends that the surgery was done without any anaesthesia.

'He just really insisted on getting it done without it,' said one of his friends.

'Under what pretext?' Anmol was horrified.

'Even the doctor was amazed, Uncle. But Abhinav stuck to

his argument that he wanted to feel the pain and see whether it was humanly tolerable.'

'Didn't the doctor advise him to the contrary? He should have known better.' Anmol was angry, though he didn't know with whom, his son or the surgeon.

'Well, Abhinav argued and argued till the doctor gave way reluctantly.'

Anmol summoned his son, who was then in the kitchen. 'Abhinav, you kept us in the dark,' he said sternly. 'And you should have listened to the doctor.'

'Papa, I wanted to be like all my other patients when we tell them to be brave. And now I know the quantum of pain much better!' Abhinav even managed to smile at his father, who seemed to still be seething with anger.

Shobhna, who simply listened silently to the conversation, thought suddenly of her father, Ganpat Rai. She thought her son had certainly inherited his grandfather's patience and endurance. Her face acquired a serene look and her lips stretched into a smile.

'What are you thinking, Shobhna?' Anmol was looking closely at her face.

'I was wondering who our son took after.'

'Well, after you, certainly!' beamed Anmol. His anger over Abhinav's stubbornness had gone away. 'Like mother, like son!'

It was this same instinct that helped Abhinav to complete his internship, which then led him to the next step, which was the house job. It was while doing this that many students thought of charting out their next line of study or joining the active field. Abhinav, along with his close friends, decided to appear for the entrance exams for the short service commission of the Armed Forces. He took his sister and mother into confidence and decided that he would tell his father only if he made it to the list of successful candidates. By the time the results would be declared, they would have almost completed their house job. They could certainly wait and watch and take life as it came normally to them. His life revolved around home, the hospital, and patients. It was a tough schedule but he came back home with a sense of immense satisfaction.

'It certainly feels like the medical profession is the noblest of them all, Mother,' he told Shobhna. 'One can really serve humanity without any vested interest if one wants to!'

Shobhna smiled and gave him her blessings with all her heart. It was only a couple of months more and he would complete his house job. Abhinav rushed back home in great excitement one afternoon. He wanted to share with his parents the greatest news of his life.

'Papa! Mother! I have been chosen to join the Army as a short service commission doctor!' He hugged them both as Nayantara came running from the other room.

Anmol thought he misheard his son. 'Did you say you're joining the Army?'

'Yes, Papa! I would like to serve my country as a uniformed servant.'

Anmol did not ride his son's enthusiasm. Measuring his words, he said, 'Son, I think you should go abroad to do your post-graduation in medicine. Besides, an Army career involves a lot of dangers and I would not like you to take those risks.'

'What risks, Father?' Anmol replied. 'Life itself is a big risk! Men come in this world to face challenges and overcome them with their courage and strength.'

'Idealism is all very well, my son, but life has a practical aspect too. I would suggest you take some time in thinking things over. Don't be too over-enthusiastic in joining the army. Consider other options too!'

'Papa, I have thought this over! Mothers send their sons to fight for their country on the front as soldiers. It is their patriotic zeal that prompts them to take such tough decisions. They brave it all.'

'Is it necessary to argue, my son?'

'I would like to serve my nation and humanity as a doctor in the Armed Forces, Father.'

'But surely there are other ways to serve your country.'

'And this is the best and the most challenging way for me.'

'When do you have to take a decision? How much time do they allow?' asked Anmol.

'About two months. But I have made my decision.'

'We will see later on!'

'No, Father. I really want this. I have set my heart on it.' Abhinav made his inclination clear.

'And I have told you about my reservations about it. You keep that in mind. I am your father.' Anmol wanted to end the conversation at that.

'Remember, Father.' Anmol's eyes were sad. 'I will never do anything unless you give me your permission willingly.'

A war of wills was on between the father and the son. Shobhna and Nayantara were mute spectators.

33

Nayantara was doing just as well as her brother. During two years of her college life, she had become actively involved in various societies and book clubs besides continuing her teaching job. Her passion for reading and writing took her to many seminars and conferences that were organized in other local colleges. She participated by reading out her research papers and showed a lot of interest in academic work. She had also been entrusted with the responsibility of directing the dramatics society in the college and the poetry-reading sessions. She was asked to accompany students whenever they participated in a theatrical performance in other colleges as part of their cultural programmes. She came in contact with other colleagues from various colleges who had also come for the same purpose.

The annual youth festival in the host college was like a big party and the colleagues often met one another at their houses for meals or a cup of coffee. Nayantara, immaculately dressed always in simple but elegant clothes, was clearly a favourite. She was beautiful and had a very social nature. A core group of like-minded colleagues had evolved into a private book club, developing intimate friendships that were carried out outside the college, too. They went to movies together or shopped. The group was a mix of young boys and girls and it was but natural that mutual affections were being formed and developing into stronger relationships.

Among them, a couple of boys were showing interest in Nayantara but she remained elusive. She would always talk of books or poetry or getting more and more involved in active research work and shied away from getting emotionally involved with any of her colleagues or friends. Many of them, in fact, did not even appeal to her standards. There was one boy though who attracted her attention, albeit mildly. He was tall, well-built, dark and handsome. Not overtly articulate, he liked to keep mostly to himself and rarely got agitated over anything, be it a quarrel or a discussion. His eyes were large and brooding and his gaze keen and unnerving. He taught literature at St. Stephen's college and was also preparing to appear for the All India Civil Services examination. Though reserved and restrained in demeanour, his personality oozed out a kind of determined charm that made others take notice of him. Nayantara liked talking to him; he could be intellectual and witty if he was in a mood to talk and his words showed his depth of feeling and comprehension. Both could relate on a mental level and shared the same interests. Nayantara, at times, had become aware of his gaze that followed her whenever she was around. She herself was not averse to a level of friendship with him. He attracted her to some extent and she thought that he too, reciprocated her feelings in his own subtle and subdued manner. In a way, the whole group looked forward to their meetings which were becoming increasingly frequent. The opportunities were many since the college session was always full of activities of some kind or the other.

Most of this Shobhna was aware of, as Nayantara was in the habit of sharing with her the details of her life in college. Shobhna had always been her daughter's confidante. It was their routine to take out about half an hour in the evening and share their intimate thoughts with each other over a cup of tea.

Once during one such conversation, Shobhna asked Nayantara, 'How large is your group of friends outside college?'

'We are about ten of us, a mix of boys and girls. They are all so cool, Mom!'

'What do you mean by cool, my dear?'

'Well, cool can mean unconventional as well as easygoing too. They like to enjoy whatever they are doing at the moment and don't take tension or pressure over anything. They like to experiment with new ideas and their heads are full of them.'

'Give me examples?'

'Like one of my friends paints so well that we have advised him to put up an exhibition of his works. We will all collaborate and help him do that. Two of the girls are involved in serious theatre and would like to make documentaries in the future. There is another one who plays the mouth organ. Another friend wants to take up acting and is planning to join the National School of Drama. Somebody else wants to go abroad for doing research and a couple of them are preparing for the civil services exams. See? We are a group of young individuals with varied interests who like to dream big!'

'And what about you, Nayantara?'

'I would like to be a writer one day.'

'May I ask if you are fond of anyone in particular in your group? Does anyone give you special attention in any way?'

'Yes, Ma, there is one boy who is preparing seriously for the Civil Services' examination. He is very sober and shares the same interests as me. I like his company. I think he also has soft feelings for me.'

'Where do you see yourself, Nayantara, five years down the line?'

The subtlety of the thought put forth with utter casualness hit Nayantara with a bang and forced her to think of an answer.

She was quiet for a few moments and looked for the right words. She certainly had not thought that far ahead, least of all about her relationships.

'Ma, on what front, five years down the line?'

'On every front, my dear! It is time you think seriously what you want to make of your life. Even settling down should figure somewhere on your priority list.'

'As far as my profession is concerned, I would like to stick to teaching and indulge in some writing. And regarding the other issue; isn't it too early, Ma?'

'Why is it too early? I think it is just the right time you start thinking about it. We must know what kind of boy would interest you and in what profession. We can also start looking around.'

'Ma, did you know my father before getting married to him? Was it totally arranged or did my *nani* allow you to meet my father occasionally before marriage also?'

'Yes, of course, Nayantara! We knew each other before getting married also but not too well. Even though he was a frequent visitor to our house, I would meet him under the watchful eye of your *nani*. It was kind of interesting really.'

'What was the reason behind his frequent visits, Ma?'

'He would come to help your *nani* with her English lessons!'

'Oh, really!' Nayantara's eyes went wide with surprise.

'Your *nani* was a great votary of education, particularly for women, Naina. Her whole life centred on this passion of hers. She lived and died for the cause of education. The sole aim of her life was to spread awareness among womenfolk about their right to acquire knowledge and its power to uplift their status and lay the foundation for an enlightened environment for their family.'

'My *nani* was indeed a great Indian woman and a noble soul!'

'Undoubtedly she was! She chose your father for me precisely because he was highly educated as compared to those who were rich but lacked the natural graces that come only with education. Now tell me what kind of a life partner would you like to have for yourself?'

'Ma, he should be well-read, kind, gracious and very well-settled in a respectable profession. I should be able to relate to him mentally and emotionally. I would like to know him beforehand. I just won't marry a stranger.' Nayantara made her mind quite clear before her mother.

'Would you like to consider this boy in your group you were talking about? Do you want us to look around? There are quite a few options from the side of relatives too.'

'Ma, there is no hurry as yet. Give us some more time. The boy I told you about would first like to become an officer in the Civil Services which will take about a year or so. Meanwhile, we would get to know each other too. There is still a long way to go!'

'What do I do about the other options?'

'Defer them for the time being and let me concentrate on my career, Mother.'

'What is the name of the boy?'

'Bijoy!'

The mother and daughter left it at that.

As for Abhinav, the time eventually came for him to decide whether or not he was joining the Armed Forces as a doctor. The stalemate at home had been continuing and his father had been unyielding. The father and the son had succeeded in avoiding a direct confrontation on the issue but were rather firm on their positions. Neither of them wanted to relent and yet wanted to honour the wishes of the other party. On the last day when Abhinav had to decide, he came to his mother. 'Mother I really want to join the Army and serve my country. What shall I do? How shall I prevail upon my father? It can wait no longer.'

'I suggest you sit down with your father and make him see

your point of view. He might not be as opposed to the idea now as he was when you had mentioned it first. His second response is usually different from the first one. He must have thought about the whole issue again and again. He loves you a lot and might agree. Take your chance!'

'All right, Ma! I will talk to him. Tell me, do you support me in this?'

'With my whole heart! There is no service better than one where one gets a chance to serve humanity as well as one's country also. You have my blessings! Your *nani*, too, would have been too happy, if she were alive.'

As soon as Anmol came home, Abhinav approached him. He pleaded, 'Papa, I will never join the Army unless you give me your willing permission to do so. The time has come when I have to take a call. Make my decision a happy one, Father.'

Anmol looked into the eyes of his son and saw quiet determination. How could he refuse his son? He so ardently wished for this. Yet his heart was not ready; a huge fear loomed there and he felt a growing pain as if his sacrifice for the country had already begun. Sensing his thoughts, Abhinav ventured to ask, 'What might your reservations be, Father?'

'It can be dangerous at times!'

'How can it be dangerous, Father? A doctor only has to treat and give medical help, even in times of war. And we have no war coming up in the near future. Many of my friends have already decided to join the Army. Papa, please give me permission!'

Anmol was silent for a long time.

'Can you please make my father understand?' Abhinav cried out in despair to his mother.

Shobhna looked at her husband with pleading eyes. She knew he would understand and never deny his son anything he wanted so wholeheartedly.

'I suppose I will have to allow you to have your way, my son,' said Anmol at last. He wiped the tears welling up in his eyes and clutched Abhinav's hands desperately. 'May God always be by your side and save you from all danger.'

The decision was a hard one for Anmol but once he had made it, he was proud of it for the sake of his son.

Abhinav was overjoyed. His wish had been granted. His father had finally come to understand the yearning of his heart. Now he would be able to give himself to his profession wholeheartedly and without guilt. He touched the feet of his parents before bursting into loud shouts of joy which brought Nayantara come running from the kitchen, 'Why are you shouting, Abhinav? Have the heavens fallen or what?' she gasped with consternation.

'Oh! My dear sister and buddy!' chuckled Abhinav taking her hands into his. 'Father has agreed, finally. I am joining the Armed Forces as a doctor. God is great! I must offer my services for the cause of humanity and serve God's will.'

'How nice. Abhinav you will look great in that olive coloured uniform. Besides, you will be a prized catch for anyone!' Nayantara laughed.

'Can you girls think of anything else also in life?' Abhinav's face glowed with joy and excitement.

'Of course! We don't lag behind you in anything,' said Nayantara. 'You wait and see! There will be a number of girls too, joining as doctors in the Army.'

'Oh, yes! I am sure there will be quiet a few even from my own college.'

'How about your immediate friends Ajay, Ashwani and Dharamveer?'

'We all are joining together!' Abhinav could not contain his excitement.

'What is the drill now, Abhinav?' asked Anmol in a sombre tone.

'Don't worry about it, Father. We will take care of all such formalities. I will keep you informed at every step.' Abhinav picked up his bag and told his mother, 'I am going to meet my friends for a while. I will be back for dinner, Ma!'

'Drop me on the way,' said Nayantara to Abhinav. 'I also have to meet my friends. I shall also be back around the same time.' Nayantara looked at her mother who nodded at both of them.

Left alone, Shobhna and Anmol sat in silence and pondered what was to come next. 'So, you finally gave Abhinav your permission,' said Shobhna. 'You really didn't have much of a choice, given his intense longing.'

'May God fulfil all his wishes and bring glory in the path he has chosen for himself!' Anmol said, his heart heavy.

'God has been so kind to us all so far. Our children are doing so well professionally and they are good human beings,' said Shobhna.

'The credit goes largely to you, Shobhna,' Anmol took her hands into his. 'You sacrificed your career for the welfare of the children. Your own learning and knowledge helped them a lot and shaped their mindset as well as personality. There is no substitute for a mother and an educated one, no doubt, lays the foundation for a civilized society where new ideas can flourish.'

'Enough is enough, now,' smiled Shobhna. 'Your single-minded devotion towards the children has equal credit.' She paused before getting up. 'Now let me prepare dinner. The children will be back soon.'

'Sit for some more time?' Anmol said, taking her hand and setting her down next to him once again.

'We have come a long way in life, haven't we, dear?' she said.

Anmol nodded. 'Do you feel old, at times?'

'I can still visualize very well the day I got married. It is as if it were only yesterday. Everything seems so real and near even now. I have lost track of time.'

'You are an eternal romantic, Shobhna!'

'Aren't you?'

'I couldn't be anything else with you beside me, my dear!'

Anmol looked deep into her eyes.

'Only if my mother were alive to see this day!' Shobhna wiped a tear from her eyes.

Anmol knew these could only be tears of happiness.

34

Nayantara's friendship with Bijoy slowly matured into a stronger relationship. They enjoyed each other's company and looked for occasions to spend time with each other after college hours. Their group, too, was very active with their own interests. Weekends were reserved for all such activities. They met over coffee, had long chats, and discussed everything under the sun that interested them. Moments spent in such carefree relaxation were precious to them and often gave way to serious discussions about life and love, where they could peep into each other's mind and heart. Similarity of thoughts, a deep perception of life around them and an acute awareness of the fleeting moments of happiness had brought them together and cemented their relationship with one another.

'You know, Nayantara!' said Bijoy to her over one such occasion. 'Though I aspire to be a civil servant and am working hard towards that goal, frankly, I don't want to belong to that elite class that is not grounded in reality. My heart belongs to the common people; their concerns and welfare interests me the most.'

'I agree with you,' replied Nayantara. 'Common people acquire an extraordinary strength of character only by going through the mill of life relentlessly. They are the ones who really empathise with others and their problems. A touch of warmth is what distinguishes them from the upper middle classes, the elite.'

'I am sure you must have read Steinbeck's *Grapes of Wrath*,' said Bijoy in earnest. 'Ma Joad says, "If you're in trouble or hurt or need—go to poor people. They're the only ones that'll help—the only ones." She is such a powerful character in the novel, isn't she?'

'Oh, surely she is. It is only the common people who constitute various shades of life, as we see it. You can actually feel them undergo a whole range of emotions. Upper middle classes may put forth innovative ideas but the common people actually live life.'

Bijoy was starting to open up before Nayantara. He would tell her everything about his life at home and work. He shared with her his thoughts and feelings. He even wanted to introduce her to the members of his family and invite her home for a meal.

'Come along with me for dinner tonight, Nayantara,' said Bijoy. 'My family would love to meet you.'

Nayantara was not sure. 'I would feel so awkward. Invite the whole group and I'll come along for free!' she laughed.

'But I want you to meet them as much as they want to meet you.'

'What do they want to meet me for?'

'To know you better, what else for!'

'I hope I haven't committed a crime, have I?' Nayantara tried to laugh and make light of the conversation.

'You have influenced their son much more than they thought anyone could. So they want to meet the actual person.'

'I will have to ask my mother about it, first.'

'Please do. By all means!'

The matter rested there for the time being. But it convinced Nayantara about the kind of feelings he harboured for her, which didn't surprise her. She had suspected it for the last few months. She, herself, had been undergoing such emotions for quite some time. She had always felt attracted towards him; rather the attraction seemed mutual and they couldn't help it. The more they tried to divert their attention in favour of other things, the more they came back to it with greater force and fondness. They had already become close companions and wished to take their relationship to the next level. They wanted to belong to each other, irrespective of the obstacles in their way, if any. On the surface there seemed none. That Nayantara was focused on her career and reasonably ambitious when it came to her profession, he was well aware. Though steeped in middle-class morality and its value system, she was not the kind of girl who would neglect her career in order to confine herself to domestic life. And Bijoy seemed to have no problem with that. Besides, she shared the same interests as he did and provided a stimulus to his imagination and thought process with her charm and intellect. Her easy manners often made others feel at home. She was friendly and combined in her persona a rare blend of traditional values and a streak of modernity. Bijoy was not only impressed but clearly charmed.

Nayantara, too, had a great tenderness for Bijoy. She had never felt for anyone else the way she felt for him. His level-headedness and gracious manners fascinated her and filled her heart with desire. She fancied him in her leisure time and preferred to be alone at home whenever free from work. Her eyes bore a dreamy look and she would often smile to herself. Shobhna was quick to notice such changes in her behaviour and guessed the reason behind it.

'So, Naina, how often does your group meet these days? Do you have any news for me?' asked Shobhna one day.

'Oh, we do still meet on weekends and sometimes during the week too.'

'And how is Bijoy?' Shobhna smiled.

'He is fine and doing very well.'

'He appeared for his Civil Services examinations, didn't he? When is his result expected?'

'A couple of months, I think.'

'How has he done his papers?'

'Quite well, I am sure! The rest, the result will tell.'

'Are you only friends or has the level of fondness between both of you increased?' Shobhna laughed.

'Ma! How can you be so blunt?' Nayantara felt a little embarrassed.

'Naina, I am an old hand at guessing these little secrets, my dear. No one can fool one's mother when it comes to these things.' Shobhna looked at her daughter affectionately.

'Mother, he really is a nice guy. He wants me to meet his parents in a casual way first. Should I say yes?'

'You can meet them in a group first and then we will see later on.' Shobhna's tone had become serious. 'You can call him home also for an informal cup of tea, in fact, your whole group.'

'Yes, Ma! That would be fine. Why not?' Nayantara was happy.

Two weeks passed before Nayantara and Bijoy met again. They went to Lodi Garden for a walk. Its quaint, wild beauty charmed them both. They liked the garden for what it was; unkempt, casual and ancient. It was a mixture of history and the beauty of nature. Perhaps it was this that enchanted people to visit. Old people came for a walk while the children loved to run around the dilapidated tombs and play games. It also served as a romantic rendezvous for young couples who were looking forward to some solitary moments away from the curious eyes of friends and relatives. Bijoy and Nayantara both found beauty even in the little, mundane things; for instance, this garden. It gave a stimulus to their imagination besides providing an excellent backdrop where they could express their soft feelings for each other without any inhibitions.

'Shall we go a little further ahead of the walkers' track?' asked Bijoy as they crossed the ancient monument and went past the shrubs where the leaf-buds were almost ready to blossom. Tiny beds of seasonal flowers lay on both the sides of the hedges that led finally to a huge tree at the end of the track. They went forward in silence and came to a point from where they could see the luminous rays of the sun making the greenery around flush with a brilliant radiance.

'Isn't it beautiful?' exclaimed Nayantara.

'Everything looks beautiful when one is accompanied by a loved one!' said Bijoy.

Nayantara was stunned by the sudden articulation of his feelings. She hadn't the faintest notion that it would come this way. She realized in a flash why Bijoy had insisted upon this meeting and chose this venue. She bowed to pluck a flower in order to avoid his intense gaze.

'Let us sit here for a while, Nayantara,' said Bijoy. He put his arms around her waist and looked at her with lovelorn eyes. They sat under the lush tree from where they could see the sun going down slowly in the west and the sky getting mellow with the receding rays. A golden glow, however, was still spread over the beds of flowers that lay behind them.

'Nayantara, I am in love with you.' Bijoy took her hands in his own. 'I fell in love with you the moment I saw you. I would love to spend my life with you beside me always. Will you marry me?' His words came out bold and clear.

Nayantara was just as sure. 'Why did you take so long in saying it? I thought it would never come!' Her eyes filled with love.

'Tell me honestly, didn't you ever expect it?'

'I don't know!' Nayantara continued to stroke the flower in her hand.

'Do you love me?' Bijoy lifted her chin and tried to look into her eyes.

'Aren't we too young to marry?'

'Do you love me?'

'With all my heart!'

'When did you first realize it?'

'I have always known. I always knew. But I thought that you were distant and not interested in anybody, the least in me.'

'Why did you think so? Aren't appearances always deceptive?'

'But you were so obsessed with your career!'

'So I am even now. That is a man's first call always. But one needs a soulmate too and of one's own choice!'

'The family, too, is important and so are their views.'

'My family is very liberal that way. They will go by my choice always. What about your family?'

'My parents knew each other before their marriage. They would just like their daughter to be happy. I don't see any problem on that front. But you aren't settled yet according to your own standards.'

'Where is the hurry, my dear? Let things take their own course and unfold themselves. Let's enjoy our moments of love! We will broach the issue before our parents when the time is ripe.'

'You mean we should wait till your result for the civil services is declared.'

'Do you agree?'

'Yes, of course!'

Bijoy began courting her like a lover. They were still very much a part of the group but also ventured to meet on their own. Nayantara made sure to keep her mother informed of her growing affection for Bijoy and their meetings, too, which had gotten more frequent. Lodi Garden became their favourite hangout. They loved to sit under the tree under which Bijoy had first professed his love for her; they would sit hand in hand with fingers clutched and look into each other's eyes. Gently, Bijoy would draw her closer and kiss her hands passionately. In the perfect stillness of the surroundings, they could feel their hearts throbbing.

'What are you thinking about?' Nayantara asked, breaking the silence.

'Nayantara, we belong to each other, do you agree?'

'Yes, of course. I trust you fully.'

'I am glad I found you. We know each other so well now. We don't have any pretensions between us any more. I wait for the time when we shall belong to each other entirely.'

Nayantara was overwhelmed by the intensity of Bijoy's feelings for her. She closed her eyes as she sat next to him and let him run his fingers all over her face before he kissed her passionately again and again.

'Shall we walk a little farther?' Nayantara tried to break away from his firm embrace.

Reluctantly he slackened his grasp of her arm and got up.

'Why not? It is also getting dark. Time for you to go home.'

'My mother will be worried about me.'

'Does she know much about us?'

'I have never kept my mother in the dark about anything I think or do.'

'Does she approve?'

'She tries to view things from my point of view. How about your family, Bijoy?'

'Oh they will love the girl I choose for myself. They have always been very supportive in anything I have ever wanted to do. You don't need to worry.'

'I do get apprehensive at times. I come from a simple, middle-class family and cherish those values.'

'You will be pleasantly surprised to find us strangely similar.'

'Why strangely?'

'You will find that out yourself one day, my dear!'

'I see a long road ahead, Bijoy. Nothing concrete seems visible to me in the near future.'

'Why so?'

'Your Civil Services result seems to stand between us. Am I right?'

'Do you regret it? Or object to it?'

'Oh, no not at all! I admire you for your lofty dreams and your persistent efforts to attain your goal.'

'Then where is the hitch?'

'I lose your companionship for a short while in both situations.'

'What do you mean?'

'God-willing, if you are successful, I lose you to the Academy for two years till you complete your training and get your posting. If, God forbid, you have to avail of another chance, you will get busier working harder still, and I wouldn't want to be an obstacle.'

'Oh God, you and your reasoning! Both seem incorrigible.' Bijoy was laughing. 'I have always considered you a support and a morale-booster. Take it from me, you both, civil services and you, are going to give each other a hell of a competition. You have been rivals from day one.'

'Who would you choose?'

'There is no question of a choice. I want both and wholeheartedly, no doubt. I can't live without either, my dear.'

'I know, Bijoy. I pray to God for your success every moment, in the first attempt itself.'

'You may not have to wait for long, Naina. I hear that the results may be announced very soon.'

'It makes me jittery!'

'I look forward to it, with you beside me, darling.' Bijoy led her back to the exit gate.

They walked back with dreams and aspirations in mind and a song of love on their lips. Ignoring the uncertainties and hassles on their chosen path, they threw the doubts out of their minds for the time being and loved to bask in the intensity of their love. They leaned against a heavy tree that stood near the gate and hugged each other warmly before saying goodbye to each other.

'We must go now,' said Nayantara.

'Yes.' But he kept her in his embrace.

Nayantara put her hands over his shoulders, then on his hair, caressing him gently and whispered in his ear, 'We must wait, sweetheart!'

'Yes, dreams stand between us for now! But they will help us come together in the long run.'

'They are beautiful and attainable, Bijoy!'

'Like us, don't you think?'

'Yes, just like us.'

35

The news of Abhinav's first posting at the high-altitude region of Leh reached Anmol and Shobhna through his letter while he was still completing his training in Lucknow. It had come suddenly. They were surprised as well as concerned about the problems involved in the posting at a difficult terrain. Abhinav, however, in his letter had tried to put them at ease and told them how excited he was about the challenges involved. He had always loved adventure and the sense of thrill involved in it; and so his parents were not surprised about his optimistic attitude. He had been given a tough task in the beginning of his career and he hoped to excel in it by dint of his merit, hard work and devotion to duty. His mood was upbeat and he eagerly looked forward to his assignment.

Before that he came home for a couple of days and sought the blessings of his parents. Anmol and Shobhna were happy to see him and so was Nayantara. They were all so proud of one another and their achievements. Their get-together quickly turned into a nostalgic trip down memory lane where they viewed their lives with an objective eye that helped them to trace their roots and see whether they had been able to take their family tree forward in life. Each member of the family pondered over their contribution towards a larger goal. Anmol and Shobhna had built up their home from a scratch; they had come to Delhi as a struggling middle-class couple in the aftermath of the Partition and dealt with the day-to-day difficulties with their never-say-die attitude and a resilience that was typical of their generation. A futuristic vision and an inexhaustible perseverance had enabled them to put their family on a strong foundation from where their children had taken up the mantle and wrought a success story with their talent, energy, and positive attitude to life. The circumstances as well as their destiny had joined hands to imbue them with the right qualities as well as opportunities and set them on the path of success.

'Papa, I am very happy today,' said Abhinav to his father. 'It was great that you finally allowed me to join the Armed Forces despite your reservations. Wait and see! I will make you all so proud one day.'

'You are going to an area where troubles will shoot up at every step,' said Anmol. 'And physical hardships will prove to be an add-on when it will come to other responsibilities.'

'Isn't it best, Father, that one's youth is spent on facing challenges and emerging victorious? Our whole training was geared towards acquiring that attitude. The Armed Forces succeed in instilling that positive approach with a daredevil instinct. I can't wait to join.' Abhinav's eyes blazed while expressing his patriotic sentiments.

'How often will you be able to visit home, Abhinav?' asked Shobhna.

'We get two months' annual leave, Ma. I will try not to keep you waiting too long.'

'Leh is known for its picturesque beauty, Abhinav,' barged in Nayantara while putting piping hot snacks on the table and laying napkins for serving tea.

'I am going to buy a good camera from the Army Canteen and take a lot of photographs to show to you. First, I shall have to discover the natural beauty of the region on my own. It is going to be a wonderful experience, a once-in-a-lifetime experience for me and a tremendous learning opportunity, no doubt.'

'Let us all sit round the table and have these delicacies,' beckoned Shobhna.

They sat till late; talking, laughing, eating and discussing everything under the sun. The happy hours stretched till late in the evening and no one was in a mood to get up or give up chatting with one another. The present moment mingled beautifully with their past when Anmol and Shobhna started relating anecdotes from their Lahore days. No one seemed to be in a hurry. They regaled each other with stories and were mad with happiness in one another's company. Spending carefree time together had already become a luxury for them and the beautiful backdrop of home gave them a feeling of intimate belonging that put periods of suffering and struggle far from their minds. This was their time of rejoicing and emotional bonding; they would not let anything or anybody mar its sacredness. Feelings reigned supreme in their speech and demeanour; they felt drugged with happiness and excitement. They wanted to make the most of the precious moments that were left to be spent with each other. God knew when they would be together again like this!

The next few evenings were spent the same way. Nothing else interested the family except spending time together.

One evening Anmol reminded Abhinav, 'You better watch out for your health properly at Leh, Abhinav.'

Abhinav nodded as his father continued, 'The high altitude area comes with its own share of problems. You will need more than just routine nutrition.'

'Papa, you forget that I am a qualified doctor,' replied Abhinav, smiling at Shobhna.

'I have heard that you get really warm shawls there, the rough, coarse *Pashmina* that is typical of the mountainous range?' Nayantara asked.

'Let me reach there first, Naina!' said Abhinav lovingly to her. 'You can then give me a whole list of your demands. Rest assured, I shall fulfil them all.'

The leisurely week passed in the blink of an eye. The last couple of days were spent in putting things together. The warmest woollens were taken out of the cupboards, exposed to the direct sunlight and suitably packed in the suitcases along with other necessities. Abhinav, otherwise used to travelling light, seemed quite perplexed at the ever increasing luggage. The day of departure was drawing near; the mood of the family was getting more solemn; the hurried atmosphere was ebbing, with the family members receding into their own cocoons and turning more silent. Nayantara tried to shake off spells of dejection with her trivial talk and an excited manner of speech.

At last the day arrived when Abhinav was all set to leave home to make a new beginning in his life. Shobhna had specially asked Abhinav and Nayantara to sit along with her when she undertook her daily *havan* in the morning. Their day started with an invocation to God to bless Abhinav who stood ready to embark on his professional journey. Shobhna, like her mother Kaushalya, always performed the sacred *havan* with special *ahutis* before starting any auspicious work or event. The *havan* was completed in an hour when Shobhna, Anmol and Nayantara showered rose petals on Abhinav amidst chanting of *mantras*, bringing the ceremony to a close. Abhinav got up and touched the feet of his parents, asking for their blessings. Anmol and Shobhna hugged their son warmly, making an effort to control their feelings and not allow their tears to well up.

Nayantara, silent till now, cheered him up with a loud uproar. 'Best of luck in all your future ventures!' she wished her brother. 'And you must not forget your promise, dear brother!'

'I won't.'

'And now it is getting late for you. Your army discipline expects you to be punctual to the minute!'

A cab stood waiting at the door. Abhinav picked up his luggage and came out. He had made a special request to his parents not to accompany him to the railway station. He did not want to trouble them and risk getting sentimental. As the cab left for the station, Shobhna and Nayantara burst into tears while Anmol escorted them inside the house wearing a shattered look. Life had come full circle.

Nayantara tried to shake off the sadness of seeing her brother leave. Besides, she was also thinking of Bijoy, who was waiting for the result of his Civil Service examinations. They had heard about the possibility of the declaration of the result that very evening. Bijoy had tried to put up a brave front the whole day but was nervous and jittery. Nayantara gave him constant company after college hours and tried to ease the situation by appearing calm and jovial. She took him to have a cup of coffee at a nearby restaurant before deciding to go the UPSC building and find out the latest news. The time spent over a cup of coffee, otherwise a pleasure for both of them, was wrought with anxiety this time.

Though engaged in routine conversation for a show, their minds were occupied with only one issue, 'Will Bijoy make it to the prestigious Services? Will he be lucky enough? Will his hard work be rewarded in the first attempt itself? How will things shape up if he failed to cross the benchmark? Their plans would go awry for at least another year if he didn't make it. Their future life revolved around this result. What was going to be the outcome of this great risk?'

'Oh God!' prayed Nayantara fervently again and again. 'Let Bijoy be successful in this attempt. He has put his heart and soul into this effort. Many others also have! Oh God! But Bijoy is truly a deserving candidate. Driven by a zeal for doing public good always, he would make a very fine officer and do the society proud!'

Bijoy was uttering his own prayers, 'Please God! Help me if you think I deserve it. It is my heartfelt desire to serve humanity in my own way. And I think this service gives one ample opportunities to do so. Oh God! I shall always be sincere to my job as well as my own self. I shall always listen to the voice of my conscience. I shall endeavour never to fail my own countrymen! Please make me successful if you think I deserve it on my own merit. Give me that extra bit of luck without which one can never be successful. Chart out my destiny for me, oh God! And give me your blessings along with the companionship of Nayantara!'

They looked at their watch frequently but deliberately avoided looking at each other. Neither wanted to broach the issue that was on their minds. The coffee over, they decided to go to the UPSC building to find out the latest news. As they neared the building, they saw a crowd gathered; their faces wrought with tension and tempers running high, and people jostling in the front to have a look at the sheets of papers that were displayed on the official notice board. The results were out. The ink on the papers held the key to their success or its deferment till the next year. The eyes of the aspirants and their parents or friends were glued to the wall; a few would burst into shouts of merriment occasionally while others walked back with dismal eyes trying to control their tears. People were in a tumult; the excitement of the successful candidates was getting out of hand; they were unable to control their emotions, successful or unsuccessful. This examination had always seemed to be almost a matter of life and death.

Nayantara and Bijoy inched forward as they found some space through the crowd. Misty-eyed, they clutched each other's hands and could feel their blood throbbing in their veins. The moment had finally arrived when they would have to confront reality and accept their fate. Their eyes ran through the list; their pupils dilating upwards and then descending downward almost in a similar fashion till their eyes got stuck on a name. Too dumbfounded to react immediately, they turned sideways to look at each other before turning their attention to the notice-board once again.

They brought their fingers to the covered board and directed them to the name they wanted to be sure about.

'Bijoy!' shouted Nayantara.

'Yeah, dear!' answered Bijoy.

'You have made it, my dear!' Nayantara's face was already smeared with tears.

'Yeah! I think so. Nayantara, I can't thank God enough. He has been very kind, sweetheart!' Bijoy pulled her closer and hugged her hard trying to put her head on his shoulders so that she wouldn't see a trickle of a tear in his eyes.

'Make way for us now, please,' cried an anxious voice from behind, 'and yes, congratulations to you both!'

'And best of luck to all of you! May God give the same happiness to all of you,' said Bijoy while holding Nayantara close and making way for others.

Nayantara and Bijoy came out and stood at the gate of the UPSC building; elated and full of stars in their eyes. The happiness had still to sink in; they were numb with pleasure; too drugged with sweet dreams. They looked at the most frequented building again and again; couldn't have enough of it, remembered their past longings whenever they passed by it or were required to visit it for fulfilling various formalities. Their eyes were full of awe, wonder and a feeling of satiation that had come naturally in them. They felt themselves an integral part of the whole process that was arduous, no doubt, and posed the toughest challenge in life. They looked at the other side of the road from where they were standing and lo and behold! They saw another very familiar face, of that of the *chaat-wallah* whose shed had stood there for many, many years catering to the appetites of all the aspirants who came there with a longing to try their fortunes in the civil-services. It was almost a ritual for all of them to have a plate of his delicious *chaat* which he offered with a lavish hand and a warm smile while wishing them good luck always.

'Bijoy! Won't you offer me *chaat* today, dear?'

'How can we go from here without having this to our hearts' content?'

'For old-time's sake, right?' Nayantara was delirious with joy.

'Yes! And for all times to come also! We will come specially to have this whenever we think of this day.'

'Which will be quite often. As of now, let us tell this amazing guy our wonderful news which will include him also in our happiness.'

'His delicious *chaat* offered with dollops of affection certainly has a role to play…'

'Before we hurry home to share this ecstatic moment with our respective families, right?'

'By all means!'

Nayantara and Bijoy walked hand in hand with a spring in their step and deep love in their eyes, oblivious of the whole cosmos around them.

The whole universe, they believed, had come together to make them happy. So happy!

36

Nayantara's marriage to Bijoy was on the cards. The Civil Services result had filled both their households with immense pleasure and made sure that they speeded up the process. Bijoy had found the right opportunity to broach the subject and introduce his lady-love to his family. They were as enthusiastic as Bijoy, in a hurry to finalise the arrangements and share the happiness with Nayantara's parents. Already aware of their son's marked emotional leanings, they had full confidence in his choice when it came to the decision of a life partner. It would still be a couple of months before he would start his training at the Mussoorie Academy and the nuptials could take place before he joined, if Nayantara's parents agreed. It was just the right time!

Nayantara, on Shobhna's asking, had invited Bijoy home for a casual evening of tea. They wanted Anmol to meet and speak to the boy. Anmol had given his consent and was willing to meet the young man before he pursued the matter further with his parents. Bijoy came on the dot and was ushered into the drawing room with both Shobhna and Nayantara. Catching a glimpse of Nayantara, Bijoy winked at her before taking a seat on the sofa and engaging Shobhna in casual conversation. They had barely talked for five minutes before Anmol walked in. He smiled at Bijoy, 'Congratulations once again, my boy! You have brought laurels to your family. It is indeed a great achievement.'

'Thank you, sir! God has been very kind to me. Nayantara, too, has been a great support. I am indebted to her.'

'Oh, I am sure she must have been. She has always been headstrong when it comes to matters that touch her heart.'

'Pitted against odds, it can be a virtue indeed.'

'And in times of peace, my dear boy?'

'A determined approach can always produce great positive results if channelized in the right direction, sir!'

Shobhna and Anmol burst out laughing while looking at their daughter all the time, who by then had blushed deeply.

'You don't see any fault in Nayantara, my boy, do you?'

'Sir, I prefer to look at the positive points, be it a person or a situation. Nothing or nobody in life can be absolutely virtuous or villainous. Life or situations are an amazing mix of opposites. It depends how one takes them, responds to them or gears them towards a direction.' Bijoy was in his element; Nayantara beamed with pride. She could see that her father was slowly falling under Bijoy's charm, something she herself was familiar with.

And then came another question from Anmol, 'Bijoy, tell me son, what is it that you like the most about Nayantara?'

Bijoy was silent for a few seconds. He wanted to measure his words. He did not want to appear too enthusiastic or ruffled. Yet he wanted to be as truthful as possible, while appearing to be totally objective.

'Sir, she is totally genuine, rather incapable of putting on any artificial behaviour. Besides, I love her for her sincerity and an ability to empathize with others. She is a wonderful person and would make a great companion. We both look at life with a similar approach. Life suddenly appears beautiful when I am with her. I shall always keep her happy to the best of my ability….' Bijoy was getting sentimental.

'Nayantara, do you have anything to say about Bijoy?' asked Anmol.

'Papa, he is an amazing person. I shall always be happy with him...' Nayantara was just a little hesitant; she wanted nothing else than to be truthful before her parents.

'Shobhna,' Anmol addressed his wife, smiling. 'What are we waiting for then? Let's take the relationship forward.'

Shobhna smiled back. 'We waited patiently for you to say that.'

Anmol asked Bijoy, 'Bijoy, when can we meet your parents?'

'Sir, we will fix up everything and then proceed. I will get back to you as soon as possible.' He paused and waited for a reply from Nayantara's parents. Hearing none, he then said, 'In the meantime, may I take your daughter for a cup of coffee, with your permission?'

'Sure, you may,' said Anmol. He got up and gave Bijoy a warm hug. Bijoy bent forward to touch his feet.

The very next day Shobhna made sure to send a letter to Abhinav, informing him of the plans for his sister's impending engagement.

At that time, Abhinav had been doing quite well in Leh, where he was posted. He had endeared himself to his Army seniors as well as *jawans* who came to him for all sorts of medical concerns. The high-altitude, mountainous area was conspicuous both for its picturesque beauty as well as its meandering tough terrain. Abhinav was mesmerized by the pristine beauty of the snow-clad Himalayan range, the crystal clear water of its integral lakes, the lush greenery of the flora around and the calm, pure air. Ah, the pure air! Something he could never hope to have in a big city!

Abhinav was on the top of the world, literally, emotionally and spiritually. His hectic day schedule would be followed by an evening of peaceful seclusion when he would sit for an hour or two pondering over the days of his childhood and youth and his well-loved upbringing under the watchful eyes of his parents.

He had all the time in the world to meditate over the role of his parents and their sacrifices in order to give them a solid foundation for their career. He had also got into the virtuous habit of writing a letter to his father every day, describing his activities as well as his innermost thoughts. He would always end his letter by writing a separate note to his mother where he would enquire about her *Arya Samaj* activities and also news about Nayantara. While the tone of letter to his father was rather sober and respectful, the manner of addressing his mother was always humorous and witty. The bond that he shared with his father was subtle and soulful whereas his mother always wrote about mundane things, giving him information about everything at home in a nutshell. They greatly looked forward to each other's letters which was like a union of minds and feelings.

It was one such letter that carried the news to Anmol and Shobhna that their son had been nominated to receive the *Vishisht Sewa* Medal for showing exemplary courage, resilience and devotion to duty. It was clear to his superiors that Abhinav, at his young age and early days as an Army doctor, had far exceeded the limits of his duty by participating actively in almost all the fields of his regiment. His name lay imprinted on the highest bridge that had been constructed in that region by the Army authorities. His dedicated participation towards the engineering services of his fellow officers had earned him their appreciation as well as the inclusion of his name on the foundation stone of the bridge. And this was indeed one of his many achievements. Abhinav had always been a well-rounded personality which made him a versatile officer as well. Looking at his contribution in almost every sphere, his commanding officer had recommended his name for the prestigious VSM at the threshold of his career itself which would be awarded to him on the celebration of the Army Day in the national capital.

The news, though hinted only casually by Abhinav in his letter, was read by Anmol, Shobhna and Nayantara with great merriment.

'Look Shobhna!' said Anmol. 'Our son is a real gem of the family. May God bless him with a lot of name and fame!'

'May God give him a very long and healthy life! May he do his country proud one day!' beamed Shobhna.

'I always knew my brother would be the star of the family,' Nayantara said. 'He will bring many more laurels, no doubt!' She was most excited.

Meanwhile in Leh, Abhinav was just as excited about Nayantara's impending engagement. He beamed with happiness for his sister. He had been Nayantara's confidant and he had already known about her blossoming friendship with Bijoy. The letter from his parents also asked him to explore the possibility of saving his annual leave for the event of Nayantara's marriage. They would let him know the exact details about the ceremonies as soon as they were fixed.

Abhinav could not be happier. His sister had made, he felt, the right choice in her career as well as for her life partner. He had met Bijoy a couple of times in Delhi on Nayantara's insistence and had instantly liked him. He found his future brother-in-law to be intelligent, and sincere, sober yet warm and caring.

At last, the happy day arrived amidst great aplomb and high expectations. All expected relatives arrived and celebrations were in full swing. The atmosphere was one of jubilation and nostalgia. Anmol and Shobhna were overwhelmed that they had indeed come a long way in their lives. Memories of their Lahore days where they lived in comfort and luxury; the Partition phase, settling down in Dhanbad and picking up the pieces of life once again; working in schools and finally getting married and starting a new life in Delhi in a very nondescript manner: everything was fresh in their minds. Shobhna remembered herself as a bride even now. That phase of life had come full circle; her daughter was ready to settle down in matrimony and bear new responsibilities. Like herself, she too would be the pivot of a new generation. It could only be the handiwork of God, the eternal creator who balances everything with his poetic justice, thought Shobhna. Her heart was heavy with emotions. She missed her mother, Kaushalya Devi, the most during this time. Her mind again and again visited her mother's lovely and affectionate face that always radiated with warmth and confidence. Shobhna's soul wanted to reach out to her mother and thank her for all that she had done for her. It was only now that she understood finally the role of a mother in the lives of children and her contribution as the progenitor of a dynasty.

'Mother,' she whispered a prayer, her hands folded. 'How I wish you were here with me at this stage of my life. You would have made things so much easier. Oh, mother, how will I send Nayantara away from me without you beside me?' As she closed her eyes, she felt a wave of calmness creep over her; her spirits lifted like leaves with the rustle of a serene wind flowing in a wood. She felt herself being blessed by her mother. 'Oh! Ma, I feel your presence. You must be somewhere around. You cannot be very far away from me. See, your granddaughter Nayantara is getting married. I know you have blessed her too. I can just feel you and your presence here along with me!'

Shobhna had regained her equilibrium. She felt light, calm and happy once again.

All the arrangements were complete: simple, tasteful, and aesthetically decorative. Shobhna had ensured that all ceremonies were to be undertaken according to the Vedic rituals, very much how her own mother would have liked. The *haldi* ceremony was performed in the morning a day before the wedding where Nayantara was given a bath with a paste of turmeric and milk. 'This will cleanse and purify as well as lend a beautiful glow to your whole body,' one of the elderly aunts explained to Nayantara before the rites started. The same evening was reserved for the *mehndi* as well as *sangeet,* where all of them were expected to let go of their inhibitions and sing and dance till the wee hours of the morning.

Abhinav and Nayantara's friends had prepared special songs and dance sequences for the occasion. Everybody was dressed in their best: girls shone in ornate *lehngas,* saris and jewellery; smartly dressed boys were in an upbeat mood, ready to coax and woo the girls with their eyes shining with mischief. The music was loud, their feet were dancing, the snacks were aplenty, piping hot and delicious. Relatives, friends and youngsters were all together, ready to mingle and sway to the lilting tunes. They made Nayantara dance along with them, with Abhinav taking the lead and making everybody dance and enjoy till everybody was dead tired.

If this was going to be Nayantara's last evening in her parental home, thought Abhinav, then he would make sure that it would be absolutely memorable so that whenever she would think of this day, her heart would fill up with happiness and nostalgia.

They retired to their rooms at midnight, ready to drop into their beds with limbs aching, longing for rest. The next day was also going to be hectic. They needed to sleep well and look their best on the most important day.

Nayantara, in her elegant, embellished bridal outfit looked naturally the best. She was wearing the same gold set that Shobhna, her mother, had worn on her wedding day and which her *nani* had got specially made for her, giving her own design to the gold artisans. Her earthly beauty and dainty persona richly complimented and enhanced the beauty of the flower decorations all around. The soft, doleful music, alternating between the tones of the *shahnai* and popular numbers added greatly to the romance of the moment. The *baraat* arrived in time bringing Bijoy along, the handsome bridegroom, who had waited for so long to take his lady-love home and begin a new chapter in their life.

The marriage ceremony, beginning with the *jaimala* was short, crisp and sweet. Bijoy, the eternal romantic and a non-believer in long rituals, had instructed the *purohit* to carry them out in a non-ostentatious way but strictly according to the *vidhi* as Shobhna had always wanted. He also requested for an explanation of the seven *pheras* and their sanctity in married life when both of them got up to walk around the sacred fire. As he put *sindoor* (vermilion) on Nayantara's forehead, relatives and friends showered rose petals amidst the chanting of blessings from every corner. The *purohit* declared them husband and wife.

Nayantara and Bijoy rose to touch the feet of their parents and seek their blessings. Their friends broke out in song and dance. Bijoy, Abhinav, Nayantara and their friends had decided that the *vidai* ceremony of the bride would be amidst happy fanfare and without any tears.

'Let emotions rule but with smiles and laughter, mother,' Bijoy had requested Shobhna, who promised to make it so and respect the wishes of her son-in-law.

As the car moved slowly carrying Bijoy and Nayantara as the happily married couple, the family and guests all waved to them, shouting in unison, 'Best of luck!' The guests bid the couple goodbye, laughed heartily and broke into steps of *bhangra*.

While Shobhna and Anmol tried their best to put up a happy facade, Abhinav was quick to spot the tears that had started to well up in his mother's eyes as he escorted her inside their home. A phase of life seemed to be over in their lives: Nayantara, the star of their eyes, had left home to make her new beginning.

Their only prayer to God now was to give her everything she desired.

37

Abhinav's high-altitude posting at Leh was about to come to an end. It was close to three years and he was due for a change in station. He had spent a wonderful time there; learning and serving as well as enjoying the picturesque beauty of the Himalayan range. He had endeared himself to his seniors, juniors and *jawans* and had become a role model for the officers of his regiment. They swore by his name as far as his devotion to duty was concerned. It was a moment of great pride for the regiment that their medical officer had been selected for the *Vishisht Sewa* Medal, right in his first posting. It was time for celebration and taking stock of the life spent there. The air was rife with the speculation that Capt. Abhinav's next station was going to be Secunderabad in southern India but it still took about a week for the news to reach their regiment. The confirmation of posting led to a number of farewell dinners. Systems in the Army are based on protocol and etiquette which are followed by a strict sense of discipline.

'A toast to Captain Abhinav's new assignment!' cheered his commanding officer as he raised his glass of liquor and the rest of the party joined in. 'May he be as successful as he has been here and bring glory to his next regiment in the same way!'

Another officer chimed in, 'May God bless him!'

In the next fortnight or so, most evenings were spent in the same way. The atmosphere was relaxed and convivial, with good food, plenty of drinks, the singing of popular songs, and even dancing. Abhinav was well-loved both for his dedication to his job and his warm and outgoing personality. He was often the centre of attention and would surely be missed.

'Captain Abhinav, you are going to a family station now,' said one of his colleagues. 'It is time for you to get married.'

'Maybe his parents are looking for a suitable bride already!' said another.

'Captain, what kind of a girl would you prefer?' the commanding officer's wife asked. 'Working, non-working, or a professional like you?'

'Ma'am, it is really for my parents to decide,' said Abhinav respectfully. 'I don't care much about working or non-working but she should, first of all, respect my parents and make a good home. We must also share the same value system.'

'Captain!' called out one officer from the other side of the room. 'Why be so serious? Life is short, enjoy it fully!'

'Oh yes, I agree!' Abhinav smiled. 'That's one thing one learns in the Army... never to take life for granted, enjoy the present moment and hope for the best always.'

And so the Army men enjoyed their moments whenever the occasion warranted or peace prevailed at the national level. They were always expected to strike a wilful balance between the call of duty, the responsibilities at home or their societal obligations. The tightrope-walk made them more mature, dependable and ready to make the most of carefree moments whenever allowed.

'Well, we hope you never forget the wonderful times you spent here with us,' his commanding officer said. 'And in such beautiful surroundings, too!'

'Sir, I will never forget my stint here. I think a soldier's first posting is like his first crush. The memory always remains fresh. The warmth, love and the respect I got from all of you is deep-rooted in my heart. I learnt a lot from you, Sir, and Ma'am has always been like a mother to me here. I am indeed indebted to you all.'

'Abhinav, you have left your mark on everything here. We are all so proud of you!' There was loud cheering.

Soon the transfer orders came through and it was time for Abhinav to join his posting at Secunderabad. He took a detour through Delhi to meet his parents and Nayantara. It was just like the old times before Abhinav and Nayantara had joined their professional careers. Bijoy wasn't around, though, as he was training at the LBS Mussoorie Academy.

Having Abhinav in their family home was a great moment for Anmol and Shobhna. They counted their blessings and realised they could not ask for more from God. With their children largely settled in their own lives, they both had resolved in their minds to contribute their bit and give it back to society in their own way. And what better way to do so than the dissemination of knowledge and that too, free of cost, to those little children around who needed it badly? Shobhna had come up with a novel idea. She started a *bal-sabha* at her home for an hour in the evening everyday when the children from their neighbourhood would come and she would teach them to recite the *gayatri mantra* while explaining its meaning along with some other teachings from the sacred texts, like the Vedas. Anmol, at times, would quote stories from *Panchtantra* and give them moral education in a very witty manner. Children would greatly enjoy such sessions while learning everything willingly and happily.

Abhinav and Nayantara were full of pride for their parents, their remarkable agility and courage of convictions even at this stage of their lives. Their life had always been a source of inspiration. They had themselves built their own lives from scratch and had inculcated the same values in their children. Abhinav and

Nayantara both had taken after them and respected them highly for their middle-class roots and value system.

As quickly as Abhinav came, he left, too, in equal haste. As he went off to Secunderabad, Nayantara decided to visit Bijoy in Mussoorie for about a week since her college happened to be closed. She loved visiting the Academy whenever she found time; this was the only way she could meet her husband except when they were communicating through letters. Their relationship, too, was undergoing several stages since their marriage. Their union, though cemented in the eyes of society, had resulted in physical distance owing to Bijoy's training at the Academy. They held their days of courtship as precious; at least they could be together whenever they wanted or go out for a cup of coffee or could talk leisurely about anything or everything during that time. Those days of romance and proximity were gone and were rather replaced with increased responsibilities, added work, unnecessary travel and periods of long waiting. They longed to be together always, hoped against hope that they would meet soon, away from their family setup for sometime at least. It wasn't easy for Bijoy to take leave from his Academy and come often to meet Nayantara and his own family. So, it had automatically befallen on Nayantara to juggle her time and responsibilities between her job, family and travel, in order to go to to Mussoorie whenever possible. They both looked forward to such solitary moments away from the snooping eyes of the world when they could enjoy each other's company in the cool environment of the hills.

Their long awaited union rekindled their moments of thrill, joy and romance. For Nayantara it was a break from the drudgery of routine; for Bijoy it was a pleasant diversion from the backbreaking process of the learning of the tenets of administration and its gruelling training. Their pent-up feelings found a release in each other's company and filled them with fresh vigour. They soon forgot about their moments of uncertainty and began dreaming about their future life and home when Bijoy would finish his training.

'I am so glad you have come, Nayantara, my love!' exclaimed Bijoy. He kissed her and folded his arms to bring her closer.

'Yes, I am happy too,' whispered Nayantara, tears welling up in her eyes suddenly. 'I am happiest when I am with you. I just wait and wait for the time when we will be together always.'

They were walking from the library point towards the Academy after having a quiet candlelit dinner at the Whispering Willows, a popular place frequented by officer-trainees on the weekends. As they walked hand in hand in the dark by the roadside, Bijoy, flooded by passion for his beautiful, young wife, clasped her very close and showered her with kisses.

'We belong to each other,' whispered Nayantara, her heart full of warm feelings for Bijoy, now her husband. She pressed her head against his chest and clenched her body stiff.

'Bijoy! Isn't the night beautiful?' she said, pointing towards the moon that peeped through the tall pine trees, its cool rays lending a shimmer to the dark atmosphere.

'Yes, it is, my dear and you are as beautiful and as soothing as the moon!'

'I always knew I could trust you, Bijoy. Ever since I laid my eyes on you, I have never ever had an iota of doubt about your sincerity. Only if you would speak more and express yourself!' laughed Nayantara gently.

'Who could have thought, at that time, that we would end up like this? God granted me both my wishes: you and an entry into this prestigious service. I couldn't have done better. When I get the chance, I must pay back my bit to the welfare of society as best as I can. As for now, you are mine, absolutely mine.'

All their strong emotions were concentrated on each other as they made their way to the government resthouse where Bijoy had booked a room for both of them. Completely engrossed with each other, they walked at leisure to their destination, soaking in the fresh, fragrant air around, their eyes full of love and desire. The rest house was true to its name, literally and symbolically. Situated in peaceful surroundings, it offered *'Aikaant'* (perfect solitude) to those who came seeking it and in the lap of nature. A side road with a meandering pathway a few feet downwards on one side was where the rest house stood, looking quite majestic. As they walked carefully on the zigzag pathway, they looked around and were fascinated to see the Dehradun Valley twinkling with glimmering lights down below. The darkness of the night stood in stark contrast against the soft, yet powerful shine of the Moon on one side and the glittering, tiny lights of the houses of habitation down below that pierced the darkness, like fireflies in a dense jungle. Bijoy and Nayantara stood mesmerized at the spectacle.

'Look at the scene, sweetheart! How beautiful!' exclaimed Nayantara.

'Shall we sit here for a while and look at this wonder of nature?' murmured Bijoy.

As they came down they spotted a bench on the terrace outside the structured building and sat there in silence. The dark night, the cool breeze, the solitary surroundings and the glamour of the moment; all combined to make them forget the rest of the world except their own which was full of feelings, emotions and passion for each other. It was almost half an hour later that they got up and went back to the house hand in hand. They ordered a hot cup of coffee before locking their door, having the little cottage all to themselves.

The night of love had come after a long wait and they longed to be with each other, to love and be loved.

When Nayantara came back to Delhi after spending a week with Bijoy in such a peaceful environment, she came to know from her parents about Abhinav and his new posting. He was settled and felt happy in his new surroundings, too. He would take some time, as he wrote in a letter to his father, to adjust to a different climate as well as cuisine but they were all trained very well to deal with such situations. He spoke highly of his colleagues and their efforts to make him feel comfortable and welcome. He had already invited his parents to come and visit him as he was sure to get a sufficiently big accommodation soon.

And so Anmol and Shobhna visited their son after a couple of months and were treated to a warm welcome by the members of his regiment. Each day was a treat to them as one after the other officer of their unit invited them home for a meal. A great feeling of comradeship prevailed among the officers and they vied with each other to show their utmost respect to the parents of the doctor of their regiment.

One evening Anmol said to Shobhna, 'I have no bitterness against God any longer for giving me such a troubled childhood and snatching my parents away in my infancy. He has more than compensated me for everything.'

'I am so happy to hear these words from you,' replied Shobhna, beaming with pride. The lifestyle of her son reminded her of their Lahore days when they were carefree, wealthy and full of happiness. She was nostalgic. Anmol, as if reading her thoughts said, 'You know, Shobhna, the days spent here with my son are indeed the glorious days of my life. It is a golden chapter in my life. May God give such happiness to everyone!' Anmol's voice choked with emotion.

A month was spent thus in perfect happiness, their conversations alternating between reminiscences of the past and contentment with the present moment.

A few weeks after they got back home to New Delhi, the national government had taken a decision to send their troops to Sri Lanka to poke their nose in an easily avoidable debacle.

Abhinav, too, now a major, accompanied the troops as a member of the Indian Peace Keeping Force. The news cast a shadow of doubt not only in the household of Anmol and Shobhna but those of the other Indian soldiers, too.

38

Everybody in the house was silent. A deep sense of gloom pervaded the atmosphere as never before. A great hush had descended over the stone walls as well as its inhabitants. Their eyes sported a look of bleak temerity trying to pierce through the vacuum of unanswered questions. It appeared as if the agony of the troubled souls, which remained stifled for want of expression, wanted to gush out through monosyllabic shrieks.

The atmosphere was full of emotions, depression and tension. Tears welled up intermittently in the eyes of those present with a fear of the unknown looming large. A huge crowd had gathered outside the house and looked askance at the inhabitants. A black crow, perched listlessly on the roof of the house and unaware of the human saga that was to unfold before them, cawed relentlessly.

Somebody had heard…somebody had read a newspaper report…some others had been watching the TV network…when a report had trickled in. The report was yet to be confirmed but eyes were moist and throats choked. The mind and the spirit were too numb to pray and the words escaped their lips. Everyone was in a daze and feared unknown tidings. Still, they kept their fingers crossed and hoped for the best. Perhaps…yes, perhaps!

And then, the telephone rang, piercing the pin-drop silence in the house. Nobody wanted to pick up the receiver. Somebody said, 'Hello' at the other end and then…two silent tears rolled down the face of the listener. The moment of suspended animation seemed like a century. It was apparent that cruel fate had struck her blow. The suspicion was confirmed.

Loud shrieks pierced the air. Anmol fell unconscious on the floor, and Shobhna, too. Nayantara sat in a stupor, unable to register anything in her mind. Bijoy stood dishevelled. People wailed at the top of their voices, invoking the mercy of God. Only a few gathered their wits and tried to take control of the situation.

Major Abhinav had made the supreme sacrifice for his country! He was gone, dead.

The wait for the body had begun. Relatives and friends started pouring in to offer their condolences. Some were crying, others trying to control themselves, while a few were trying to console the parents and sister, all of them sitting with a stoic expression on their faces.

The coffin arrived as expected, draped in the tricolour and carried by the pall-bearers. The departed soldier was accorded a hero's welcome. The air ranted with the shouts of 'Major Abhinav *amar rahe!*' (Long live Major Abhinav!). The kith and kin wailed inconsolably. The uncontrolled emotions of people had let go of all inhibitions, banishing any sense of reason, if any, at that point of time. The mob sentiments and fury was at its peak. Everyone wanted a glimpse of the 'valiant' who had made the supreme sacrifice for his motherland.

The father, through reticent till now, failed to control his feelings on seeing the face of his dead son. The mother had turned to stone as she looked at her beloved son. A volcano was ready to erupt from her heart. The sister wailed uncontrollably, bewildered and flabbergasted at the turn of events. Not an eye was dry...not a heart grieved less! What was left behind was a chain of human memories and a pool of tears to draw the recesses of strength from!

It was time to move on. The last post was sounding, the bugle playing a solitary tune. The body was placed on the carriage. Columns of the Army stood on both sides of the road with their guns reversed as a mark of respect for the departed soldier. The carriage was decked with flowers, homage had been paid, debts of this life cleared. It was time for the last journey.

The caravan started moving slowly, inch by inch, for the final post. People, with folded hands, gathered on both the sides of the road, showering flower petals on their martyred hero. Hearts were breaking, tears were rolling down the cheeks, yet a sense of pride had enveloped all...pride that the son of the family had made the supreme sacrifice, had brought honour and glory not only to the family but to the nation. He had made mankind proud by his valour, his resolve, determination and his legendary devotion to duty.

The final destination was reached after a journey of three hours. Traffic on the road had come to a standstill, as if the whole town had lined up to pay tribute to the great son of the land. Many envied their hero his hour of glory and wanted to exchange their insignificant lives for such a glorious death.

The funeral pyre was lit. Amid the chanting of 'mantras', the priest was giving a sermon... 'One should not shed tears in the memory of those who sacrifice their lives at the altar of duty. Such men are rare and their deeds stand unparalleled. Their names are written in golden letters in the annals of their nation. They live for their country...they die happily for it, thus bringing glory to the land where they were born. Snow fails to dampen their spirits and imminent death doesn't scare them at all. Each and every drop of their blood serves their motherland... Nothing is impossible for them to achieve and nothing stands between them and their motto of "do or die". They fight undaunted and display exemplary courage in living up to the highest ideals of humanity and mankind.'

Shobhna found the words striking her like the strokes of a hammer. Their impact thawed into her senses and conscience, slowly but surely. The priest had said, 'humanity'... 'But where is humanity? Is it a relative term? Is it to be found only in a relative context? Is it a prerogative of the powerful or an easy alternate for the helpless or weak? Or is it simply a cliché of the politicians to suit their ends? Or is it the mania of the policy makers, which crumbles at the ruthless hands of the rule breakers?'

There was no one to answer her questions! Was she thinking in the wilderness? Shobhna wondered as to where 'humanity' had hidden its guileless face when the LTTE snipers, perched high in the tree branches, had shot Abhinav down while he was providing medical cover right on the warfront to his injured commanding officer. This was in gross violation of the principles of humanity so well enshrined in the Geneva Convention declaration forbidding attack on medical personnel. Many others had met the same fate and died unsung in the enemy's custody, badly injured, starved, tortured, mutilated and what not?

It seemed that Nayantara, too, had lost balance and turned cynical! The euphoria surrounding the funeral procession had begun to sink in and started taking its toll. She felt like shouting at the top of her voice, 'Are we humans! Are we civilized? Do we qualify to be humans and civilized? Can animals be worse? Was primitive man any worse than the so-called modern creature? Is the Geneva Convention a toothless declaration... made only to be flouted by those who do not believe in the religion of human conventions? Do they stand only on paper? What accountability awaits those who defy them to fulfil their gory ideas? Is there any depth of the bottomless pit in which we have fallen?'

No one answered! No one had the answer! Nayantara sought the answer in Mark Twain's essay, 'The Lowest Animal' when he wrote that man was a lowly animal, rather, the lowest in the hierarchy of animals. She was yet reminded of his other master creation, *Adventures of Huckleberry Finn* in which the visionary, Huck Finn, disgusted at the treatment meted out to the Duke and the Dauphin, observed stoically yet thoughtfully that '...human beings can be awful cruel to one another!' Yes, Perhaps! No... Surely, when it suited them and their evil designs.

The funeral pyre was ablaze! It was all over! The soul had broken human bondage to take abode in greener pastures...much above the cruel world! The thin thread tying life and death was beyond repair now.

The crowd had started dispersing. People walked out of the cremation ground, a bit wiser, a lot sadder, dreaming still about world peace.

Anmol, Shobhna and Nayantara couldn't bear to look at each other. Day after day they sat in the drawing room listening to the mourners who thronged their home to share their grief. They sat motionless, listening without comprehending or caring what was being said to them. They did not utter a word, just stared back or wore a cynical smile. Anmol had lost all interest in life; he seemed to have aged twenty years in about a week; his eyes bore a blank expression most of the time except when, in bouts of depression, he raved and ranted against the injustice meted out to him by God, 'What is it that you have always held against me? Oh God! You could never see my happiness! Whenever I heaved a sigh of relief or felt ecstatic, you struck your blow. What did I ever do in this life to deserve tragedy like this? You took away the brightest gem of my family without batting an eyelid; you showed no mercy on me or my family. How will we bear this loss?'

It had fallen on Bijoy to take care of the family members as well as oversee the arrangements. Sensitive and efficient as he was, he tried to pour all his warmth and comfort into the lives of the people he loved so much. Nayantara, too, many times, seemed to him totally devastated though she tried hard to put up a brave front before her parents.

'Mother!' she said to Shobhna, tears rolling down her cheeks. 'Life will never be the same for me ever again. I don't think I will ever be as happy as I have been till now. Something in me has died, just died! God may give me all the happiness in the world but there will always be a void somewhere in my heart…it will never be filled.'

Bijoy, heartbroken to see her crying, would try to comfort her in his own way, 'Naina, nobody in life has ever been able to understand why things happen the way they do. We human beings have no control over things we don't understand.' He, too, couldn't help an occasional sigh or tear.

Anmol, with sunken eyes and an aimless demeanour, drifted about the house talking to himself, 'God, cruel God! Why did you take my son away? You could have taken me instead. I am so old, have lived my life already. It was my time to go; I would have gone happily with you. Why did you take my son away from all of us! He was in the prime of his life and had a long way to go. Oh God! You have been cruel, extremely cruel. You don't exist for me anymore. I will not have faith in you any longer! Where is your poetic justice…?' He collapsed on the floor, overcome with emotions.

Shobhna was mute. She looked around with empty eyes.

'Those God loves, die young! Our son has brought glory to his motherland. People remember only those who sacrifice their lives for the welfare of mankind. Everyone lives a normal life. Who remembers them anyway? Our son is a true martyr! His name will go down in the history of our nation in golden letters. We should not shed tears and demean his sacrifice. Rather, we should take pride and feel lucky that he was born to us. He must have been a saint in his previous life; he came to this world, fulfilled his role on this earth and now has gone back to his eternal home. This mundane world didn't deserve him. He will be happier in the home of God....,' Shobhna tried to come to terms with the tragedy with her usual composure, grit and remarkable equilibrium.

'Mother! As it is who can fight with God? We are all puppets in his hands...He can make us dance the way he wants... Do we have an alternative but to accept his Will? Where is the question of eternal choice? We have none, in anything.'

'Naina, God only knows what is right or wrong. The rest is all conjecture. He puts us on this earth in circumstances and situations determined by the deeds of our previous life; gives us a chance to react or respond according to our mindset or *sanskars*, exposes us to a number of alternatives and allows us to make a choice. The course of our destiny is thus determined by this choice that we have made or make. Having chosen a path, he guides us by our nose and helps us run through this life and relationships, rewarding us for our virtues and punishing us for our sins. Anyone who is born on this earth has to die one day. The difference may lie in the contribution we have made to mankind in general. We have to let go of our personal interests and embrace humanity and its pain...'

Shobhna's mind suddenly went back to the gentle and calm face of her father, Ganpat Rai, when he had sat unnerved by the side of the dead body of his second son, Anand Prakash. Shobhna found that it was only now that she could actually comprehend the significance of her father's words in totality when he had uttered, 'Every fruit falls from the tree on the earth; some fall ripe, others are shaken or snatched away by the forces of nature, incomprehensible to mankind.'

Nayantara looked at the weather-worn face of her aging mother and admired her cool strength of character; a mix of the qualities of her grandparents; gentle, god-fearing, vivacious, strong, tenacious, marvellous, extraordinary and full of grace when under pressure. Yes! Shobhna had become a mirror image of her mother, Kaushalya Devi, ready to fight or live life on her own terms without crumbling under pressure from the cruel hand of fate.

'What extraordinary women and what interesting lives!' thought Nayantara, herself firmly on the same path as shown by her mother and grandmother both!

'All said and done, life is still worth living and fascinating. I would like to be born again and again and live, live and just live…,' Nayantara got up and hugged her mother tightly as Anmol and Bijoy looked at them silently, trying to understand the unbreakable bond that had always existed between the mother and daughter of this extraordinary dynasty.

Perhaps they never would.

Praise for the author's earlier books

Indian Memsahib

'Indian Memsahib *gives a peep into the well-guarded world of civil servants...*'

—Ruskin Bond

'*The good times and the bad times, the lonely battle fought by Sunaina as a bahu, wife and mother make* Indian Memsahib *an impressive debut.*'

—The Statesman

'*Suchita Malik's debut novel,* Indian Memsahib, *weaves fact and fiction to tell the untold story of a bureaucrat's wife.*'

—The Indian Express

Memsahib's Chronicles: A Story of Grit and Glamour

'*The author has demystified the powerful elite, making the characters enviable yet relatable. The book puts a human face to the sacrosanct, all powerful bureaucracy, both envied and maligned in equal measures. At the end of the day, it is not a story of careers, parties or society; it is a tale of people ...*'

—The Tribune

'*... reading of this book of Suchita Malik is like showing civil servants in a glass house.*'

—Shekhar Gupta, Edior-in-Chief, The Indian Express

Made in the USA
Monee, IL
03 May 2026

49438699R00177